Caroline

TIED UP IN
heartstrings

With lots
of love!

xoxo
Felicia
Lynn ♡

FELICIA LYNN

Published by Felicia Lynn
Copyright © 2013 Felicia Lynn
Second Edition: 2013
Cover Art By: Cassy Roop of Pink Ink Designs
Editing by: Book Peddler's Editing
Proofreading by: Tabitha Jorgensen
Formatting by: Cassy Roop
Song lyrics written by: Raymond Jorgensen

PINK INK
D E S I G N S

To the ones who make my life worth living:

Michael & Skylar

You will never know the depths of my love for you two.
Thank you for making me smile every day.

Prologue

MY QUIET HOUSE NOW HAS a revolving door. People are bringing more food than anyone could ever use. Most of them seem to have forgotten that they never really liked me! I've always been a little too outspoken with my thoughts and opinions. Some consider it a character flaw, since the input isn't well received, usually. But, I'm okay with it, because I refuse to be a rug for people to walk all over. I know who my real friends are. Everyone else, who wishes to stand beside me acting as if they're supportive in this tragedy, I could totally do without. I'm not even sure why they're here. Is it the media coverage, the drama, or do they need someone to feel sorry for? I'm not sure how much more of this I can take. I have a few close friends, and I have my family! That's all I need right now, except... I need to get out of here...NOW!

I cross the expanse of this far too big home that Jed designed for us. I've loved every minute of living in it for the past five years, but now I feel like I'm drowning in it. It's filled with memories; memories which crash into me like a wave with a massive undertow, dragging me under. This house is my dream home...*or was.* Who gets to build their dream home for their very first home? Jed, the perfectionist, does.

He always strived to give us everything we wanted or wished for, sacrificing time with Sierra and me to provide it all. That precious man didn't have it in him to say no to us. He wasn't wired to reject us in any way. I wish he could've been satisfied providing a more simple life for us. Maybe if he hadn't been so obsessed with building his career, being more and more successful, he would be here now. We would all be whole and complete.

I walk into the kitchen, where my brother, Jason, and his wife, Kate, are sitting at the farm table talking softly. I know they're talking about me, since they stop speaking as soon as they notice me walking into the room.

"What's up, babe? How was your nap? It doesn't look like you slept any!"

Really, who could possibly sleep when their entire world has just crumbled around them? I feel like I'm buried in the rubble of that plane crash, too. Yet, all I hear from those around me is how important it is to take care of myself. What Idiots! They have no idea what I'm going through, and if they do, then they're just asses for suggesting such a thing.

"Jason, I need to leave. I need to get out of town for a little while." Jason, who has been my white knight forever, is the perfect example of an overprotective big brother. I'm usually opposed to his control freak tendencies, but I'm happy he's here with me dealing with this nightmare. A nightmare is the only way to describe it. Only when I wake up, it's still very much real. I have a hole in my heart the size of Texas, and there's no way to fill it. Continually explaining to a three year old that Daddy isn't coming home is hard and mentally draining. She doesn't understand. I'm not sure she will anytime soon.

"Alexis Nicole, you can't escape this. I get that you need some time to pull yourself together, but, babe…you've got a little girl who will be coming home from Cami's any minute. You can't just run away like the old days. She needs you. She just lost her daddy. She can't lose you, too. You're what she's clinging to. Hold it together, even if you have to fake it. Damn it, you're staying, no running! Got it?"

Ah shit…he used my full name. I know he's serious and very worried. Our mother and father have always been absentee parents, assholes really. Having Jason as a big brother meant I was never really alone. Right now, he's my gate-keeper. I've only had to speak to a few people since the funeral, and I'm so very grateful for that.

"UGH…I know that! I would *NEVER* leave her behind, no matter how badly I want to run away. But she needs an escape too. We can't just stay here and wait for him to walk thru the door every night, Jason. He's not coming back. Do you realize what it's like for us every night? *We* can't do this anymore."

The look on his face tells me he's trying to understand. He's crushed too, not just for Sierra and me. He's hurting because Jed was his best friend, as well his brother in law. They were best friends in college and worked at the same architectural firm up until…well…the crash. Yet, here he is, as always, holding me up when he's hurting. He's so strong, too strong, the strongest and most loyal person I know.

"Yes, babe, I know. I wish I could fix this. I would do anything for this nightmare not to be our reality. I hate seeing my sister falling apart. I can count on one hand the number of times you've cried over the years. Now, I can only remember the few times, over this past week and a half, I haven't seen tears staining your face. I get it, you're grieving. We all are, but YOU CAN'T ESCAPE THIS PAIN by running. It's going where your heart goes, because that's what's broken, sweetie. Our best chance of surviving this is to be strong together. Because when you're falling down, you have all of us here for you to pick you up. I promise you, I'll be here to help you! But, when I'm missing my best friend, I'm hoping you'll be strong enough to help me out, baby girl. I loved him, too."

I feel more tears overflowing my eyes. I'm convinced that the phrase 'all cried out' is a load of crap! I had no idea my body contained this ungodly amount of fluid. I'm sick of being so broken and weak.

Twelve days ago we woke up to a normal day. My sweet little girl, Jed, and I all went to the park. Sierra played, while Jed and I sat in the grass watching. We were talking about all the things going on with his work, my stuff, and planning our summer vacation. This was when Jed and I excelled. Being best friends made us great parents. Don't get me wrong, we had our challenges and we had to work on our relationship constantly, but we were committed and loved each other very much. It was a great morning and afternoon with just us, the fab 3, as Jed called us.

He had to leave that evening for a west coast business trip. He traveled often. We were used to it, but still it sucked. Sometimes it felt like we played second fiddle to his career. He was so focused on making up for what my childhood lacked materially. I was more concerned with making sure our life didn't suffer from the lack of love that was prevalent during my childhood. We'd always tried to make the most of the time he was home. West coast trips were most challenging, because of the time change, but we learned to manage and adapted.

Then the phone rang at 2:47 a.m. and my entire world flipped on its axis. The time will be eternally ingrained in my mind, because I actually said, out loud, as I looked at the clock, *'Someone better be dead!'* I'm not even sure what happened after the dreaded words came across the phone lines. Can you imagine a worse thing to say before you hear that kind of news? I'll never forgive myself for saying that. Yep, I am the major bitch everyone perceives me to be.

Before I knew it Jason, Kate, and Whitney were here, and then I just existed. For the last twelve days I've only engaged in things pertaining to Sierra. She and I are what's left of the fab 3. She needs me and she's the only light in my whole world now. Three years old without a daddy. This is not the life I wanted for my little girl. I know what it's like to grow up without a daddy. I'll never be able to compensate enough for his loss. How can we ever get back to anything normal?

Chapter One

Alexis
Present Day

> For all tragedy there is a miracle to make up for it,
> just somewhere else.
>
> **-Unknown**

IT'S A BEAUTIFUL MORNING, my favorite time, besides Sierra's bedtime when I sing to her. Sitting on the lanai with a great book and a cup of tea provides the peaceful start I need to my day. I normally use this time to clear my head and prepare myself for putting on that proverbial 'happy face' so that I can actually 'fake it, till I make it' as they say. Believe me, I know how insane that sounds! Although, today it feels a little more like creative avoidance. I *should* be packing. I *should* be headed toward a resort in St. Pete Beach in an hour.

My tri-annual girls' weekend with my best friends from college is this weekend. We're heading for some beach time. It's supposed to be relaxing and healing and all that jazz. At least that's what the girls said. My mind is wandering all over the place. The anxiety of leaving Sierra is a bit crippling for me, not so much for her. She's thrilled to be spending the long weekend with Uncle Jason and Auntie Kate. They have three adorable little spawn, and Sierra loves spending time with her cousins. I'm contemplating possible excuses to back out of the trip when I hear the chime of my iPhone alerting me that I have a text.

> **Kate: Hey sweets! I'm scooping Sierra from school with my lot this afternoon. Enjoy your time. You deserve this! I'll pick up her bag later. Just leave it in the entryway.**

Shit. I guess the idea that Kate would cancel was a bit out of the range of possibility.

> **Me: UGH…I don't know Kate. What am I doing? I have no desire to leave town for a girls' weekend. I'm just not ready to be social. I can handle the girls, but I don't want to put a damper on their plans. I think I'm going to stay behind. Plus, I really don't want to leave Sierra.**

I'm actually not really concerned about leaving Sierra. She'll be in the best hands possible with Kate and Jason. She's stayed with them many times and loves being there. It's me… I'm afraid of moving on with my life and doing anything normal. Whitney keeps telling me I can't continue to use Sierra as an excuse to not proceed with life. She's worried that by me always using Sierra as an excuse to avoid doing things, I'm going to hold Sierra back from having a normal life. I hope that's not what I'm doing.

Kate: I knew you were going to need a kick in the ass this morning. I'm coming over. NOW!

Great, this isn't going to end well. My sister in-law is the epitome of a mama-tiger. She is mama-tiger to not only my brother and their children, but to everyone she loves! To be fair, there are very few of us in that category, but my daughter and I are blessed, and *sometimes cursed,* enough to reside on that list. There's no way she's letting me off the hook!

I should never have mentioned this girls' trip to her. Truthfully, I was never planning to go. The girls and I have done these trips three times a year since our freshman year of college. I haven't attended any since the accident. I think it was the guilt of abandoning them that made me bring it up in the first place.

I really do miss being with them for these special weekends. And they have done so much for me over the last eighteen months. I hate abandoning them…again!

The thing is, where there's a group of ladies there's always some kind of drama or issue going on. I've been living in my own bubble, praying by the grace of God that we don't run into any sharp corners. I'm not really ready to deal with anyone else's issues yet. *Yep, just call me the selfish ass bitch!*

My friends have mostly kept me out of the loop with all their troubles over the last several months. They call, or stop by to visit often, and always tell me the latest gossip just leaving out all the things they know I'm not capable of dealing with in their lives. I'm not stupid. We all have stuff going on.

I know things are happening with all of them. In spite of that plane crash that turned my world upside down, life has gone on. For me as well, Sierra is just about to turn five and has started pre-k. Even without a daddy around, she's still thriving and growing.

I've been friends with them for years and I know these girls…too well. We've stood behind each other in good and bad times, through marriages, children, and the numerous life-craps (as we call them) that we wouldn't want to re-live. There are four of us in our little group.

Whitney, my best friend, has a heart of gold. She's funny, beautiful in every way, and of course she doesn't realize it. She's the life of every party, and everyone wants to be her friend. I literally wouldn't have survived the last eighteen months without her in my life. It amazes me that she isn't head over heels in love with some wonderful man. God knows, that there have been plenty of men head over heels for her, and more lining up for the chance. But that's just not her thing. When Whit loves, she loves with her whole heart. It'll take a really special man to capture her heart. I know it'll happen someday, she's a definite romantic. She's feisty as hell, and will defend you with her life if necessary, no questions asked. She and I are most alike in that case. However, unlike me, she likely wouldn't hurt a fly, but has a damn good poker face about it. Throughout our friendship I can't recount the number of times she and I have gone after catty bitches for mistreating or taking advantage of Cami and Kelsey!

Then there's Kelsey. She's a piece of work. She's been married and quickly divorced, no kiddos, thankfully. He was a complete idiot. She loves to fall in love. I really think it's the hunt and chase that gets her. She's stunning and knows how to work it to get what she wants. The girl can find the man of her dreams anywhere, and make all the men think she's the only girl in the room. Jed used to say she carried some sort of love potion in her pheromones, because the men she dated always fell in love with her fast, like proposals and all. I think it has something to do with her bedroom activities…just sayin'. Kelsey is crazy, but she is the most amazing friend anyone could ask for. She'll stop whatever she's doing to be there for you whenever you need her.

Cami is the most quiet and reserved of us all. She's the mom of the group. She always takes care of us. She has been married for a decade. We're only just now in our late twenties. Who does that? But she is over the top in love with her husband, Drake, and he loves her just as much. They were high school sweethearts. Cami & Drake have four little people, who are a perfect combination of the two of them. It's actually unbelievable. I cannot think of two more perfectly matched people. Cami brings balance to the group and always makes sure we all stay together, hence, why we always call her the mother hen.

Then there's me…completely broken when my safety blanket was ripped from me. I wasn't always this way. Jed and I would have been married for just over five years, or I should say were just celebrating four years when the plane went down. Now, I'm a shell of who I used to be. Slowly I'm seeing glimmers of my old self. But they're just that, glimmers. Enough that I have hope of someday piecing together my very broken self. The sunshine, and primary light in my world, comes from Sierra.

Sierra has her daddy's blond hair and bright blue eyes, and my feisty personality. Thankfully, she can bat those gorgeous baby blues when her cute little mouth finds her in trouble, which is often these days, since four and a half year olds know way more than the greater population of the world. She's strong and amazing. I think about how proud Jed would be of her resilience every day. She and I often talk about Jed. I sing her pretty songs that remind me of her daddy all the time. Sometimes, singing is easier than telling stories, so I try to do both, often.

I haven't gone on the last few girls' trips, because I really didn't want the girls taking care of me and not doing the things they all enjoy. Barely holding myself together, I'm seriously lacking the ability to think of great advice for their stuff going on.

I swear I couldn't bear to hear any more about how much fun it would be to go to the spa for the weekend. They don't want to be at a spa all weekend, any more than I do, but obviously they thought it would be the easiest place to ease me back into the real world. Definitely easier than going out dancing and seeing a lot of happy couples around having fun. So I just kept cancelling, using Sierra as an excuse, until they wouldn't take no for an answer.

They let it slide for a little bit, but Whitney wasn't having it this time. She planned this trip and chose all things she knew the old me would love. That girl is damn well determined to bring some joy and happiness back to my life, and she refuses to miss a minute of it. My therapist, Dr. Powell, agrees and is pushing me to start rebuilding my social life. I'm young, only twenty-nine, but I suppose I'm acting more like an old maid. I just can't bear the idea of moving on. This wasn't ever the plan. I was supposed to live happily ever after.

"WHAT—IN—THE—HELL—Is this I'm hearing from

Kate that you're thinking about bagging out of the beach trip with us this weekend?" Whit yells, as she barges into my house and starts stomping her pretty little shoes, that likely cost more than half my wardrobe combined across my tile floor.

"Whit, Listen..." I try, but she points her finger at me and plasters that 'I mean business face' on.

"NO! Listen nothing! I have NO MORE listening tolerance. No desire at all to hear all the reasons why you can't go. JUST. SHUT. UP. Get your ass up out of that chair and into the shower before I drag your stubborn ass out of here with that greasy, just worked-out hair, and sweaty clothes. People are waiting on YOU. We have a great day planned at the resort. Move your ass, sister! Where are your bags?"

Oh no…Crap! Why did Kate call her? We could've talked this through without Whit here forcing my hand. Kate knows I won't bail on Whit face to face. Ahhh…That's exactly why she called her.

"Umm…I haven't packed yet. I was just..."

"Alexis, get in the shower," she yells, then continues without missing a step on her way to find a suitcase. "Kate is on the way. She and I will handle packing for you, and I'm sure for Sierra, too. I'll never understand why you are choosing to hide your head in the sand. This is not you, Alexis. Go get showered and dressed."

Sometimes, when you know you cannot win, you just have to shut your mouth and do as you're told. This is one of those times. I'll never be able to reason with these women. I'm going on this trip whether I want to or not.

"Alexis, Whitney, where are you guys?" Kate calls from the foyer, arriving to double team me into agreement. Whitney tugs me out of my cozy chair and into the house toward the family room where Kate meets us. Jed designed our home after I accepted his proposal six years ago and we started construction almost immediately. Our house is not small, but by no means is it a mini mansion. He designed it so that we could have three kids max and live comfortably. For just Sierra and me, this house is way too big. I can't imagine anyone else living here, though. He designed this for us.

"We're coming. Traitor!" I quip. They both laugh at my scowl, as I'm dragged up the stairs to the master suite. They shove me toward the bathroom with very stern looks. Whitney asks Kate to get out my overnight bag, explaining that I haven't begun to pack for myself or Sierra; as if I thought that was going to be the deal breaker for those two. No chance. That was just a small obstacle to get me out the door. I'm sunk!

Chapter Two

Alexis

WE WALK INTO THE MOST beautiful two-bedroom suite overlooking the ocean on St. Petersburg Beach, near Tampa. The view is breathtaking. I immediately take a deep breath and scan the room for our friends. The resort is close enough to home that I don't feel disconnected from Sierra, which is good, but far enough that it feels like I'm away from the realities of the world. I'll certainly sleep better knowing I'm close enough. Cami and Kelsey are supposed to be here, but it's very quiet when we enter. I'm feeling a little anxious and will be much more settled when we get this weekend started.

The resort is gorgeous. It's a historic hotel that has been impeccably rebuilt and maintained. It has everything we'll need, or want, over the next few days. I love the ocean. It's so peaceful. The beach has always been my place of respite. And since my best friends knew that the location was key to me joining them, they chose this place. The resort is only an hour away from our home outside of Tampa.

"Yay, you're finally here!" Cami calls from the balcony. "I'm so happy to see you. It hasn't been the same without you on these trips," she says, jumping up from the chaise lounge she's sitting on. She looks so pretty in her long maxi dress with the chevron print that's so popular now days. I have no idea how she has time to put cute outfits together with four busy kids.

"Thanks, Cami, I'm glad I'm here, too!" I say, hugging her. Whitney smirks and snorts behind me, eyeing me with sarcasm. "Whit, I am really happy to be here. I'm sorry I made this morning hard for you." Cami glares at Whit, issuing a silent warning for her to drop it and not start our weekend with an argument.

I do feel really bad for always putting Whitney in a position where she always has to push me to do anything different than what I'm accustomed to. "All right, girlies, we're all here now. It doesn't really matter what it took to get us here. Let's just be glad we're here now." She says, trying to keep the peace. Cami's role is caretaker and peacemaker. She goes out of her way to make sure everyone is comfortable. She's helped me adjust to parenting on my own, and telling Sierra the really tough stuff. I look up to her.

Kate and Cami have been incredible role models for me. They're both tremendous assets, since my upbringing didn't provide anything to be mimicked in the way of parenting. Well, I could have mimicked my mother's life, but would have likely ended up behind bars or cracked out on someone's couch somewhere - leaving Sierra God knows where.

I survived my childhood because of Jason and other assorted family members or friends that let us move in when my mother decided partying was a more suitable lifestyle than being a mom. They forced our mother to handle the basic needs we couldn't provide for ourselves for as long as I can remember. *The squeaky wheel gets the oil,* Jason would say, even though, he is only four years older than me. I have no idea where he learned it, but he made use of it to his satisfaction.

To this day, I rarely have to deal with our mother. Our father is long gone. I'm really not sure if he is still walking this planet. Jason doesn't allow our mother to come around at all, but he does still keep in contact with her. I know he hopes that one day she'll be better and can be part of our lives. I have long since lost any hope that she'll ever be someone I want a relationship with. Even if she's well, our relationship is too damaged for me to trust her. She calls him mainly when she's in trouble, but never me. He keeps her at bay.

"Where's Kelsey?" Whitney asks, thankfully breaking my thoughts before I start rehashing all the crap that's better left in the past. I really need to get to a place where everything doesn't remind me of the rocky foundation my crumbled world rests on.

"She's downstairs making appointments for massages on the beach," Cami says with a hint of sarcasm and a wink of the eye.

"Couldn't she have done that by phone?" I ask.

"Yeah, but she wanted to scope out the hottest massage therapists. This is Kelsey we're talking about, ladies."

We're all belly laughing when the door to the suite opens and Kelsey walks in with a room service waiter pushing a cart full of sandwich trays, fruit, sparkling waters, and two pitchers of peach Sangria. Oh happy day…liquid courage.

"Hey, Alexis and Whit. Glad you guys finally made it!" She says as she walks over hugging us both and doing a little dance. "This is going to be such a fun weekend. I can feel it!" She smiles. "I thought we could eat in the room before getting ready for the beach. Let's hurry up! I'm so ready to get this weekend started," Kelsey excitedly proclaims as she kisses both my cheeks and rushes over to sign the waiter's bill. He slips out of the room, leaving us to our catching up.

We all eat and visit a bit about our current happenings, but it's a light hearted, totally mindless conversation as we consume the tasty grouper sandwiches with sweet potato chips. I sip the Sangria, which is delightful, and just what I needed to relax into this weekend. Kelsey looks over at me and winks. She knew I would need this drink to loosen me up. I love that girl!

We all retreat to our bedrooms without any conversation about who's rooming with whom. I always room with Whit, and Kelsey and Cami room together. This is exactly the way we roomed all those years ago in the sorority house. It's nice that we never have to think about it. We all go to our corners to unpack our luggage and get ready for the beach.

I choose my simple strapless navy tankini and nautical blue and white cover-up. After I tie my long brown hair back in a low ponytail, I plop my favorite floppy hat on my head. I swipe some sheer lip moisturizer across my lips and apply a little waterproof mascara. I grab my canvas pool bag with sunscreen, the latest People magazine, my Kindle, and phone and I'm ready to go.

Kelsey has reserved a beach hut, so we don't have to search for chairs or rent beach umbrellas. The beach hut has a private butler. Leave it to Kelsey to set up the VIP service everywhere we go. It's a wooden platform with a pergola built around and sheer draperies provide just a hint of shade. It definitely provides a nice ambiance. We're all situated and enjoying the sunshine with mojitos in hand. Whitney's iPod is playing her beach themed playlist. I'm truly relaxed, more than I have been in months, sitting, reading, and hanging out with friends. The ocean is refreshing, unlike how it will be in a few weeks. I hate it when the temperature rises and the water starts to resemble bath water temperatures.

Who knew this is what I needed? Apparently Whit, hence, why she basically carried me out of the house this morning. I'm so grateful she did, though. I'll likely never admit it. She, like Jason, has a compulsive need to jump in and take over my life when they feel like I can't handle it on my own. They perceive me to be much weaker than I actually am. It's been an ongoing battle over the years, but I love them both so much that most of the time I just suck it up, which says a lot, since I'm not much of a sucker-upper.

"Kelsey, what's going on with you and the baseball player? It looked serious the last time I saw you guys together. I was a little surprised to see you looking at him so endearingly," Cami asks, but everyone is looking at me out of the corner of their eyes, trying to gage my reaction to the conversation.

I really don't want my best friends walking on eggshells, so to lighten the mood I respond quickly, making sure my smile reaches my eyes, so they know I really am okay. "Wow, Kels, I haven't heard a word about you dating a baseball player. Why are you holding out on me? Please tell me he's not a Ray's player. You know the only team worth a damn is the Red Sox! How's his ass?" I ramble, trying to come across teasingly.

My friends all visibly relax. Whitney lets out a breath she clearly didn't realize she was holding. They laugh, and Kelsey spends the next hour telling us everything about this new guy. He is indeed a Ray's player, which I figured. It's still the very early stages of their relationship, but they're having fun and it's taking her mind off her loser ex-husband. Her ex was the biggest ASS. We all hated him. I personally threatened his life on several occasions for the way he talked to Kelsey. She needs some joy in her life, and if this guy is what's making her smile, I'll support that relationship with all that I can.

I don't want any of my friends to experience the emotional angst that seems to have followed me through this life, starting with my childhood and my insanely irresponsible parents.

Everything was better after I left home for good to go to college. Jason was a senior when I entered college. He's always been my best friend and I knew I'd always be safe when he was close by. It wasn't that I wasn't safe without him. By the time he left home for college, I was capable of taking care of myself when my mother ran off with whoever was occupying her time, and Jason was always close enough by that he could be there in fifteen minutes if I really needed him.

During college, I lived in the dorm, but Jason and Jed's apartment was close. They spent a lot of time on campus anyway. That's how I met Jed. He and Jason were best friends and roommates. Jed and I immediately became close friends. Our relationship kind of developed because we were always hanging out together. It wasn't ever an instant, head-over-heels attraction. I grew to love Jed very much, and like Jason, he took care of me even when I didn't want him or need him to. But he made me feel secure and I was desperate for that in my life.

Our life together was perfectly…imperfect.

If I'm honest with myself, there were many days and nights that I felt lonely and unconnected to Jed, even when he was in the same room. Sometimes he was so focused on his career ambitions and other times because we struggled to connect intimately and physically. We were best friends, deeply supportive and protective of one another, but the physical part of our marriage never came easily. We had sex very sporadically, usually scheduled or requested to fulfill a need in each of us. Once it was over, we were back to best friends with occasional benefits.

We were masters at every other aspect of our marriage and life together. We were happy enough. There was never a day that I didn't feel safe and provided for, and for a girl like me with a rocky start in life, that meant a lot. I loved Jed so much for the way he cared for me that I was willing to take him in whatever capacity he was willing to give. The fact that Jason approved and supported our relationship was key. Jason trusted Jed and knew he would be loyal and take care of me. So at the end of the day, what Jed offered was enough for me.

I trusted Jason's judgment, so when he gave Jed his blessing to marry me that told me that I was making a good decision in saying yes…I did, and I mostly never regretted it. Jed provided an amazing life for me from the beginning and soon after for Sierra, when she finally made her surprise entrance into the world. Even after his death, he made sure all his bases were covered in the event of his demise. That made me a little mad, I must say. I know it's the responsible thing to do, but to put so much thought into life going on without him seems crazy. And the fact is he was right…it does go on.

Sierra and I will never have to worry about losing our

home, me having to work to pay the bills, pay for college, or frankly anything else. We're all set financially, but emotionally we're a disaster! Well, I should say I'm a disaster. Sierra is great and strong. I think she would like to have a man in our life to do the things daddy's do. She used to ask if we could go to the store and pick out a new daddy. Strangers would sigh and say how cute it was without knowing the real situation, but to me, it was just another knife in the heart. Now, she asks about it less and less. I try to be both, and when I can't, I have my brother, Kate, and great friends to help fill Jed's shoes. Let me tell you, we can pack the house at a dance recital. She may not have her daddy, but she still has a ton of people who love her. That has to count for something!

We spent a couple more hours on the beach, catching up on life. Cami tells us all about the kids and all their extracurricular activities and achievements. She really is supermom! "Overachiever," I say sarcastically. She's beaming with a huge smile on her face. She's so proud of her family.

We go upstairs to freshen up before dinner at the resort restaurant. As Whitney and I are walking towards the elevators, we overhear a group of college girls excitedly discussing some hot country artist who is staying in the resort. Whitney and I are laughing at their insane plots to bed that poor, unsuspecting man. Though, he likely isn't so unsuspecting. He would probably be thrilled to take any of these ladies into the bedroom! They're all very nice looking and have paid careful attention to how they look.

"Was there ever a time in my life that plotting to take some rock star to bed was appealing?" I ask Whitney.

"Please, like you would have had to plot. Garrett McKenna would have done a lot more than just take you to bed, back in the day. That boy was as obsessed as they come," she says, laughing at me!

Garrett McKenna was an amazingly talented musician we went to college with. We were all good friends, and although I had a major crush on him, we never really made it past the friend stage. I never, ever saw him with the same girl twice the whole year we hung out. "Whatever, who didn't think Garrett was the hottest thing on two legs? That boy was never going to be the settle down type and I'm pretty sure that hasn't changed, from what the gossip magazines say. Don't pretend we had something we didn't. You know he just liked to hang out and sing with me."

We're both giggling like school-girls and reminiscing as we walk down the hall to our suite. I feel normal for the first time in months. I'm so happy that I'm stepping out of my comfort zone and doing something for myself. Just when I think I'll never get back to normal again, I see a glimmer of the old Alexis peek through the darkness. But I'm careful not to be too hopeful that the darkness is ceasing. I can't set myself up to fail.

We make it back to the room and scurry off to the showers. "Thank God for two bathrooms. Four girls and one bathroom would have been a nightmare!" I say after Whitney gets out of the shower twenty-five minutes later. She's always been a bathroom hog. I guess that's why we made perfect roomies. I'm completely showered and dressed in the time it takes her to wash her hair!

I'm wearing a white eyelet, sleeveless cotton dress with brown sandals, and my hair is braided over my shoulder. It's a comfortable beach outfit for dinner, and then later, since I'm pretty sure we'll end in a local bar. I'm also hoping to escape these ladies at some point and have a bit of quiet time on the beach. We'll have to see. Before leaving for dinner I grab my cell and head out to the balcony to call my baby girl. I'm sure Kate is feeding the kids before getting them ready for bed, but I need to hear her voice and sing her special bedtime song. I dial the number.

"Hey, sis, how's the beach?" Jason answers on the first ring.

"It's great, warm and sunny. Believe it or not, I think this may be just what the doctor ordered. I'm really relaxed, and it's nice to catch up with the girls. How's my little mini-me? I miss her like crazy!" I whine a little at the last sentence.

He snickers, "Well, I'm not convinced that feeling is mutual. She's having a blast torturing the boys! Poor little bastards don't stand a chance with Sierra and Lyla. They're ruling this roost! The boys are all being forced to play some game of house. The little brats are all wearing tutus and barking. I'm not really sure what's going on in their storyline. I was just wondering if I was going to need to bill you for the therapy that I'm sure they will need after today."

I'm laughing at what my daughter's idea of playing house could be - turning my twin nephews into tutu-wearing animals or whatever else she's come up with. "Wow, sounds like Sierra. She is dog obsessed, lately. She's been asking me for a puppy every day. Thank you for giving her that! I definitely owe you and Kate a few days away. Let me know when I can cover and stay with the kiddos. Can I hear my baby girl's voice before we head out to dinner?" I ask.

"No problem, sis. We'll let you stay with these rug rats anytime! But for now, just go and have a great night. Love you," he says right before he passes the phone to a squealing little girl.

"Hi, Mama, we're playing house and I bought a dog and named her Petals. She wears a pink ballerina dress." She fills me in, talking so fast she barely takes a breath.

"Nice, sweet girl, remember to be super sweet to that puppy. I would hate for the little rascal to bite you!" I say, with hopes she gets the message that picking on her older twin cousins isn't acceptable.

I know she understands when she responds, giggling, "Mama, I know how to take care of puppies, silly."

Oh how I love the sound of my giggling girl. "I love you as high as the sky, precious girl! Sleep well and I'll call you after breakfast tomorrow. Do you want me to sing your song before we hang up?" I ask, but she sounds a bit distracted.

"No, thanks, Mama. You can sing to me at breakfast. I gotta go. Auntie Kate wants to talk to you. Love you, Mama," she exclaims, and that's it as she hands the phone off to Kate.

Kate fills me in on their plans for the weekend. I know my baby will have a great time. Kate is like another super-mom. Since she has three of her own, adding Sierra to her group doesn't really cramp her style. I'm so grateful that my brother chose this woman to spend his life with. She really is amazing. I remind him all the time that he's a lucky bastard. We talk for a little while about the beach and what we girls are up to. Then I disconnect to finish getting ready for our night out.

We enjoyed a fantastic dinner at the hotel. Now the girls and I are walking to a little bar down the street. There's a big wedding at the resort this weekend, so we thought it best to escape the wedding crowd.

Apparently, that country music star we heard the girls

talking about this morning is attending the wedding, so there are tons of fangirls hanging out in the hotel bar and restaurant trying to catch a peek. I haven't been interested enough to ask who it is. I'm trying to escape the crowds, not go toward them. I have no interest in chasing some star down for an autograph or anything else. I'm all too happy to find another bar that's not too crowded.

"Hey…it's open mic night, Alexis. It's about time you get back up on a little stage, don't you think?" I give Kelsey a look that will clearly state my intolerance of her peer pressure, but it seems my look has no effect.

"No chance, my friend. There's not enough beer in this bar to get me on that stage!" We walk into the quaint bar that overlooks the ocean. In the corner is a small little stage with a mic and what looks like a few performers prepping to sing. There's even a Martin guitar in the corner. I really like the feeling of this place. We find a table on the deck so we can look at the ocean. We place our orders with the waiter, and then settle in to listen to several performers, enjoying the entertainment.

The mood takes a little bit of a dive when Kelsey tells us about her ex's most recent refusal to meet the requirements of their divorce decree. He's really put her through the ringer. I have a lot of pent up frustrations that I would very much enjoy releasing on him, but I won't, since I don't want to cause any more issues for Kels.

I really do want to cheer her up, so maybe, I think, I could sing her a song to put a smile on her face. There's a cute song on Whit's playlist that we were all singing to today. We've made it our honorary weekend theme song. I'll sing that for her.

I get up from my seat, taking my Blue Moon with me, and approach the audio tech beside the stage. I ask him if he has the instrumentals for the song I'd like to sing and he tells me he doesn't. I'm trying to think of another song when I feel someone beside me, a little too close. "Alexis Phillips, is that you?" He asks inquisitively. "My God—it—is—you," mystery guy stutters before I can turn around.

Oh my...right beside me is Garrett McKenna. Like *THE Garrett McKenna*. He has a hat and sunglasses on, even though it's dusk. I'd recognize him anywhere. How could I ever forget that face? I feel like I'm floating as he stares at me with those mesmerizing gray eyes. Damn...he's still so beautiful. I know men don't want to be referred to as beautiful, but damn I'm not sure of another word to describe him.

I was a freshman when we used to sit in the park on campus and sing together. Really, he would play guitar and write his songs and I mostly harmonized with him. It was all in good fun, because I liked hanging out with him and he allowed me to be me, *not* because I kind of had a major crush on him. We lost touch years ago, after he left college to pursue his music career in Nashville.

He got a recording contract and is doing really well for himself. I'm shocked to see him in this bar. I know he notices my reaction, since my mouth seems to have stopped working and is hanging wide open. "Um...hi," that's it...that's all I can say. Yep, I officially look like the biggest loser!

"Alexis, stop looking at me like that. You're going to blow my cover and, right now, that wouldn't work out very well. It's just me, the same ole Garrett!" He lightly slugs me on the shoulder, trying to reassure me.

"Garrett! Oh my God. I can't believe you're here. How

are you? Never mind, I know how you are. I see your face on the cover of magazines all the time," I ramble like those crazy fangirls we saw earlier. He flinches slightly, but then his gorgeous smile sweeps across his face.

He takes my hand, guiding me away from the stage and over to a less crowded corner of the bar. The butterflies that one would usually feel fluttering in your stomach are sweeping though my entire body, and it feels much more like an elephant stampede than butterfly flight. What's wrong with me and why am I so star struck? Isn't this the same guy I used to hang with on the west lawn? Nope, this is Garrett McKenna. The Garrett McKenna. The CMA artist of the year, the playboy that's constantly surrounded by screaming fangirls and different beautiful celebrities at the red carpet events. I wonder where all the fans are?

He's wearing an expression I don't quite recognize. It looks happy, but at the same time concerned. Maybe he's worried about being recognized with me beside him. "Alexis, I'm so happy to see you. What are you doing here?" he asks. I tell him I'm great and that I'm here with the girls, pointing over to our table outside. "How are you, sweetheart? I think about you all the time. I heard about Jed, but I wasn't really sure the best way to handle contacting you. I couldn't really show up at the funeral without bringing a lot of unnecessary attention. I did think about you and wonder how you were."

Wow…I can hear the concern in his voice. But I don't need anyone else feeling sorry for me. Not even superstar Garrett McKenna. Besides, he couldn't send a card, a letter, or pick up the phone? I'm at a loss as to what to say. "I'm actually doing okay, Garrett. Sierra, my daughter, is growing up and that's fun to watch. The girls and I are here for a little beach getaway," I reply with my 'Fake it till you make it' attitude. "I was going to sing a song for Kelsey, but they don't have the instrumentals for the song. Why don't you come back to the table with me and say hello to everyone? I know they would love to say hi to you, too." I say, reaching for his arm to pull him toward the girls.

He stops me, wearing a huge grin. "You were going to sing, Alexis?" he asks.

"Yeah, but I can't now. I wanted to sing our weekend anthem and they don't have it. This isn't really a country music kind of crowd, I suppose. Please, come over with me," I implore him again, knowing this would make their night just as it's done for me.

"Not yet, Alexis. What song did you want to sing?" I have no idea why he is so interested in what I was going to sing. I'm obviously not singing it now.

"*Killing Little Umbrellas* by Sarah Darling. Kels is kind of in a funk. She's just gone through an insane divorce from an idiot, and I wanted to cheer her up. No biggie…now I have you to cheer her up," I say, feeling like I've hit the goldmine of cheer-ups for Kelsey.

"No, lady, you want to sing that song and I want to hear it, so I'll play guitar for you. Just don't say who's accompanying you. It'll start all kinds of craziness, and I'm happy to catch up with you girls tonight without all that nonsense. I don't want a bigger crowd getting in the way," he explains, pulling me back toward the stage. "Come on. Let's do this!"

How could he possibly jump on stage with me and play a song we've never done together. Is he insane? "Wait, Garrett! Do you know that song? Hold on, I can't go on that stage with you. Let's just go to the table. Kelsey will be so happy to see you that she'll forget all about her mood." I'm pleading with him.

"No way, Lex. I haven't heard your voice in years and that's a crime by my standard. Up you go." He lifts me by the hips and sets me on the stage, then leans over chatting in the tech's ear. The lights on the back of the stage dim and he pulls the bill of his hat down even lower to mask his identity before he jumps up on the stage. He grabs the guitar in the corner and stands waiting for my signal, but doesn't say anything.

I speak to the crowd. "Hey, I'm here with my best friends in the world. We've all kinda had a rough year or so and we're here celebrating our friendships this week," I say holding up my beer, saluting in their direction. "This song has kind of become our weekend anthem and one of my girls needs a little pick me up tonight. Thanks to my longtime friend back there for playing the acoustics, so I can sing to my Kelsey girl!" I inform the crowd, looking over at my three friends and their shocked, but overjoyed expressions.

I nod my head in Garrett's direction, desperately trying to avoid eye contact with him. He begins playing the chords for the song. I'm completely awestruck. But right on time, I sing to the crowd, looking towards my friends, who are all wearing huge-ass grins. It's obvious they've figured out who's on stage with me. He's the only longtime friend that I have that I've sung with. They're all jumping up and down and singing along. When the song ends, Garrett quickly jumps off stage and heads in the direction of our table. I thank everyone for listening and follow right behind him.

Chapter Three

Garrett

TO SAY I'M SHOCKED to see Alexis here would be the understatement of the century. This is…THE GIRL! By 'The Girl' I mean, the girl I used to compare all others against for years, and frankly still do. Shit, honestly, no one has even come close to making me feel the way that she did. I haven't seen her in, what's it been, nine years? But hot damn, she looks amazing. Better than she did in college. I thought the ladies were supposed to lose their bodies as they got older. Not this girl. She's got a little more to love on her bottom than I remember, but damn do I love it. Lex is simply the most beautiful woman in this bar. I noticed her immediately when she walked to the stage. The energy in the whole room changed. It was like a bunch of twinkling star lights shining around her. Even across the room she makes me feel light-headed and dazed. How is that?

I can't believe the song she wants to sing is one that I know, since it happens to be Courtney's favorite. Drew and I are constantly playing it for her to sing, as well. It's a chic, boy hater song, but I don't care. I'd play Alanis Morissette if Alexis wanted. I'm glad to play it for her. She's got the voice of an angel. I haven't heard her sing since I left college.

Going to Nashville and leaving my friends behind isn't something I'm proud of. When I got to Nashville, it was hard work to get noticed. Playing in lousy dive bars, my chances of being successful in the beginning were very slim. Everyone told me I was making a huge mistake leaving Florida and college to do this, but it was something I just couldn't ever look back on and regret. I lost touch with my friends. In the beginning, the thought of calling and telling them I hadn't hit it big yet was a knock to my ego. Then, when I did start getting my name out there, I was just busy. That and I didn't want to call because at that point, it felt like I was bragging. It sucked either way. So I lost all of my friends, along with my privacy, and other things I wasn't expecting to go along with this life.

Listening to Alexis sing about 'Killing Little Umbrellas' is adorable. She looks a little like she killed a few too many today, to be honest. Her face is flush and she seems like her words are lost in conversation. But, that's okay, because she is slamming the lyrics while she sings, never missing a key. I should have taken her to Nashville with me. She wouldn't have had to work nearly as hard as I did to get a recording contract.

I'm not worried about getting noticed up on stage because everyone in the bar is staring at Alexis. Even if my cover did get blown, I wouldn't care. Being on stage with her would make it worth it.

After the song ends, I dash off the stage before anyone notices me. I head in the direction of Alexis' best friends. I knew all these girls back in the day. Not quite as well as I knew Alexis, but well enough.

The five of us sit on the deck out back, hanging out and talking for a while. I was desperate to get away from the resort, and I found this little dive bar to hide out in. I'm so glad I came out alone. I wouldn't want to share this time with anyone else. It actually feels like old times. They don't treat me very differently, aside from asking a few questions about 'star life'. The time catching up with Alexis has flown by. I didn't even notice the time, until I see Alexis covering her sweet lips behind her hand, try to disguise a yawn.

"Wow, it's one in the morning, ladies. Let me walk you guys back to the hotel." I signal the waiter for our check. Alexis is reaching for her wallet, too. "Put it away, lady, I got this. I can't even remember the last time I had this much fun with a bunch of girls."

Alexis turns bright red and whips her head around to stare daggers at me. "Garrett, we don't want to hear about your play-boyish ways. Leave it." She's pissed.

Damn, that's hot, but I don't want her mad. "Wait, Alexis, that's not what I meant. I meant, when I'm around ladies, they usually don't want to talk…they...UGH… Never mind, this isn't going to sound the way I mean it, no matter how I phrase it." I smile at her, hoping she sees that I really wasn't trying to sound like an ass.

I pay the check and we all walk out onto the sidewalk, heading back toward the huge pink hotel. I can't believe the girls are staying at the same resort. What are the chances? I'm here for my cousin's wedding. I thought it would be nice to come a couple days early and get a little R&R, while hanging out with my family. Someone in the bridal party let it slip that I was going to be here performing, so there have been a lot of fans and photographers hanging around snapping pictures. I was sick of being holed up in my hotel room, and decided to go out and have a beer. Shit, am I happy I did! Seeing Alexis here tonight has been fantastic.

I've been concerned about her since I heard about the plane crash that killed her husband. It was widely televised in Tampa. My parents still live there and told me about it, since they knew Alexis and I were friends in college. In spite of all that she's been through, she looks okay, not deeply devastated, but a little derailed. I know it's been over a year. I have no idea how long it takes for life to be okay again after a loss like that. I haven't ever lost anyone close to me. I tend to try and keep most people at arm's length, anyway.

Jed and I weren't friends, per say, we knew each other because we ran in the same crowd. When he and Alexis started dating, I tried to stay away from him as much as possible. He was a nice enough guy, but shit, I was crazy jealous. He had the most amazing girl I'd ever met and there was no way I wanted to ever hear how happy she made him. So, I just hung with Alexis in between her classes, when she could fit me in, and tried to avoid social situations where I would be forced to see them together. I could never have handled seeing her wrapped around another guy.

Lex and I would sit on the west lawn where I would play the guitar and sing with her. It was my favorite college pastime. Many guys would say they loved the time they spent partying, picking up the chicks, or hanging with the frat brothers, but me, hell no. My time singing with Alexis was the best time ever. Hell, I think I would still choose that over packing the house at Madison Square Garden.

The girls are leading the way to their suite. I'm in the suite directly above them. Damn, how the universe works sometimes!

We reach the door to their room. Before they walk into the room I hug each of them and tell them I'll see them around this weekend. The door closes gently behind them, as Alexis steps up to give me a hug. Now that I know Alexis is here, I know I won't be able to stay away. When she gets close, I sweep her up and swing her around in a big bear hug. It feels so nice to be close to her. "Sweetheart, I knew I missed you, but even I didn't realize how much until tonight."

I see her cell phone poking out of the front pocket of her purse. I pull it out and quickly program my number into her phone, then dial my own number from her phone, so I can save it. I vow to myself at that point, never again will I let her get away from me.

Even though I'll never have her in the capacity I once wanted her in, and still do frankly, I refuse to live a life without her. "Tomorrow morning, let's go for a walk on the beach. We can go early. We have a lot of catching up to do. I'll get you back here before the girls wake up, so that I don't trample all over that girl time." I intended it to be a question or invitation, but it came out as a statement and order. I realize my mistake, but still continue with my words. "Call me, as early as possible. I'll be waiting."

She looks confused, but her facial expressions change from a funny little scowl to what I'm hoping is a look of acceptance. She pauses and takes a deep breath, "Okay, Garrett. Thanks for tonight, the drinks, the performance, and mostly for hanging out with us. It was a lot of fun. It's…" She hesitates, and I'm still stuck on that she said okay. "Yeah, it's been a fun night, Garrett. Thanks, again. We'll chat tomorrow morning. If you don't hear from me, you can call me, now that you have my phone number," she says, pointing out the obvious fact that I took it without asking. I shrug unrepentantly.

Yes, I do have her number, and damn it, I'm going to burn those digits into my brain. Shit, if it were up to me, she wouldn't be going to sleep at all tonight. I would drag her cute little ass down to the beach, and make her tell me every damn thing that she has done since we've lost touch. But since that sounds insane, and I want a little bit of her time tomorrow, I'll try and be reasonable. I gently brush the back of my fingers across her cheek. She's so damn soft. "Yeah, sweetheart. Tomorrow. Goodnight, Lex." I bend down and kiss her cheek. Then I open her door for her and she walks in. I can't wait to get back to my room and dream about her resting directly under me, nestled snugly into her bed.

Chapter Four

Alexis

ICLOSE THE DOOR TO the suite and fall against the wall, sighing. I wanted to tell him how happy I was to see him, but he's only here a couple days before he has to go back to his superstardom, real life. I don't want to come across as the desperate blast from the past. Seeing him again leaves a very unfamiliar feeling in my body. You know, that feeling when you can't seem to get close enough to that special someone because every millimeter closer feels so much better than the last? Only, I shouldn't want that with Garrett. He's just my friend. He's always been just my friend, yet, when he bent down to kiss my cheek, my heart was fluttering and I desperately wanted his touch on my lips, not my cheek. What is wrong with me? I really need to pull myself together.

Garrett's here for his cousin's wedding. His gift to the couple is to sing the song for their first dance. He has hired the band for the wedding, too. Apparently they're incredible musicians, a local indie band. Since the wedding is in a couple days he's hoping to hang out on the beach and get some R&R before going back out on tour. I'm not sure how that's going to happen with all these fangirls hanging around plotting sexcapades with him. What I thought was funny earlier, when those girls were talking about some unknown star, now infuriates me! They can all keep their nasty little hands off him.

The girls have gone to their separate rooms for bed. I walk quietly into the bedroom I'm sharing with Whit. She's in the bathroom brushing her teeth, so I quickly dress in my favorite pj pants and tank and climb into bed. I'm exhausted. Yet I can't stop thinking about this evening. I'm actually comforted by seeing Garrett again after all these years. It's always made me a little sad that our friendship was disposable to him, but I guess that comes with fame and fortune. You have to leave the little people behind. That's alright, at the end of the day I'll be happy to have had a few hours with him to reminisce and hear about his life.

"Do you really think I'm going to let you drift off to dreamland without discussing what went down tonight?" Whitney says, marching into the room and plopping herself down on my bed. "Spill it, Lex. What happened tonight?"

Like I know what the hell is happening. I never expected the stampede of butterflies, or to perform with him like we'd been doing it for years. The shiver when his lips touched my face, and the desire to have him closer than I've ever wanted anyone, was even more unexpected. How the hell can I answer her questions when I don't know myself?

"Whitney, it's almost two in the morning. I don't know what you're talking about. We met up with an old friend, had a great night full of reminiscing and conversation. That's it. You were there the whole time. Did you see something I didn't?" I ask, my voice laced with annoyance.

"Yes, I suppose I did, since my brain-dead best friend didn't see the man sitting at our table, staring longingly at her all night, and completely taken with every single syllable that escaped her mouth. What the hell is wrong with you, Lex? How could you not see it?" she asks.

"No, Whitney, leave it! We're just friends. It's always been just friends. Stop trying to make it into something it's not, stop imagining things. I haven't even set eyes on the man in almost a decade," I say sternly, and to make my point very clear I throw in a nasty look before walking into the bathroom and firmly closing the door.

"Be pissed at me all you want, but I wasn't imagining shit and YOU KNOW IT, Alexis," she says through the door, while I completely ignore her. That'll show her. I'll pretend I didn't hear.

I stand staring at myself in the mirror, begging for a reason from myself for the feelings that stirred tonight. I haven't ever had that angsty, can't-get-close-enough-to-your-touch feeling, ever. What's different about tonight? What's different about now? What's different about him and me, together? I had a crush on him in college and got butterflies when he was around, but this, this is very different.

When I leave the bathroom after washing my face and brushing my teeth, I see that Whitney is sound asleep. Thankfully round one of that conversation is over, but my guess is round two will begin before I've had a chance to find the answers to my own questions.

I close my eyes, willing myself to get some sleep, but rest

escapes me. I wonder what early means to him. Early to me is 5 a.m. Sierra is an early riser. She likes to wake up when she hears the birds start chirping at around 6:30ish. Should I call him at my early? or wait until a more reasonable 8 a.m.? He's a superstar; I'm pretty sure 5 a.m. is much too early, especially since we didn't make it back to the hotel until after 1:30 a.m.

It's now 2:30 in the morning, and sleep still escapes me. I decide to do a little reading on the balcony outside. I grab my phone and my Kindle and head outside. Hoping the fresh air, and an escape into the fictional world of lovers I don't know, will make my brain too tired to think.

After an hour of reading, daydreaming, and listening to the ocean, I finally feel myself relax enough to drift off to sleep. I really don't want to move and this chaise lounge is getting more comfortable by the second. I decide to stay where I am.

The next thing I hear is my iPhone chime, alerting me I have a text. It's from Garrett.

Garrett: Are you awake yet? Early was an hour ago. I'm outside your suite. I have a Chai for you. If you're awake, open up.

I check the time. Oh my, 6:30 a.m. Well, at least I know we both have the same definition of early, for future reference. I respond before heading to the room to quickly get dressed and meet him in the hall.

Me: Just waking up. Sorry…had a hard time falling asleep. I'll be out in a few minutes.

Garrett: Alexis, stop texting me and open the door!

Oh my, but I'm wearing pajamas. Great. Well, I guess it won't be the first time he's seen a woman in pjs. My guess, he usually sees his lady loves in much less than pajama pants and tank tops. I walk over to the door and look through the peep hole. He looks directly at the door and waves. How does he know I'm looking?

"Sweetheart, I know you're there. Open up. I have Starbucks for you," he says, as if he can read my mind and expression through the door.

I open the door, and he hands me a venti, non-fat, no water, no foam, Chai Tea Latte. Oh my goodness, my drink. How did he know? He couldn't possibly have remembered it after all these years. It's not like it's a simple order.

"How did you know what I drink?" I ask.

"I took a chance that your drink order hadn't changed. I remember that's what you used to order when we hung out back in the day. But I wasn't sure if your taste buds had matured. I guess not," he laughs.

"What the hell! You were winning major cool points for remembering my drink and bringing it to me. That totally went out the window when you insulted my palate. You ASS!" I smack his arm, and it's hard, *really hard*. It hurts my hand. Shaking out the throb, I flinch. "Ow. That hurt."

He smirks, "Don't hit that babe. It's like rock! You should know better. Let me see," he says jokingly, but with concern seeing that I'm still shaking my hand. "You okay?" he asks while inspecting each finger, then placing a kiss on my palm.

The throb immediately dissipates. All I can feel is the tingle of his touch.

"Yeah, I'm okay. Let me put some real clothes on," I say, running off to the room to change. "I'll be back in a second."

The beach is empty when we make our way downstairs. There are a few workers out setting up cushions on the chairs and stocking the bars. This early it's not too warm. We're walking side-by-side sipping our drinks, not really saying much. The silence isn't uncomfortable. It's pleasant, but I still feel the need to fill the silence.

There are so many things I want to ask him. "Garrett, can I ask you a question?"

He looks over at me. "Anything you like, lady," he replies with a smile.

"Why didn't you keep in touch with us after you left?" I ask and he looks remorseful.

"Oh, I was afraid you'd want to talk about that…well…I guess, I was afraid to tell you guys how hard it was to survive up there. I was afraid to be a failure in everyone's eyes. So, I just didn't call. I'm sorry. I was an ass and that was wrong. I thought of you all the time, Lex."

Huh, but he wasn't a failure. I never would have thought of him that way. I was proud of him before he was a superstar. "But, you weren't a failure. You did what you sought out to accomplish. You're successful. Congratulations on making all your dreams come true! I'm really proud of you. I always have been, even before you made it, Garrett. I've always known how special you are." Okay, that was deep, but it needed to be said. Didn't I ever tell him how amazing he is, even back then? I know I told him. I must have.

He looks at me, and his gorgeous gray eyes melt me to

the core. "Sweetheart, not all my dreams have come true. My biggest dreams have yet to see the light of day."

What more could he want? He's a superstar musician, he's rich, he travels the world, and he has adoring fans who worship him. He can have any woman he wants. Yet, he wants more? I can't even imagine.

"Tell me about your life, Lex. What are your days like? What have you been up to for the past nine years?" he asks.

"Well, I'll give you the CliffsNotes version. Jed and I married, I'm not sure if you know, just over five years ago. I have the most adorable little girl in the world. She's four and a half, and keeps me so busy. My brother and his wife, Kate, live about two miles from me in Tampa, which is great, since I'm alone now. When Jed died…it was really hard…but I'm getting better and Sierra is so great!" I say, wondering if he's heard enough, but he's just looking over at me waiting for more details. I continue, "I guess since she was still so little when Jed died, she doesn't really remember what it was like when he was around. It's a double-edged sword, because I want her to remember him, yet it's nice that she isn't sad. That sounds bad, but I guess there's not a better way to describe it. Do you know what I mean?" Having to explain that is awful.

Garrett looks at me with eyes full of sadness. I'm hoping not to see the pitying look I've come to know so well. I hate that look. I'm sick of people feeling sorry for me. "Lex, when I heard about Jed, I want you to know, I wanted to call you so badly. I wanted to rush here and hold you. I wanted to assure you it was going to be okay. But, after being away so long, I knew that would be wrong. I wasn't the one you needed to console you. So I stayed in Nashville and just prayed. I actually went to church for three Sundays in a row, praying for you to be okay, to be strong. And then I saw your picture in the newspaper my mom sent me. I could see your strength in that picture, even through your tears, as you were holding Sierra." He smiles. It's not a pitying face, but one that holds a great deal of regret. I've learned to see the difference.

He stops walking and looks me directly in the eyes. "She's really beautiful, by the way. She looks so much like you." He takes me by the hand and we continue walking, as he rubs circles into my palm. It's almost like he's trying to comfort me. He knows how hard that was for me to admit. I have never told anyone that I am grateful Sierra doesn't re-member much of what it was like to have a daddy. Yet, still I hope someday we'll have someone in our life who wants to take on that role.

No one will ever replace Jed, but a little girl needs a daddy growing up. Believe me, this is something I do know about. Growing up without a dad was hard for me. I remember being so envious of other little girls, whose dads took them to the father/daughter dances in elementary school, who took them for doughnuts on Saturday mornings so the moms could sleep, who taught them how to ride a bike and drive a car-- all the things that I either did without or learned from Jason.

Jason and I survived in spite of our parents' failures. I want something different for my little girl. I want her to have those special memories with a daddy and feel what it's like to be the sunshine in a daddy's world. But I don't know how to do that without feeling like I'm replacing or discounting Jed. Maybe I'm just not ready. Will I ever be ready?

"Where'd you go, beautiful?" he asks, looking at me cu-riously.

"Oh, I'm sorry. I guess I got lost in my thoughts. I do that a lot. I'm sorry." He nods, allowing me time to snap out of my wandering thoughts.

We reach the pier. I think we've been walking a while, but I have no idea what time it is. I reach for my phone and realize it's almost eight o'clock. I need to call Sierra. I promised I'd call at breakfast. "I'm sorry, Garrett, can you give me a few minutes? I need to make a call." He's puzzled, but says no problem.

I walk over to sit in the sand under the pier and dial Jason. "Hey, sis. Sierra just said mommy's gonna call soon. That kid has you on her radar."

Yep, that's my girl. At least she has learned that when I say I'm going to do something, I'll always come through! It's the one thing I always want her to know. Good or bad, I'll always be there for my girl.

"Yeah, she does. Did I tell you what she told the teacher last week when she got in trouble?" I ask him.

"Your kid, in trouble, I'm shocked to hear that," he says, laughing.

"Well, apparently she wasn't following the instructions Ms. Davis gave, so she issued an ultimatum, telling Sierra that if she didn't listen, she was going to have to call her mommy. Sierra told Ms. Davis that would be great! Please call her mama and tell her how much she hated school. Needless to say, I have to go to a parent/teacher conference this week, *again*. This is the part of being a single parent I hate."

He's still laughing at me. And although I too thought it was funny, I'm not looking forward to another meeting. "Well, sis, you raised that little monster to say whatever she feels. *What comes up, comes out!* Aren't those your words? Good luck with *that* conference. I can go with you, if you want me to. I know it's hard to always do these things alone."

He's always so supportive and willing to step in at any time. But I'm trying so hard to prove I can do this on my own. "No, Jason, I'll be fine. Thanks, though. Can I talk to Sierra, before y'all run off on your day?" I ask.

"Yep. Here she is. Love ya!"

"Love you, too!"

He calls Sierra in a sing song voice. I hear her running in the background. "Hi, Mama," she says loudly. "I had Mickey Mouse pancakes with chocolate chips for breakfast. Uncle Jason made them special. Can we go to Disney World soon?"

God, I love that kid. My heart just soars, hearing her precious voice. I miss her. "Of course, baby girl. We can go soon. Maybe we can even stay at the hotel that the monorail rides through that you love so much. Tell me what you're doing today." She's very excited, and it makes me happy that she enjoys spending time with our only family.

"Auntie Kate says we're going to the zoo and the splash park. I'm wearing my new bathing suit. She made me a towel with a hood and it has my name on it!" My overachieving sister in-law can't help herself when it comes to making me feel less than competent. She doesn't mean to do it, but she freaking sews and makes gourmet dinners, while working full-time at the kids' school. She's class mom, and whatever else she can fit into the last six minutes of her day. But I love her dearly. Even though, I'm convinced she's likely undercover, testing some pharmaceutical, to make herself super-mom!

"Oh, that sounds fun. You'll have to tell me all about it when I call you tonight. Do you want to hear your song now?"

"Yes, Mama. I changed my mind at bedtime. I wanted you to sing, but Uncle Jason sang instead. He's not as good as you, Mama." I knew that would happen, but I find it fascinating that Jason sang to her. He has an amazing voice, but doesn't really enjoy singing very much.

"Hey, I heard that," Jason says in the background and Sierra's giggles explode, music to my ears.

"Okay, baby girl, listen up!" I sing part of the song from *Butterfly Fly Away* by Miley & Billy Ray Cyrus to her while I sit on the beach, watching the waves gently caress the shoreline. She loves hearing about the caterpillars and butterflies. It's really a precious song. I've been singing it to her for years. It used to be she only wanted to hear *Puff the Magic Dragon*, but now it's *Butterfly Fly Away*.

As I finish singing and say my "I love yous", I realize that Garrett is sitting there staring at me. His beautiful gray eyes are glowing. He looks so peaceful. He was listening to me sing.

"Garrett, did you enjoy the song about caterpillars? Do you need someone to sing to you every day, too?" I'm being silly and trying to tease him.

Instead of deflecting, he says, "Sweetheart, I would give anything in this world to hear you sing to me every day. And you can sing about whatever you want. You're quite amazing, Lex! What you're giving to Sierra is priceless. Those memories are irreplaceable."

Tears…I feel them coming. Oh no, I haven't cried in a while. I was doing so good! Not now, I plead with myself. But it's happening, and I can't stop them. The dam has opened.

"Lex, you're the best mom. I thought my mom was pretty amazing, and she is, but what I just heard, sweetheart. *You* really are special. I've never experienced anything quite like that."

Yep, big tears are streaming down my face. I'm not sure what to say. I hate when people see me cry, but this time they aren't sad tears. I try so hard to be not just a good mom, but the best mom, and so often I feel inadequate. I want to fill Jed's shoes, too, so I work twice as hard to compensate sometimes. It's exhausting, but I love Sierra so much it makes it all worth it. The fact that Garrett sees what I wish I could see, makes me happy but also makes me wonder how it's possible he got that from overhearing a ten minute conversation.

"Thank you, Garrett, for saying that. You don't know how much that means to me." He just lifts me off the sand and holds me banishing my tears, as he wipes them away one by one with the tip of his pointer finger.

It's getting late and I told Whitney before I left that I'd be back for breakfast. They're all probably just waking up. We start walking back toward the resort, in the comfortable silence of before, but this time my mind is consumed with thoughts of saying goodbye to Garrett and not seeing him for God knows how long. Now that I've spent this time with him, it feels like a huge loss all over again. I don't want to be an overzealous blast from the past. I'll walk away with a smile, even though my heart will break a little on the inside.

Right before we reach the resort he stops abruptly and pulls me into him. "Lex, I'm not ready to say goodbye to you. It's too hard. I know this is a girls' weekend, and I can't hijack all your time, but please, will you come to the wedding with me tonight? I need to spend more time with you. Nine years is a very long time to make up for in a few hours."

His beautiful gray eyes are pleading with me, but there's no fighting on this end. I'm relieved that he was thinking the same thing as me. He's not ready to walk away either. How can I possibly deny him, or myself for that matter? He's right. This little amount of time is nowhere near enough.

"Yes, Garrett, I'd love to go to the wedding with you. I'll go upstairs and raid the girls' closets. I'm sure I can come up with something to wear to a wedding between all our wardrobes."

His face lights up like the Fourth of July. "Thank you so much, sweetheart. I'll pick you up at 4:30. I'll have my phone with me if you want to call and say 'hi' today, or if you need anything. *You* have my number so *use* it, Alexis." He winks at me and then we walk into the resort.

Chapter Five

Garrett

SHE'S COMING TO THE wedding with me! She said she'd come. I never expected her to agree, but she didn't even hesitate. I'm shocked, yet so damn excited! I wanted to kiss her. I wanted to do more than kiss her. I felt like I'd just hit the jackpot. The idea of having to spend time with her in a room full of people doesn't thrill me as much as having her all to myself, but as long as I get to be close to her, I really don't care. I'll take what I can get.

I'm performing a song for the bride and groom's first dance tonight. They chose the song *Marry Me* by Train. Now I have a better idea. I pull out my phone and text Alexis.

> **Me: Do you know the song Marry Me by Train?**

She responds right away. Nice! I like that.

Alexis: Of course, who doesn't?

She's such a smart ass sometimes. I kind of like it, but it evokes a need I can't quite take care of with her, unfortunately. Down, boy!

Me: Have you ever heard the version by Martina McBride & Pat Monahan?

Fingers are crossed. I want to sing with her again, badly.

Alexis: Yes. It's my favorite version. I'm a country girl through and through. You should know that!

She is a country girl. It was one of the first things I loved about her, and clearly she hasn't strayed from her roots. That makes me proud.

Me: Will you sing it with me, tonight? For the bride and groom's first dance? It's supposed to be my gift to them.

Alexis: Garrett, they want to hear you, not me. I'll just stand by the stage and try to look pretty.

Oh please, she thinks if she stands by the stage she'll go unnoticed. I know better. Every eye in the room will be on her. Guaranteed!

Me: Please? It'll be so much better if you sing with me. It's been too long. What can I do to convince you, Lex? Name it? Any price, deed or favor.

I'm begging her, and damn well praying she wants a deed or a favor, but I'd pay any price. I know her too well, though. She'll do it if she wants to, but if she doesn't want to, there'll be nothing I can do to convince her.

Alexis: Ugh! Only if you come up to my room with your guitar so we can practice. I don't want to wing it and I'll need LOTS of practice so I don't make a fool out of you, which will likely happen anyway. You've been warned!

Fan-Fucking-Tastic! I'm a lucky-ass guy! This girl hasn't let me down yet!

Me: Sweetheart, you could never make me look foolish! I'm on my way up. See you in a few! BTW…THANKS and I meant it when I said, name your price, deed or favor!

I grab my Martin case and bolt to the end of the hall. I take the stairs, since I only have to go down one flight. When I reach her door, I knock once before Kelsey opens up.

"Well, good morning, early riser! I hear you're taking our girl to a snazzy wedding tonight. Thanks for the heads up. If you would've told us before, we could've acquired more appropriate wedding attire."

I reach for my cellphone dialing Josh, my assistant. I

briefly instruct him to make arrangements for the ladies to shop on my account anywhere they'd like. I have Kelsey relay her cell phone number to Josh then reach into my wallet and hand over my black Amex to Kelsey, flippantly telling her, "Go buy her whatever she would want. Pamper her. Her coming to this wedding with me is the best news I've had in years. Buy her whatever will make her happy to be there. Josh will make arrangements for you. Be sure to call him if you need anything." I've learned over the years that giving a chic a credit card and telling her to buy whatever she wants makes them go a bit starry eyed, just like Kelsey is doing now.

"Eeeeeekkkk! Whit, Cami, let's go. We have some shopping to do to get our girl ready for her ball tonight," she says, mock dancing and twirling around.

Alexis looks at me with concern pooling in her eyes and…anger. Those emotions are quickly gone and replaced with feisty.

"ABSOLUTELY NOT! Kels, give him back that card, right now! I can buy my own clothes," she says, reaching for her purse and snatching out her wallet. "Here, take my credit card and get me a nice dress that I can perform in, and shoes that I'll be able to stand in."

Kelsey looks from me to Alexis and shrugs, ignoring Lex's nasty snarl and tone. Kelsey, Cami, and Whit blow kisses toward Alexis and say their goodbyes without taking her credit card. I'm thrilled that I get to spoil this little lady. I've never wanted to spend my money on a dress and shoes before, but damn if this doesn't feel great!

I walk past Lex to sit in the chair in the corner with my guitar case. She's scowling at me, not nearly as happy as I am about me buying her a dress. She may be the only girl I've met who didn't want me to buy her anything. She didn't even want me picking up the tab at the bar last night. She knows how much money I make, and that I can afford to splurge on her a little.

She's frustrated and giving me this adorable little dirty scowl. I know she's trying to intimidate me, but damn if she's not making my cock twitch. She's failing miserably at staying mad. She's too damn cute for her own good. So, I just sit and smile at her. I can wait this out. I know she can't stay mad. I've smiled more in the last twelve hours than I have in the last twelve days. She's the only one I want right now, so I'll take her happy, mad, frustrated, content, or any other way! I start playing the chords to the song and she finally relents.

"Garrett, you and I are going to come to some agreements. Got it?" she says, as I laugh. She's just throwing a little fit because she didn't win the argument of who's paying for the dress. That's okay. She can throw as big a fit as she wants, as long as she wears the dress I pay for.

"Whatever you say, lady," I tell her. Knowing the bell for end of the round has been rung and my arm is held high!

We start rehearsing the song we're singing at the wedding tonight. I feel pretty confident in her ability to wing it, but if this makes her more comfortable, and allows me more time in the same room with her, I'll do whatever she wants. We sing in perfect harmony. I knew we would. Her voice is very well suited to the song. I think she could probably sing anything she wanted. She's quite talented, but has no interest in pursuing music as a career. She never has.

Watching her sing to Sierra this morning just about brought me to my knees. The look on her face was one of great joy. You could hear so much love and pride in her voice.

She would do anything for her child, and I suspect becoming a single parent hasn't been easy. She is strong, though. I'm not sure there is much in this world she can't overcome.

I overheard her talking to her brother about having to go to another parent/teacher conference alone. I wish she didn't have another hurdle to overcome. It's not like she's led a charmed life. She's always had struggles, but I've never heard her complain about them or make excuses because of them. Damn Jed, I didn't want him to have Alexis all those years ago, but he got her, and now I'm pissed at him for not being here to go to that conference and hold her hand. Great, now I'm putting my frustrations on her dead husband. I'm an ass!

We sing together for a little while, and talk a lot about music. She still enjoys talking about music. She asks about my career, my writing, and touring. She's under the impression that all artists love the fame, and is quite surprised when I tell her that's my least favorite part of the job. If I could make music, perform, and have people leave me alone off stage, I would be so happy. It's not that I don't appreciate the fans. I do, I love them, I just don't like the stalking and lack of privacy. I miss being able to sit in a restaurant, or take a walk in the park, without constantly looking over my shoulder for who's snapping photos and what they'll say when they're posted online. The rumors are torture.

I heard Alexis talk to Sierra about going to Disney World. Will I ever have a life where doing something so public is possible? I haven't been to Disney in years. I guess I didn't know I wanted to go until I found out Alexis would be going with Sierra. Now, I want to go really bad, too.

Alexis thinks all my dreams have come true because I'm doing what I always strived for all those years. But I'm thirty-two, I want a family, I want my house to have handprints on the walls, and my swimming pool to be full of toys. I want to watch my kids hang on the fences as they watch horses in the pasture. I'm not sure any of those dreams will ever happen. Who would want to be part of a life where I can't take them anywhere? Living a very public life is hard.

Chapter Six

Alexis

THE GIRLS ARE BACK from their shopping adventure; although, I'm still pissed that they didn't take my card and are walking in the door with *bags* and *bags* of crap. It was nice spending time with Garrett talking about music, life, and everything in between.

"Seriously, I'm going to a wedding, not freaking getting married! What the hell is all that?" I ask as they walk into the room with huge smiles, completely ignoring me. Kelsey walks to Garrett and tells him he needs to get lost for a few hours. She returns his credit card, letting him know she did some real damage. He laughs, replying, "Glad to hear it!" Real damage…shit! What in the world are those idiot best friends of mine thinking? I know what I'm thinking. I'm going to kill them all with very little remorse! UGH…

He walks over to me, and bends to kiss my cheek. I feel

the stampede again. "Don't be mad, sweetheart. They want to spoil you and take care of you as much as I do. Humor us for a minute, okay?"

Okay, let me say when he looks at me like that, I think I'd agree to anything he wants. I lift my arms and wrap them around his shoulders, giving him a tight squeeze, before willing myself not to stay there too long. Embracing him is so comfortable it takes all I have not climb up his body and hoist myself into his arm. "Garrett, thank you for whatever's in those bags," I say, trying to appear nonchalant, "but mostly, thank you for hanging out with me all day instead of the other more important people you need to spend time with." He sacrificed his day to be with me, and although, I do feel a bit guilty, I really am grateful. Today I forgot how hard the last eighteen months have been. I remembered myself, my hobbies, my friends. I saw more than just a glimmer of the old Alexis. She was here…front and center, hanging out. It was a great day!

After Garrett leaves, I not so successfully chastise my best friends for taking advantage of Garrett's generosity and buying out Nordstrom. They must have spent thousands of dollars. There are multiple dresses, shoes, outfits, handbags, and all kinds of cosmetics. I don't even wear much makeup, only a little gloss and some eye shadow. Ugh, these girls are going to be the death of me.

It doesn't take long for me to get ready. If I must say, the girls chose the perfect lace, fitted and flared sleeveless dress in taupe with a black velvet belt around the waist by Adrianna Papell. They bought a pair of Jimmy Choo wedge pumps in black. My hair is in soft curls, tied low, and draped over my shoulder with a beaded hair accessory. It's all beautiful, comfortable, and I feel very pretty in it. It's me, not too dressy, but girly and fun.

I make sure to call Sierra before leaving, since I'm not really sure when I'll have a few minutes to talk to her later. I promised I would call. I'll never break a promise to her.

Garrett knocks on the door to escort me down to the wedding ceremony, which is being held on the beach, while I'm still trying to calm myself in the bedroom. I'm really nervous. I'm not completely sure why, but part of me knows that I don't come close to measuring up to the actresses and models I've seen him with in magazines. I'm not sure it matters. It's not like he wants me beside him as anything more than a friend from the past. He's definitely not charting a course to get in bed with me. I'd never compare in that way.

I walk out to the entry room where Kelsey and Cami are chatting with him about the events of the evening. Whit takes my arm and whispers in my ear, "Whatever happens tonight let it be. Don't try to evade feelings and emotions you know you can't avoid."

I look to her and stop and whisper, "What are you talking about, Whitney?" What does she see? It's obviously clear to her, yet not at all to me.

"Sweets, that man is all wrapped up in you, and you deserve to be happy and treated like a princess. Try not to over think this. You have a tendency to self-destruct when you're scared."

Wrapped up in me? Doubtful. He needed a date. I happened to be here. We like talking and hanging out, but this is a friendly thing. I'm not sure my brain could handle if it were more, but my body is another story. It warms at the sight of him.

I walk over to Garrett, who looks at me with those beautiful gray eyes that light up the room when he smiles. "Look at you, beautiful girl. Wow. I guess I won't have to be worried at cameras pointing at me tonight." He says. The girls all laugh.

"You like, Garrett? Money well spent?" Cami asks, knowing he approves from the look on his face.

"Ladies, I'm pretty sure a hefty sack would look like a red carpet gown on this beautiful girl. Thanks for taking care of her today while she and I spent some time catching up," he says to the girls, as he takes my hand and escorts me from the room.

While walking down the hall toward the elevators, he looks over his shoulder to verify we're alone. Then he sweeps me into a little hall off to the side. "Lex, I can't wait, not another minute. You're beautiful and these lips…" he says, running the tip of his finger around the edge of my bottom lip as I'm pressed against the wall by his hips. "I'm going to kiss you now. Any objections?" he asks. But my voice box is broken. I can't muster any words. So after several seconds he says, "I take that as acceptance." And he launches an assault on my lips. It's aggressive and fiery, but precious and tender at the same time. My body comes alive. Like it's been comatose for years and is finally waking up. He's makes me feel like a real woman, a little bit strong and more myself by the minute.

When he finally releases me from his captivating kiss, he brushes his finger down my face and looks me directly in the eyes. "Lex, you're amazing, but if I don't put a little space between us for a second, I'm not sure we'll make it to this wedding." But he hasn't stepped away. I'm still pressed firmly between his hips and the wall.

"Okay, that starts with taking a step back." He does, but

groans under his breath as he retreats. He takes my hand in his, kissing it, and we walk hand in hand toward the beach.

The ceremony was beautiful. Garrett's family has been very nice and accommodating. His parents seem a bit over zealous, but it's apparent their only child is the love of their lives. They ask a lot of questions about Sierra and me in a conversational way, not interrogating. I can tell they're genuinely interested.

When we finally make it through the crowds of people waiting to say hello to Garrett, we go directly to the banquet room. Garrett and I are singing the song for the first dance then we can enjoy the rest of the party with the other attendees; although, I'd rather be alone with him. After that kiss, the one I knew I wanted, but hadn't imagined how amazing it would actually feel, I can't wait to be alone with him again.

This is my last night here. We're packing up after brunch tomorrow and heading back home. It's bittersweet. I can't wait to get my hands on my little munchkin, but it's been so nice reconnecting with Garrett, too. I'm not really ready to say goodbye for God knows how long.

I want to ask Garrett to keep in touch with me, but I don't want him to feel the pressure of one more person wanting something from him, even if it is only a phone call or text every once in a while.

We perform the song. They're all very pleased to hear Garrett sing, and they thank us, telling us how much they liked it as we work our way through the room to a table in the back. I suspect Garrett chose this table for a quick escape. I'm learning he doesn't really like crowds, which is funny since he performs at venues with tens of thousands of people all the time.

The rest of the evening passes with us eating, drinking, and sometimes dancing. Garrett likes to slow dance. He's not much for breaking it down with anything fast. That's okay. I like dancing to the slower songs, with him holding me tight in his arms. I'm dying to lean into him and kiss his face, but I know that's not appropriate since there are so many eyes on us constantly. It's been a long time since anyone has held me, dancing. Jed didn't like to dance. He actually didn't really like to listen to music, unless he was in the car. He preferred television, movies, and video games. I wasn't much for that type of noise.

That's one thing that has changed drastically in our house since Jed passed away. Now it's always filled with all kinds of music. Sierra loves to sing and dance with me. She still watches her favorite shows, but mostly we like to listen to music and read.

The night is coming to an end. The girls don't really expect me back early. I thought they might be upset with me for ditching them to hang out with Garrett all day, but they weren't. They were happy to see me doing *something out of the ordinary*, as Whit says. I guess this is yet one more glimmer of my real self coming back to life. It's just something else to be grateful to Garrett for giving me.

It was really great singing with him again. I'm not really a fan of performing publicly, but it was worth it to be on stage with Garrett. I love singing, but I would never want it to be my life. I want a family life. Even after losing Jed and my happy ever after, I still see myself with more kids someday, and a husband who thinks the sun and moon rises and sets behind me. That dream is still there living vividly inside me. I know it sounds as farfetched as, 'I wear Cinderella's slippers, have no wicked step-sisters, live in a big castle with prince charming, and we all live happily ever after.' I need to lower my expectations on what my new life will really look like. Otherwise, I'll be setting myself up for failure, and likely heartbreak, at my unachievable dreams.

We say our goodbyes to Garrett's family and friends, leaving the party behind a bit earlier than I expected. I walk a couple steps ahead of Garret toward the elevators.

"Alexis, can we go sit on the beach for a little while? I really want to spend these last few minutes of our night alone with you." Alone, yes, I want more time alone with Garrett.

"I'm only too happy to oblige, Mr. McKenna," I say, highlighting my good southern girl drawl. "Thank you, sir," I say with a curtsy.

"Why are you thanking me, sweetheart?" he asks, sweeping me in the opposite direction, toward the beach. I love it when he calls me sweetheart. I've never had a pet name like that. Jed always called me Alexis, or sometimes honey, but not very often.

"I guess I wasn't really ready for the night to end. I was thanking you for reading my mind again, Mr. McKenna. You seem to be able to do that often."

We walk out to the beach and sit on one of the double beach loungers overlooking the ocean. We're back to the comfortable silence for a bit before I hear Garrett clear his throat. "Lex, I need to tell you something."

I look over at him, mentally preparing myself to hear all the excuses as to why he can't keep in touch with me, but instead he says, "Sweetheart, seeing you these past two days has been the best thing to happen to me in a long, long time. Now that we've reconnected, I'm not sure I can let you walk out of my life. I really need to know in what capacity you have space for me in your life. I'll take whatever you have to offer, darling. If I can text or call every once in a while, that's great, but really I want to see you. I want to visit you and you visit me. I want to hear your voice on the phone when I'm on the road, and I really want to meet that beautiful little angel of yours. But I'm at your mercy. Tell me what role I can have in your life."

I feel excitement welling in my stomach. This weekend has been magical, but I'm a bit unsure of how it will translate in my real life. This is vacation life. It'll be really different when I'm home. I have responsibilities. I have Sierra, and there's no way I'll ever allow anything into her life that could cause any harm. She needs me, and it takes every ounce of time and energy I have to fill the role of two parents. This situation, although it's wonderful, exciting, and fun, isn't real. Not for me. This is a happy ending for someone else. Some-one whose life is more suited to his. I feel tears burning in the back of my eyes, but I refuse to allow my fear to overpower this situation. I want to enjoy this time.

He makes me happy with his words. No wonder he's a famous songwriter and performer. He's really good. I can't believe this man has brought me to happy tears twice in the same day. "Garrett, I'm so glad you said that. I don't want to lose contact with you either. You're a very important friend. I have missed you terribly, but I need you to know my life is complicated. With that being said, please visit me…and Sierra. If we can ever make it work, we would love to visit you. She loves horses and would love to visit your ranch in Nashville." Then in my effort to keep things fun, I slug him more gently in the stomach this time, since I hurt my hand on his bicep this morning, and say, "I did tell you this morning I would sing to you about caterpillars and butterflies if you needed me to."

I'm laughing even though a few happy tears have escaped my eyes. He's smiling when he pulls me onto his lap to hug me and hold me close. We sit looking at the ocean with my back leaning into him and his chin resting on the top of my head. I'm listening to his breath, feeling the strength of his heartbeat on my back. It's comfortable, making me want so much more. Even though, we're so close, it's not enough. It's dark out here, and the beach is thankfully empty, because before I even realize what I've done, I'm turned around grabbing his face and pulling his lips back to mine, desperate to taste him.

Chapter Seven

Garrett

THANKFULLY, SHE'S THE aggressor this time. I wouldn't have been able to hold off much longer. My heart rate is through the roof, well, it would be if we were under a roof, having her in my lap, with her perfect little ass pressing into my crotch. My cock is hurting from being lodged so tightly in these dress pants.

She's straddling my legs, doing powerful things to my tongue that strongly resemble what I want her to do to my cock. But I can't go there. Not with Lex. She's not that type of girl. I wouldn't want her to be. I'm going to have to reign this shit in right quick, before we do something I know I wouldn't regret, but I'm not sure she wouldn't.

"Lex, baby, you feel amazing, and stopping you is going to kill me, but…babe, I don't think you really want to do this now…here…we should…." I'm trying so hard to say 'stop', but I just can't do it. I grab her perfect little ass and pull her down hard against my lap. Even through my pants I feel the warmth pooling between her legs and I can imagine what she would feel like. "Sweetheart…we need to go right now."

I pull her up off the lounger and kiss her senseless, before putting my arm around her shoulder and bringing her to somewhere private. I want to get her back to my room. I can't risk letting pictures like this be taken. Not with her, not here.

When we get to the elevator, her face is pale, her cheeks are still flushed, and her perfect lips look swollen. I rub my finger around them. "Lex, do you want to go to my room? Do you need more time before going to your room?"

She shakes her head looking me, alarmed. "No, my room. Please, Garrett. I need to go," She says frantically, so I push the button for her floor.

"Lex, I didn't stop that for my benefit, sweetheart. You know that, right? I didn't want anything to happen that you'd regret, especially not in public where people like to take photos of me. Babe, I want you…in any way that you want me. That's what you need to know," pleading that she doesn't view what I did as me rejecting her. I'm not…I couldn't…I don't want to stop, but I need Alexis to tell me she wants to continue!

"I know, Garrett, but this is wrong. I don't understand these feelings, but I just lost my husband and I have a little girl, who needs my undivided attention. I can't do this. Not now. I need a minute." She steps back, putting more space between us, and as soon as the elevator doors open, she bolts down the hall.

"Alexis, wait. Please. Give me a chance. I need to tell you..." She stops, directing looks at me with scared eyes halting my words.

"No, Garrett, this is about me. You're phenomenal, amazing, and so full of love, life, and passion. I'm sorry, I let this go too far. Please, just be my friend. That's all I can do right now," she says. I reach for her, but she shakes her head. "Sorry, not now. I'll…I'll talk to you soon," she says.

What the hell does soon mean? Tonight? Tomorrow? Next week, month, year? What? So I stand there utterly confused and frustrated, because I damn well knew better than to let it go too far and I did it anyway. She's hurting, and she's walking away. I'm praying to God it won't be for too long, because I can't stay away now that I've found her after all this time. She's like a magnet drawing me closer and closer. I can't muster enough strength to not go to her, but I have to, for her sake. I'll step back and give her the minute she asked for. I'm quickly learning that I hate her long ass minutes.

I watch her walk away from me into her room. I hate this ending. It wasn't my intention, when I saw her in that bar yesterday, for this to happen. I mean, yeah, I'm no idiot, I wanted her, but I wanted it to happen the right way. I didn't expect to nose dive off a damn cliff and become head over heels into her again. I'm such a stupid ass. Of course that would happen. I never really got over her and what she meant to me then. How could I expect to feel differently now?

I take the stairs to my room. Damn! This day started so perfectly. How did it fall apart so quickly? Was it because I said we needed to get indoors? Did she take it the wrong way? Is it just too soon? Am I not the right man? I think that's it. I'm not a dad. I don't know the first thing about kids. I'm not even a real man. I don't do anything for myself. I travel the country performing, and when I'm not doing that I'm writing and sitting around a studio. I don't have a typical 9 to 5 job where I'm home for dinner. I'm not sure my life could ever be that simple.

SHIT! Why did this happen? Why now? Why her?

I lay in my room staring at my cell phone waiting…willing…pleading for answers, or any indication from her that she's okay. I get nothing. No answers, no messages or texts, no sleep, no feeling better, nothing!

Chapter Eight

Alexis

WE LEFT THE RESORT AFTER breakfast the next morning. I was quite ready to get on the road with Whit and get home to my baby girl. I said goodbye to Cami and Kelsey. We agreed to have dinner together in the next couple weeks. Whit knew, as soon as I walked into our room last night, that something went down with Garrett. I completely lost it when I finally got out of my clothes.

I wanted every second with Garrett. I didn't want to stop what was happening on the beach. I would've kept going if not for him stopping us. He has this amazing power to jolt my system back to life and make me feel like myself again. But I'm not just me. I'm Alexis Phillips, whose husband died and is now a single mother to a four year old little girl. I have to stay focused in order to keep my life from becoming derailed by these lust driven needs. I don't have time for those kinds of needs.

I hate that I hurt him. I could see the hurt in his eyes when I walked away. It was torture not to run back to him, climb into his arms, and let him make me forget. I wanted to forget it all, until I remembered who I am and the responsibilities I have, and that's when the guilt engulfed me.

Garrett met us in the lobby before we left this morning to say goodbye. He seemed to be having a hard time. He stared at me with a weird look on his face. Last night must have been a doozy for him, too. I'm not the type of girl he's usually seen with. I'm sure he realizes the mistake. He looked very stressed and anxious. I know I've caused this situation. I'm a bit worried about him, but I also know there's no way to fix it.

On the drive home Whitney was very quiet at first, but that didn't last long. "Alexis, you're twenty-nine years old. Your life doesn't have to be over because your husband died. You're young, sweetie. No one will fault you for living a fulfilling life. Garrett's a great guy. He obviously thinks you're incredible. Can you please, for the love of God, give it a chance? Give him a chance? Do something other than nothing."

This was the tone for the rest of the ride home. Whitney finally drops me off at my house after round six of the *'move on'* lecture. I'm emotionally exhausted at this point!

I'm happy to be back home with Sierra. My house smells so nice when I walk in the door. I know Kate must have gotten there before me and started dinner. As soon as I round the corner to the kitchen I see my angel with her little apron on, sitting on the counter helping Kate roll meatballs to put in the homemade sauce.

She squeals when she sees me, waving her nasty little

hands at me to come and pick her up. "Hey, sweet girl. How was your weekend? I missed you!" I wipe her hands on a dish cloth, and then scoop her up as she wraps her little body around me.

"I love you, Mama. We're making you dinner." She's what makes me better. She's what makes me forget.

"Why, thank you. You guys know just how to spoil a mama who's been away all weekend. We should probably be making dinner for Auntie."

She shakes her head, "No, Uncle Jason gots a baby sitter and they're going on a special date night!"

Kate is smiling at us. "That's right, ladies, I got a hot date with Uncle Jason in a couple hours. I'm going to scram. Enjoy dinner, Alexis. Welcome home. Hope you had a great weekend." She kisses us both on the cheek, and I tell her I'll call her tomorrow. And I will because if she finds out from anyone other than me, there'll be hell to pay. I'm sure of it.

Sierra and I spend the rest of the day together. We walk to the park to play, we have lunch on the lawn in the backyard, we read books, and we sing. Dinner is fantastic, as always. Kate made enough for a small army. She doesn't know how to cook for just two people. After dinner we start our night time routine. Since it's a school night Sierra will need to be in bed at 7:30, and then we'll read and sing until 8:00. Usually, she falls asleep while I read. I like that it relaxes her.

My phone chimes with a text from Garrett.

Garrett: Hi sweetheart, did you make it home ok?

I wasn't expecting to hear from him so soon. I wasn't 100% sure I'd ever hear from him again.

Me: Yes, thank you for checking on me. All good.

Garrett: I was hoping I could call you later. You said you would sing to me every day if I wanted and I do. Does that still apply after last night? I'm sorry…again. I hope you know that.

Why is he sorry? I'm confused. I initiated, I ran away, it was all on me. I don't want him to ever question our friendship. We can always be friends.

Me: I'm getting Sierra ready for bed. Do you want me to call you after she is in bed? Or you can call me after 8:00 whenever you're not busy.

I know his schedule is more restrictive than mine. He probably has a line of people waiting to talk to him. I can certainly wait for his call, since I'll be reading in bed, *or rehashing what went down last night and trying to sort out my thoughts.*

Garrett: Sweetheart, you will never have to wait to talk to me. You call me whenever you want to, whenever you have time. I'll always answer your call.

He shouldn't commit to things he can't follow through on. That's just crazy. I will keep my expectations low on that.

Me: ok…will call you after 8:00? Would love to talk to you if you're available. If not call me whenever. XO

Garrett: I will be available. XO I like that!

Sierra is out like a light. She's tired from her eventful weekend. Me too. I got very little sleep hanging out with Garrett. And last night Whitney kept me up forever, telling me how I need to let this happen naturally and stop trying to control and over think things. It was a marathon lecture that ended with me feeling worse than before it started.

I think I'll try and turn in early tonight. I'm not sure if I really should call Garrett tonight. He asked me to call, but I'm not sure what to say about last night. I guess I should give him a brief call, since I said I would. I won't keep him too long. I press send next to his name. He answers on the first ring.

"Hi, sweetheart, how was your day?" he asks. I tell him about my day. It feels familiar and comforting, having someone to tell about what Sierra and I have been up to. Jed used to call at night after Sierra went down to sleep and would want the rundown of what he missed.

I don't feel any of the tension in the conversation that I would have expected, and I'm grateful that we can both move past it and remain friends. "How are you? Are you back on the road? I guess, I don't know much about your tour schedule." I'm curious where he'll be, and when, or if, I'll see him again. Truthfully, I'm still craving his touch and desperately want to be close to him, although, I'll never admit it to anyone.

"I'm still in town. I'm here for the next few weeks doing some writing for the next album," he says and I'm shocked! He's never stayed around the bay area before that I know of. I've actually never heard of him being around town, except when he's here for his show once or twice a year.

"Drew's wife is going to pop any day now. We intentionally scheduled creative time, so that he could be home for Court and their baby." He says as if reading my mind again.

"Is Drew in the band?" I don't know much about the actual band, sad to say. I only know Garrett.

"Yeah, he's the drummer."

"Is the whole band from Tampa?" That would be odd, since he didn't play with these guys when he lived here. He played the guitar without a band at that time.

"No, sweetheart, just me. Court's parents live here, though, and she's been staying with them because Drew didn't want her home alone in Nashville being pregnant. He's here in town to pick her up and take her back home. Maybe you can meet them before they leave? I'll be staying here for a few weeks, even after they leave," he says.

He's staying here for a few weeks? Wow. So, does that mean I'll get to see him? Will he *want* to see me?

"Lex, you there?"

I haven't responded yet, but, shit, what do I say? Should I ask? "Yeah….Sorry….. I didn't know you were still in town, or that you were planning to stay. That's really nice, Garrett. I hope you'll get the downtime you were hoping for." I'm reclining on my bed, drinking a cup of chamomile tea. I made the tea hoping it would calm me. It's not working. Not now, anyway. He's still close to me.

He's laughing. I don't really know why, since I'm totally freaking out! "No, I'm hoping to be very busy. See, there's this girl I know from college that I saw at the beach this weekend. She happens to live in this town. She means a lot to me, and the only thing I want to do right now is find out when I can see her. Rest and downtime aren't even on my radar, right now. So…sweetheart, when can I see you?"

Oh my…pools of warmth have invaded my body. I'm nervous and anxious, but excited and hopeful at the same time. It's emotional tug-o-war.

"Whenever you want to, Garrett. I said I would make time for you. I meant it." It's not like he'll be underfoot all the time. He's a very busy man.

"Well, sweetheart, whenever I want is right now and first thing in the morning and all day every day. So you're going to have to give me a few more guidelines."

He's insane, completely lost his mind. "Where are you staying?" I ask, wondering if he is close by, but that is doubtful since he's likely at one of the five star resorts in South Tampa.

"At my parents' house in Tampa. Actually their guest house. I'd rather be here and get home cooked meals than stay at a hotel and eat room service." His parents live in Avila Golf & Country Club, and it's only like 10 minutes from my house in Carrollwood Village.

"Garrett, do you want to come over tonight to talk? I know it's getting late, but I'm not feeling very sleepy. I don't have any coffee, but I do have tea."

I hear him draw in a deep breath. "Yeah, sweetheart, I do. Don't make anything. I'll stop at Starbucks and get your favorite. I'll see you in a half hour. Is that good?"

Oh my, yes. Maybe we can sort out what happened last night. I really need to do that before I can think about anything else. "Yes, please. I'll text you my address. See you soon."

Twenty seven minutes later he arrives, wearing loose fitting jeans that rest just above his hips and a solid black t-shirt that hugs his chest, shoulders, and arms. He's in great shape. He must spend a lot of time at the gym. He's carrying a tray with our drinks and a paper bag. I reach to help him with the tray, and he leans over to kiss my cheek.

"Thank you for the XO earlier in your text message. I needed that. That held me over until I could come and get the real thing. I wasn't sure when you'd let me see you again."

With a smile I reply. "We'll work something out, Garrett." Whenever he wants, is what I wanted to say, but even I know that's not really how this will play out. However, being around him makes me feel safe and special, warm and tingly. I think that warm and tingly sensation is right between my thighs. Oh no! This cannot be happening. I gotta reign this in, or I'll be taking my clothes off before the night is over. I don't want to be just another notch in his belt. I want to be his friend, like the old days.

Chapter Nine

Garrett

SHIT…THIS GIRL HAS TOTALLY turned my world upside down. I can't sleep. When she's not beside me, I'm constantly checking my cell phone. Yesterday was an unbelievably great day, but last night took a turn when things got a bit too hot and heavy. I need to be careful.

I talked to Whitney today. She said Alexis is having a hard time feeling worthy of anything good in her life. This little lady has had a seriously hard life; and I'm ready for that shit to change. She's amazing and deserves to sit on a throne and be pampered. Maybe I'll buy her a throne.

Tonight she basically told me I could call her whenever I could fit her into my schedule. That pissed me off. At this point I would stomp on anyone who got between her and me talking. I really need to talk to her to see where her head is about us. Damn, she lost her husband last year, and I'm not sure she's ready for what I want with her.

"Lex, we need to talk about what that means. Where should we sit?"

She points to the sliding glass door off the family room. It's a beautiful house, not at all what I expected of her home. It's not really girly, but there are lots of throw pillows on a big leather sectional sofa with a flat screen TV on the wall, stacks of books everywhere, and lots of family pictures around. This house isn't like a museum. It's a home, a well-loved and lived in home. I actually like it a lot, even with all the toys around.

She leads the way out to the lanai. Her backyard over-looks a big swimming pool. Beyond that is a big pond. I wonder who helps her take care of this big house and yard. She's got to be sitting on an acre of land at least. Huh. I want to ask and I need to know, but I'm pretty sure that she wouldn't like that right now.

"Thank you for inviting me over, Lex. I wasn't expecting you to do that, but I sure am glad you did. I missed you today. I was dying to talk to you after last night. I'm sorry, again."

Her face is tense. I can see she's holding on to what happened, but we need to get past this shit and on to whatever is possible with us. She's so damn adorable. I love that she didn't try to dress up for me. She's wearing some short little sweat pants and a tank top. Her hair is in a messy bun on top of her head and she's wearing the cutest little glasses. She's kissable, so very kissable. It's going to take every ounce of strength I can muster to keep my lips off her.

"I wasn't expecting you to want to be here, Garrett. Can you please stop apologizing for last night? That was my fault. I'm the one that's sorry."

I don't want to keep bringing it up, but damn, I saw her

face and I feel bad. Now I'm ready to move on to better topics.

"I was sure you'd have more important things to do, but, I'm happy you had the time to come over. I like chillaxin' with you."

That's a funny word. "Chillaxin'…??? Sweetheart, what the hell does it mean to chillax, and tell me what I'm doing to chillax with you, so I can do it right. I love doing things you like. By the way, lady, nothing, and I do mean nothing, is more important to me than chillaxin with you!"

She giggles. I'm not sure there is a sweeter sound.

"It's chilling out and relaxing. Exactly what we're doing now. I like it a lot, only I usually don't have time," she explains.

I smirk at her. Shit! How can I make more time in the day. When I'm with her things are good, and I want to do more of it!

"Tell me what you do to fill your day. I want to know what it's like to walk a day in your shoes," I inquire, because I can only imagine how challenging it is to care for a child alone. Now that I see this big house and yard, I'm sure that takes up a good bit of time, too. Plus, I know she has some sort of job or work. She said she works from home. I'm not sure what she does, though. We never really got that far when we talked. I know for a fact she works out. No other woman in the world has a rocking body like she does, and that doesn't come without hard work.

"Well, tomorrow for example, my day will start around 6:30 in the morning. I'll get up, get ready, and take Sierra to school. When I get back I'll go for a run, come home and do some work, pick Sierra up from school, come home and do some chores, cook dinner, enjoy some quality time with

Sierra, go to bed, and then start all over the next day. Pretty simple, actually."

Damn, that doesn't sound simple. I thought my day was challenging. "That doesn't sound so simple at all. What kind of work do you do?" I ask, curious as to how she can fit it in with all the other stuff.

"I'm a writer, or trying to be, so I usually spend my day writing my manuscripts and reading others. I like it. I haven't published anything, yet. I'm not really ready for that, but I do love writing and reading. I'm not in a position to work a real job, since Sierra is still young and I want to be involved firsthand with what she is doing. Since Jed was responsible and prepared for the worst, Sierra and I are fine without my income. "

"She's lost so much, you know, me working a regular job and leaving her with a nanny doesn't seem fair," she explains. "Not to mention, I really never got around to getting a real job after college. Since I was getting married to Jed and he was working hard establishing his career, starting our family and building our home was my priority. So I'm not really sure who would even hire me now."

Damn, I knew that girl would do something creative with her life. I'd love to get my hands on her books. "I have a lot of respect for you. Creative writing is an amazing talent. I don't know many people that could commit to that. The sacrifices you're making for your family are commendable. But it makes me happy that you're pursuing something on your own, too. Crazy talent in that little body, lady." She's laughing. You have no idea how happy that makes me. "I'm sure publishing houses are lining up waiting for you. You're a catch!" I tell her, leaning in closer to run my fingers across her arm, needing to touch her beautiful soft skin.

"Garrett, shut up, you don't know if I am a catch in the literary world," she says, laughing.

"Baby, you're a catch in every world. And I know for a fact you're smart as hell, because you used to read me some of those papers you wrote in college. You're crazy smart, and you'd look great on the cover of any book!"

"Garrett, just shut up. You're embarrassing me." She's cute when she starts blushing, but I don't want her to stop talking, so I rub her leg just above her knee, telling her that I'll stop talking about her being such a catch and hottie.

She shivers and gets goose bumps when my hand brushes the inside of her knee. "Are you cold, sweetheart? Want me to get you a blanket, or we could go inside?"

"No, I'm fine," she says, but her face is very flush. We're sitting on an outdoor sofa that faces the pool and pond. The moon is bright and lights up the backyard with the refection off the pool and pond. It's warm outside.

"This is a really pretty house. You said you built it?" Her shoulders drop. She looks a little deflated.

"Yeah, Jed designed it. He was an architect. I basically gave him a list of all the things I would want in my perfect house and he tried to find a way to design it based on my wish list, with a lot of extras. At one point, I thought this house would be a family home. I wanted 3 children, so did Jed. We were just starting to think about our second child when the accident happened. But now that it's just Sierra and me, it's a lonely house. The dreams I had for us in this home seem like they may never come true. I've been thinking about selling it, but even that seems too hard to consider. I don't know. Anyway, to answer your question, we designed it and had a contractor build it. We were involved in every detail, though. This house kind of feels like my first kid." She looks so sad talking about the house, but it's a feeling I understand. Some dreams you want so badly, but you just have no idea how in the world you'll ever make them reality. That I understand all too well.

"I'm sorry, sweetheart. I know that's not what you want to hear right now, but Lex, I really am sorry. I hoped you would always lead a charmed life. I hate that you've had such hard things to deal with in this last year or so. I want you to know I'm here for you. I mean…I want to be here for you, and help out with whatever you need. I don't know if you have a go to guy in your life, but, baby doll, I want to be him." She looks like she's getting a little pissed. I'm not really sure what I said that was wrong, but I think I'm about to find out. She's not really a quiet, keep it under the lid kind of girl.

"Garrett, I'm not sure what you are asking me. I don't need a chore boy, if that's what you want to know. Remember, I have a control freak of a brother, and he makes sure the yard crew comes as scheduled. I have a fantastic housekeeper, who has been helping me since Sierra was a baby. If you think I need someone to sweep in and rescue poor little me and that's why you're here, you can leave. I'm happy to rekindle a friendship, but I'm sick to death of people wanting to take care of me. I'm perfectly capable of taking care of myself and my little girl without damn egotistical superstars sweeping in. Got it? Do you even understand how insulting what you just said *is*?" Her little fists are pumping, and her knuckles are turning red as blood, then white as milk. She's really pissed. I gotta fix this shit. I think she misunderstood what I was trying to say.

I jump out of my seat fast and kneel on the ground directly in front of her. "Lex, that's not what I meant. I just want to be here for you, too."

I grasp her face in my hands and pull her lips directly to mine, willing her to open them, so I can taste her. She struggles for less than three seconds before she gives in to her desire, which I know is as strong as my own, or I wouldn't be sitting here. I kiss her and taste her goodness.

I let go of her face and wrap my arms around her waist, lifting her up as I stand, and then sitting back down on the sofa. I place her on my lap when I sit without breaking the contact of our lips. We sit this way, kissing, while I rub her back. I'm pretty sure I feel a little moan vibrate on my tongue. My cock, which is already being crushed in my jeans, twitches and I'm sure she felt it because she jumps. "I'm sorry, sweetheart, I can't really control that when you're sitting on my lap, kissing me with those perfect little lips."

She looks a little embarrassed, "I'm sorry, Garrett. I don't want you to think I invite men over to my house all the time after Sierra goes to bed to do…to do this. I don't ever. I mean, I haven't ever. Not at all…since Jed. That's why last night was hard for me. I was enjoying doing this with you, then when you pulled away I remembered and felt so…so guilty."

Let me get this straight…she's worried I think this is a common occurrence for her, and she's feeling guilty because of her dead husband? "Baby, I know you better than that. I'm the one who's sorry. You were so mad at me and I just wanted you to not be mad. I was a bit desperate and kissing you was the best and quickest way I could think of to fix that."

I continue, "Lex, I don't want to be your chore boy, sweetheart. I want to be your guy. I want to be the one you talk to at the start and end of every day. I want to mean more to you than the damn lawn guy. Baby, I want to kiss you just like this and hold you tight every chance I get. I want to meet Sierra, and all of us go places and do things together."

My mouth is running away with words. Shit, I'm worried to death that I'm scaring her. "But, Lex, if all you'll let me be is your chore boy, honey…I'll take it. I'll do almost anything to be close to you. If you don't want any of what I just said, tell me, and I'll shut it down, but honey, walking out of your life completely will never be an option for me at this point. We can be friends, you can be my girl, I can be your guy, or …I'll just be the lawn boy. You tell me."

She's squeezing my shoulders. This conversation is making her tense, but we have to get it out there. "Garrett, I haven't been in a relationship since Jed. I'm not sure I'm ready for that. But kissing you feels nice, really nice, and I like you. Can you just give me a minute to process what's happening?"

Damn, I know how long her minutes are…her minute sucks!

"By the way, the chore boy and lawn guy positions are filled. But I don't have anyone to call me at the start or end of my day, so I guess I'll let you try that out on a trial run." She winks, laughing at me.

Oh, hell no! I tickle her on her hips and she squirms on my thighs, belly laughing. Damn, I'd kill to hear this sound every day.

I'm thrilled she partially agreed to let me into her life. "Trial run, huh, lady. I'll show you a damn trial run." I continue tickling her, until she plasters her lips directly over mine and kisses me with the will to possess me. I'm distracted from tickling her and more interested in learning all the curves of her body. I place my hands on her hips, rubbing her from her hips to her back. I hear that little moan again, and she flexes her hips forward grinding only once right on my cock. Hot damn, she is worked up and wanting to be touched. I'm the guy to do it! "Lex, baby, can I touch you here?" I ask her, my hands hovering over her perfect breasts.

"Yes," she moans.

Sliding my hands under her shirt, I lift her tank top. Her skin is so damn soft. I could spend all my days and nights caressing her and still not ever have enough.

Her hand is on my chest mimicking what I'm doing to her under her shirt. I need her hands on my bare skin desperately, so I lean back and start to lift my shirt. She's immediately game for that plan, because she jerks my shirt up over my head and throws it over her shoulder. Her lips return to mine. We're touching and caressing each other.

She leans back, looks me up and down, takes a sharp intake of breath and says. "Garrett, you're beautiful," as she rubs her little hands over my upper body. She's tracing the tattoo on my upper arm and shoulder. She's mesmerized by the look of it. It's not exactly your run of the mill tattoo. It's a tribal band with a court jester above. I'm really worked up and so is she. I'm not sure if she wants this to continue, but I know I'm towing this line carefully.

"Baby, I love doing all this with you. I don't think I've ever loved anything more, but if we don't stop this right now, I'm not sure I'll be able to control myself much longer."

She looks a little frustrated. I can see her mind is working in overdrive when she starts rambling, "Yeah, I guess you're right, but it feels so good. I like feeling this good. I haven't had this feeling in a long time. I think I got a little too excited. I'm sorry."

She's sorry? I just told her how much I love touching her and kissing her, and now she thinks I don't want to do this. "Alexis, look at me." Her hazel eyes meet mine right away. "Baby, you said you needed time. If you want me to keep touching you I will, believe me I want to. I'm trying real hard not to push you too far. You need to drive this train if you want more of this, because I don't want to screw this up by doing something you don't want." She blushes.

She's biting her bottom lip, trying to avoid saying something. I remember that about her. She's very outspoken and when she feels like she can't keep her mouth shut she bites down on it. Another thing that is so damn sexy about her. "I don't want to move too fast. But, I didn't expect to feel sad about having to stop kissing you. I just want to be close to you while I can. You're going to leave me soon and I want to have this time." LEAVE HER SOON? What the hell is she talking about? I told this girl I want her. Did she not understand that?

Chapter Ten

Alexis

WHEN I INVITED GARRETT over, never in a million years would I have thought this is what we'd be doing. I thought we'd be rehashing what happened last night and plotting how to avoid it again. But it feels too good to stop. To have someone touch me, damn near worship my body with clothes on, feels incredible. I'm not sure I've ever felt this good when a man's touched me. Garrett's touch sends this rush of joy through my body, along with the stampede of butterflies.

He wants to be my guy. I'm not really sure what that means in the grand scheme of things, but I do know I want him enough that I'll let him be whatever he wants. I'm not ready to stop what we've started tonight, and since I have to conduct this train, I will.

I reach for the hem of my tank top, lifting it over my

head. I'm not wearing a bra, since my tank had one built in. He's looking at me with glassy, lust drunken eyes. He sucks in a breath and say's, "Damn, Baby. It's on!" He stands up, carrying me with him, over to the larger outdoor sofa. He lays me down on my back, kneels beside me on the ground looking over my chest, and glides the tips of his fingers up and down my chest. "Alexis, you're the most beautiful creation I've ever seen. Baby, I'm going to kiss all over you, is that okay?"

I nod my head looking directly at him. "Yes, I need you, Garrett. Now."

"Baby, tell me what you want me to do. You say it's too soon, but then say you need me. When you need something I want to make it happen. Tell me, do you want me to kiss you here?" He asks, looking at my hardened nipple and tracing it with the tip of his finger.

"Yes, please," I whimper.

He does. He kisses and licks my breast, neck, stomach, and hips. When he reaches my hips he's caressing my lower abdomen, just below the waist band of my pants. I'm dying for him to touch me lower. I'm lifting my hips, trying to give him every clue possible, but he's being cautious. My body is hot, the warmth pooling between my thighs is throbbing. There's no way I'm letting him stop. He can't!

"Lex, I promise I won't do anything you don't want, but, sweetheart, let me take care of you and make you feel good. Is that okay?"

"Yes! Yes! *Please!*" I almost yell. He slides my pants off, leaving me in my panties and him in his jeans and sneakers. I reach for his waist band to unbutton his jeans, but he shakes his head at me.

"No, baby, this is for you. Relax for me. I need to do this

right."

I want to touch him and feel him. I can already see that he's constricted in his jeans. "*That* could be for me, too, Garrett."

He smirks, his eyes filled with lust. He slides his hand into my panties, brushing his fingers against my clit. I feel the growing sensation and know I'm going to explode. We're kissing with our eyes open. He's carefully watching me. It drives me crazy and just before I know I'm about to fall apart, he tucks a finger inside me and I finally let go. "Oh my…oh my…Garrett, please kiss me," and he does.

Picking me up as he stands, cradling me in his arms, he sits back down on the sofa. He kisses me and holds me. I'm so relaxed I could probably fall asleep right here. I want to, actually. "Baby, watching you explode in my arms is the sexiest thing I've ever seen. It doesn't get any better, but I think I need to put you to bed and go, sweetheart. You look tired and you have a very busy day tomorrow. Can I carry you to bed?" he asks.

"Only if you sing me a lullaby," I say.

He smirks and laughs softly at me. "I'll sing you whatever you want, Lex."

He reaches down for my pants and slides them up my legs, then finds my top and puts that on as well. He reaches for his shirt, but doesn't put it on. He stands with me still in his arms. I've never been carried like this by a man... Garrett does it effortlessly. He navigates his way through my house all the way to my bedroom, cradling me in his arms. He pulls back the covers and lays me in the bed. "Sweetheart, I want to tuck you in before I go. Do you need to change into pajamas?"

I wish I could be tucked into bed, but I have to lock up

the house and check on Sierra. "No, it's okay. I need to lock up the house and check on Sierra. I like that you tucked me in, but I'll walk you out."

He shakes his head. "No, baby, I need to see you tucked safely into this bed. Let's go peek in on Sierra, and then get you in bed too. I'll lock up for you."

Sitting up I take him by the hand to Sierra's room. I tiptoe into the room as Garrett waits for me by the door. I kiss her forehead and brush her hair off her sweet cheek. She sleeps like a log. She's so peaceful when she's resting. I tiptoe back out of the room, cracking the door, and walk directly into Garrett's arms. He lifts me and carries me back to my bedroom. He stands me up next to him beside the bed, so I can pull off my pants, since I usually only sleep in a tank top and panties. Then I slide into the bed. His eyes run up and down the length of my body before he reaches down and pulls the covers up over my arms. I can see that he still has unfulfilled needs. I want to fix that, but he won't let me.

"Will you sing to me, Garrett?" He looks at me with those glassy eyes again, only they aren't lust filled. There's something else there that I don't quite recognize. "My old guitar is over there," I say pointing to the corner of the room.

He walks over to pick up my old guitar case. He takes the guitar out, adjusts the keys to make sure it's in tune, and starts strumming a quick soft chord before walking back to the bed. He sits beside me, and starts playing the chords to *Wanted* by Hunter Hayes and singing to me. It's the sweetest lullaby anyone could ever sing. There is so much more to this man than I ever realized. He sings to me and I rest my hand on his knee. I'm overwhelmed with the feelings he stirs up in me. I'm not really sure how to deal with them all. I feel tears prickling the back of my eyes and then spilling down my cheeks when he finishes the song.

"Baby, please tell me those are happy tears." I nod my head, because I can't possibly speak without opening the flood gates further. He bends, quietly kissing my cheeks until all the tears are kissed away. When he's successfully completed his task he says, "Goodnight, sweetheart, thank you for tonight. I'll lock up and turn the lights off." I've trusted him with my body, with my heart, with *everything*. I can surely trust him to lock up the house so that we are safe.

"Thank you, Garrett." I see a little sparkle in his eyes before he nods his head, kisses me one more time, then he walks out of the bedroom switching off the light before he does so. I hear him checking and locking all the doors downstairs. My phone is plugged in on the nightstand beside the bed, so as soon as I hear the front door close, I pick it up and send him a text.

> **Me: Thank you for tonight. I like ending my nights with you, Ace!**
>
> **Garrett: Ace? ← I think I like that too. Aren't you supposed to be sleeping? I just tucked you in. Missing you already, lady. Wake up call in the am?**
>
> **Me: Sure, Ace ← it's fitting. Start and finish my day, remember? What time do you want me to wake you?**
>
> **Garrett: I can't wait to find out why you think that name is fitting. I want to start my day**

**when you do. Call me as soon as your eyes
flutter open. I'll be dreaming of you tonight.
Sleep well.**

I will sleep well tonight. Being tucked in, loved, kissed, and sung to before bed makes me feel cherished. I do this for Sierra every night, but I've never had anyone do this for me… not my parents when I was younger, not Jed, no one. I knew it was important time for Sierra and me, but I never understood the feeling of being on the receiving end. I feel safe and secure. Garrett is special…and he's making me feel the words of the song he sang to me tonight. I can't wait till morning.

Chapter Eleven

Garrett

MY PHONE RINGS THE next morning at 6:24. I've been awake a while, just lying in bed, staring at the device, willing it to ring.

"Good morning, Garrett!"

"Good morning, sweetheart! Did you have sweet dreams?"

I hear her dreamy little sigh through the phone. "Yes, when my night ends like last night, only sweet dreams are possible."

I had some pretty sweet ass dreams, too. Seeing her fall apart in my arms was something incredible, but tucking her sweet little body into bed and singing to her as her eyes got heavy. Damn…Damn…Damn! I want to do that again every night!

"I have to go wake up Sierra, Garrett. I hope I get to talk

to you later. Thank you again for coming over last night!"

She'll talk to me today for sure, no questions asked, whenever she damn well wants! "Baby, you call me whenever you want. Always remember what I said. Anytime." We say our quick goodbyes, and she's off and running on her crazy busy day.

I need to start my day. I have a lot of phone calls to return and I need to check up on all the guys. We haven't really talked much in the last few days, since thoughts of Alexis have consumed me. I can't very well call them this early, so I'll have to make do with my other crap first. I grab my leather messenger bag off the kitchen chair and pull out my laptop.

I spend the next couple hours returning emails and speaking with Josh, my personal assistant, regarding upcoming promotional events, tour contracts, and a bunch of other stuff that takes up far too much time that should be spent writing music.

I call Drew around 11:00 to check on Court. She's like twenty-seven hundred months pregnant, or some shit like that. They're leaving Tampa tomorrow morning to head back to Nashville. They're driving back, since she can't travel by plane anymore. I want to try and have lunch with them at that little Cuban restaurant down the street that Court loves.

I push the call button next to Drew's picture. When he answers, he sounds like he's still sleeping.

He answers the phone, "What's up, McKenna?"

"Dude, do you know it's almost eleven o'clock, and your pregnant wife has missed breakfast if y'all are still in bed. I wanted to see if we could all have lunch before y'all head out," I explain my reason for calling.

"Man, my wife didn't sleep three hours last night because she says my spawn feels like it has four arms and legs inside her belly kicking her all night. That little bugger can move and kick. I'm talking legs in her ribs, beating the hell out of her. Shit, I felt bad." I laugh at the thought of Drew's kid having all those arms and legs. "I didn't understand what she was telling me when we were on the road, but damn, I got a pretty clear picture last night. I owe this girl so much pampering, and I'm spending all my time from now until whenever this little monster pops out doing just that!" He says sympathetically.

Drew is over the top in love with Courtney, a feat for that bad boy drummer. But for Drew, Courtney's the only girl in the world worth spending any thoughts on. "We can meet up when she wakes up and feels like eating, but I'm not waking her, dude."

"Sounds like you got a future drummer on your hands. Call me when Court's ready. Believe me, we all owe her. She hasn't given us any shit for being on the road as much as we have been." She hasn't been even a little bit of the pain in the ass she deserved to be. "We can't keep doing this you know. It's not fair. We need to get this schedule under control," I say, knowing we need to start making this a priority. We're getting to an age where we need to start living our real lives and not just be musicians.

"Yeah, I know. I don't want to be leaving the family behind for months at a time, Garrett. They're both coming with me next tour. Consider this your 'Heads Up'," he says in his typical no bullshit tone.

"Yeah, got it. See you this afternoon," I say before hanging up. We can't do this to our families. Even though I am not the only single band member, I still can't allow these guys to continue making this kind of sacrifice. Anyway, I think the idea of a committed relationship just got a lot more appealing to me in the last few days.

Drew calls later that afternoon to meet up at the little Cuban place. Courtney loves Cuban sandwiches. You can't really get anything that tastes this good in Nashville, so she's making sure she gets her fill before she leaves town. She tells us all about the baby and how he's keeping her awake all night, in the bathroom a hundred times a day, and hungry all the time. We laugh and talk to her about our road stories.

Court asks where I've been the last few nights. She expected me to come hang out, like I've always done in the past. Drew's my best friend. Usually we're together in the same town when we have time off. I spend a lot of time hanging out at his house, even though I have my own house right down the road. It's lonely in that big house, so I only really ever sleep, and sometimes work, there. The fact that I'm staying in Tampa, instead of going home to Nashville with them is making them curious, I'm sure.

"Is everything okay with your 'rents?" Drew asks, prying for information.

"Yeah, dude, just putting in some quality time," I explain. "It's been a while since I've been back hanging out in the old stomping grounds and haven't been prepping for a show. You know?"

Courtney frowns. "Garrett, will you come home when the baby is born? I want you to meet him."

Court's become kind of like a sister. I don't want her to be upset by my staying away, but I need to figure this out with Alexis. "Of course, girl! Try and keep me away!" I say to her and she smiles. I feel better immediately.

I decide that I need some advice about what's happening with Alexis. I know Drew and Court are the only ones I can trust with this information, so I spill the beans. "So…there's this girl." Drew drops his fork and it clatters on his plate. "I've known her since college. We lost touch, but I ran into her a few days ago."

Courtney looks surprised, but very interested. "Tell us about her." She asks.

"Well, it's Alexis." I've mentioned her several times to the guys, but never in detail, except for one drunken night a couple years ago when I told Court I thought I loved Alexis, still, and that she was the only girl I'd ever had feelings for.

"What?" She says. "I thought you said she was married, G? You can't go breaking up families. That's wrong." She looks at me sternly.

Like I don't know that! "Court, her husband died, like over a year and something ago. She's alone. I would never want to break up any family. You should know me better. But, Court, she's more amazing than I remembered. This girl brings me to my damn knees. She's got a really cute little girl, who's turning five in a couple months. Her little girl looks just like her, but I've only seen her in pictures and when Lexi checked on her after she went to sleep. I can't wait to really meet her." I'm blabbering on and on while smiling from ear to ear, telling my best friends everything I can think of about Alexis, our college years, her singing, her as a mother, the house she helped design and did all the decorating for, how beautiful she is, everything, except the private parts from the last couple nights. I don't want to share those with anyone.

Courtney looks from Drew, to me, then back to Drew and says, "Uh, we're staying a few more days. I cannot leave town without meeting the girl he's head over heels in love with. This baby is staying put at least another few weeks, anyway."

Drew nods his head. "Yeah, Court, I was thinking the same thing." He picks up his phone and sends a quick text.

"So, when can we meet her, since we're sticking around? Tonight okay for dinner?"

"Wait, guys, I'm not sure I'm seeing her tonight. She's a single mom, and really busy. Shouldn't you wait and find out if she's even available before you go changing your schedules?"

Court laughs. "Oh, if she likes you anywhere near the amount you love her, she wants to see you and meet us. Believe me!"

I take out my phone to send a text to Alexis.

Me: Hi, sweetheart. Having a good day?

She responds within seconds.

Alexis: having a happy day. Ran too far... Legs are tired but it could be that I'm getting too accustomed to being carried around instead of walking on my own! ;) How's your day?

I loved carrying her to bed, and plan on doing it again. Many times, actually.

Me: I want to do that again, real soon. I'm at lunch with my best friends. They want to meet you. They're here for only a couple more days before they have to go home to Nashville. How would you feel about introductions? I can tell

them no if you aren't up for it.

I'm pretty sure Courtney isn't going to take no for an answer, and then Drew will be all about making his wife happy and nag the shit out of me until I make it happen. But if Lex isn't ready to meet my friends there's no way in hell I'll let them near her. I told her she was going to drive this train and I meant it.

I say goodbye to Drew and Court, and tell them I'll let them know later if we can make plans.

Alexis doesn't respond right away like before. I'm getting really concerned. Fifteen minutes pass, then thirty minutes. Finally, after thirty-seven minutes I pick up my cell and press the green send button next to her name. She answers on the second ring. I hear loud music and a very small person's voice singing at the top of her lungs in the background.

"Hi," she says. "I'm sorry I couldn't respond back right away. I had to pick up Sierra. I was driving, so I couldn't text back. My car is loud right now, but this kiddo is having too much fun to stop the party. Can you hear me okay?" She doesn't sound upset, but I'm worried that my text asking her to meet my friends was too much, too soon.

Chapter Twelve

Alexis

I DIDN'T GET A CHANCE to text Garret back before it
was my turn in the carpool line at school. I had to buckle
Sierra up, and then she was rambling about her day. I like to
hear everything about her time away from me, so I didn't want
to pause her in her rambling. I figured I would just text Garrett
back when I got home.

Sierra and I are singing along to her favorite Taylor Swift
album when my phone rings. It's Garrett. "Hi," I say "I'm sorry I couldn't respond back right away. I had to pick up Sierra.
I was driving, so I couldn't text back. My car is loud right
now, but this kiddo is having too much fun to stop the party.
Can you hear me okay?" I ask.

"Yeah, sweetheart, I can hear you. You don't have to
meet my friends if you aren't ready for that. I just thought I'd
ask before they left town," he reassures me.

I don't like meeting new people. I'm not really good at it. I'm a little nervous that if they don't like me, he'll walk away. I don't think he would ask if it weren't important to him. Maybe if we could meet in a larger gathering with people I love too, it wouldn't be so bad. I could invite my brother's family over to my house for dinner, and Garrett could come with his friends, too. Huh…

"I was thinking, maybe they could come over to my place for dinner tomorrow. I'll invite Jason's family, too. It's been a while since I've had people over, but it could be fun. Would that be okay?" I don't like to get babysitters, anyway. So if he doesn't like that plan, we probably won't be able to make one. I can count on one hand the number of people I'll allow to stay with Sierra. I really hate leaving her. We're a package deal, so her being there feels right.

"Lex, I'll do whatever you want, sweetheart, but won't that be a lot of extra work for you? I can take us all out to dinner, if you would rather."

I wouldn't rather. I would feel much more comfortable in my own home. "No, I would rather be home. That way the kids can run around and play, and we can all relax. I'll call a restaurant to have a meal brought in. I'm not really good at cooking for a lot of people. I can only cook for a few. Does that work?

They would really hate me if I poisoned them with my cooking. I'm not actually a bad cook, but I only have my few meals that I do well."

"Let me arrange the food, babe. The fact that you're willing to open your house to my friends and introduce me to the most important people in your life makes me very happy, sweetheart. I don't want you doing anything extra. What time do you want us there?" he asks.

I'm so glad he's happy with my plan, because that's really all I could offer. And the first time he meets Sierra I want us to be on her home turf. "Let's do 5:30-6ish. It's a school night, and Kate will want to get the kids home early enough for bedtime." And Sierra can't miss her bedtime either, or she'll be a holy terror.

"Sounds great. I'll let you get back to y'all's girly time. Will you call me later?"

Um…his job was to start and end my day, and I'm holding him to it. "Absolutely, Garrett. Start and end the day. Remember?"

He laughs. "Yeah, sweetheart, I remember. Call me whenever you can."

Even after filling every second of my day, it's been such a long day. I have no idea why the hours passed so slowly. I stayed busy, but it went by so slowly. Sierra is FINALLY in bed. I told her we would be having company tomorrow and that my special friend from college was looking forward to meeting her. Sierra is super outgoing and loves meeting new people, unlike me. She's happy, talkative, and an overall joy. Anyone who doesn't like this little girl is just crazy! Although, she is a bit sassy sometimes and this is why I have a parent/teacher conference tomorrow, again. Her school sometimes takes themselves a little too seriously. It's a great school, but their expectations for little kids can sometimes be a little far off the spectrum. Good thing I like her teacher a lot.

Finally, after turning off all the lights and locking the doors, I drag myself upstairs to make my end of day call to Garrett while I relax in a nice long bath. I pick up my cell phone and call him as I walk into the bathroom to fill my tub with hot water and lavender bath salts.

He answers as it rings the first time. "Hi." He's speaking softly.

"Hi," I reply in the same tone.

"Did you have a good day, sweetheart?" He asks, sounding a bit melancholic.

"It was a good day for me. Just long…how about you?"

"A good day, because I get to see you tomorrow, and I talked to you three times today. But I haven't seen you in twenty-two hours. That part sucks a bit."

He's counting hours. I am too, actually. I want to see him again, soon. "Oh Garrett, you can't see me every day. That would just spoil me," I say to him, hoping to help him out of his mood, unsure what's put him in it.

"I'm all about spoiling you, Lex. I'd do it every day if you let me. I set up a caterer for tomorrow. They'll handle everything, so you can sit back and relax. Is it okay if they come to set up at five o'clock? The food will already be prepared, except for some heating," he says. I can tell he's accustomed to telling people what to do. He's a bit powerful and controlling, and I think I might like it.

"That's fine. I'll be back home after picking Sierra up from school. I promised Sierra we could make you brownies. She's excited to meet 'my special friend from college and his friends'." I relay Sierra's excitement, smiling, thinking of my little girl and her plan.

"That's fantastic. I love brownies. Lex, I'm driving separately from Drew and Courtney tomorrow. Can I stay after Sierra goes to bed tomorrow night for a little while? I miss you, lady."

He can't possibly miss me as much as I'm missing him.

Everything about him, the way he touches me, holds me, talks to me, sings to me, carries me, and every other part of him. I'm quite addicted to this man. "Yes, I would love that. Please stay."

"What are you doing now, Alexis?" he asks.

"Getting ready to soak in the bath tub. Do you need to hang up, Garrett? If you're busy, I can talk to you tomorrow." I hate to keep him from more important things. I can only imagine how many people want a part of him each day.

"Try and hang up, Lex, and see what happens. I've been waiting by my phone for hours to talk to you. I miss you. I want to stay on the phone with you until you lay your head on your pillow to sleep." Again, there's so much more to this man than I realized. He's spoiling me a little with the amount of time and attention he's giving me. I must admit that I like it.

I slip into the tub and put my phone on speaker, so we can talk while I soak. He's in the guest house on his parents' property. Garrett parents are financially very well off, so I'm sure the guest house on their property is likely larger than the average little bungalow. Other than the wedding I've only met his parents once, during parents' week ten years ago. Jason did tell me that Garrett's mother attended Jed's memorial service, but I didn't notice or speak to anyone during that time.

We talk until my bath water is cold. He tells me stories of his adventures on the road and he sings me a song that he's working on. He asks questions about Sierra and laughs at her funny little stories. He's not shocked to hear what a handful she is or that I'm being called into the school for a conference tomorrow. He even offers to go with me to just sit there beside me. I tell him I'll be fine. I've done it plenty of times before.

After my bath, I put on my pajamas and climb into bed.

I'm exhausted, but I'm not ready to say goodnight yet, so I ask Garrett to sing to me. He does, soothing a part of me I didn't realize needed it. I feel my eyes getting heavy as he finishes the second song. "Thank you, Garrett. Goodnight."

"Goodnight, sweetheart. Tomorrow morning?" he asks.

"Yes. Always," I confirm before disconnecting the phone.

Chapter Thirteen

Garrett

I STARTED MY DAY WITH Alexis again. I like our little ritual, but she's busy in the mornings and we only have time to say good morning. It's the best two minutes of my day, until I hear her voice again, that is.

I've been working with our management team this week trying to iron out the details of the upcoming promotional tour in June and July. I'm not exactly sure how that's all going to work out. I'm not really thrilled about leaving the girls, but I guess we're going to have to figure this out. The band is supposed to be on the tour for six weeks, but we break for several days in the middle. It's a U.S. tour, so thankfully no long flights.

I'm on my way over to Alexis' house. I leave early because I want to stop at the florist and get flowers. I walk into the shop and pick a large bouquet of lilies, daisies, sunflowers, and roses. Then I pick the exact same flower combination in a smaller bouquet for Sierra, with a big pink stuffed bear and a balloon.

When I arrive at the house I'm the first one there. I'm glad no one is here yet. I didn't want Alexis to have to deal with the catering company, and I want to give the girls their flowers before everyone else arrives. I knock on the front door and ring the bell, but there's no answer. I wait a couple more minutes and ring again. I know they're here. I see her Jeep in the garage through the window. I jiggle the handle and the front door is unlocked. I peek my head in and that's when I hear it.

The sound system is blaring. I walk in and yell, "Hello," but no response. I walk cautiously around the corner, because I don't want to startle the girls, and I see the most beautiful sight in the world. Alexis and Sierra are dancing around the kitchen singing at the top of their lungs. They're laughing and having fun while making my brownies.

Sierra notices me first, coming around the corner, and with no shyness at all she says, "Hi, Mr. Garrett. Mama showed me your picture. You're famous! Want to sing and dance with us?" she asks. Her blond hair is in pig tails and her bright blue eyes sparkle. She's a happy kid. It shows that all Alexis' efforts in pulling double duty are paying off.

I place the flowers into her hand with the bear. She responds by batting her cute little eyes. "Thank you, Mr. Garrett. I like flowers, and pink is my favorite color. Want to dance now?" She asks, going back to her original question.

"Yes, sweet girl, I can't think of anything I'd like to do more. Thank you for inviting me." I join in on the fun. This has to be the coolest kid. She isn't singing songs from children's television shows. She's singing popular country music songs. I wonder if she knows any of my songs. Damn, that would be cool.

Alexis is smiling, watching the interaction as we all dance around like crazy people. I look at her and say, "Hi. I knocked. I don't think you could hear me," as I hand her the larger bouquet of flowers.

"Mama, can we listen to Taylor now?" Sierra asks.

"Again?" Lex says to her little mini me. She looks over to me and says, "I apologize in advance. She's Taylor obsessed." I look at Sierra and tell her that Taylor's one of my very favorite artists, too, and that I want to hear all her favorite songs.

Sierra jumps up and down, shouting, "Stay, Stay, Stay," until Lex puts the song on. Then little Sierra sings the whole song, word for word. We dance around, singing along, while we wait for the rest of the invitees. Lex turns the music down a bit, so we can hear the doorbell, since the caterers and the company will be arriving shortly.

Lex looks beautiful tonight. She's wearing a black strapless dress and a little apron wrapped around her waist. She's baking brownies, which smell great. The doorbell rings and Sierra runs toward the door to meet whoever has arrived.

I follow right behind her to greet the caterers. I feel so relaxed here, like this is where I'm meant to be. I feel like a real man doing these normal family things with these girls, like dancing in the kitchen, bringing home flowers, and watching the girls bake brownies. It's all a bit surreal.

We head back to the kitchen to find Alexis and introduce her to the caterers. She shows them around. After the introductions, I put my hand at the small of her back to guide her out of the kitchen. I whisper in her ear, "Baby, I hired them so you wouldn't have to do anything. Now get on out of here and let them work." She laughs and walks out with me.

Jason, his wife, Kate, and their three little ones arrive next. Jason and I hung out a bit in college, so we greet each other easily. He introduces his family and tells me how nice it is to see me again. Jason is a good guy. Taking care of his sister is a top priority in his life, you can tell. He'll always have my greatest respect for that alone. Kate is spunky and a lot of fun to be around. She too loves her sister in-law. I immediately sense her protective instincts.

Drew and Courtney arrive and introductions are comfortable and everyone seems to get along fine. I notice Alexis isn't really talking to anyone, though. She's engaging with the children, but seems to be avoiding conversations with the adults. I'm not really sure what's up with that, but damn it, I'll just hang out with the kids too. I walk over to where she is kneeling by the coffee table working on a puzzle with the kids. I kneel beside her and speak softly so that only she can hear. "Hi. You okay over here, sweetheart?" She flashes a quick smile that doesn't put that little glimmer in her eyes and nods her head. Even though, her head is signaling yes, I know she's not okay. Something's up, but I'm not really sure what. She was fine before everyone arrived. I rub her back gently and just stay beside her hanging and playing with the kids. I want her to get to know Court and Drew, but she needs to do it in her own time.

The evening progresses with simple conversations, except for Alexis, who says very little to anyone. She's very shy tonight, which is not anything I've ever seen from her. When she gets up from the dinner table to refill the pitcher of sweet tea, Jason follows her into the kitchen. Obviously, he's noticed, too. I don't immediately follow. I don't want to intrude on their private conversation, but I'm worried, so I rise from my seat excusing myself to the bathroom when enough time has passed.

After returning from the bathroom I notice they aren't back yet, so I walk toward the kitchen and overhear Alexis talking to her brother. "Yes, I like him. I like him a lot, Jason. But what the hell will people think of me for jumping into a relationship after just losing my husband? I can't be reckless about this. I have Sierra to consider. You know?" She just admitted out loud to her brother she cares about me. I'm elated, but at the same time, that's what's upsetting her so I'm pissed, too. Damn!

"Alexis Nicole, you aren't a complete idiot. You've never jumped into anything. This isn't reckless. You've known the man for years! We all have. He's a good guy. It's obvious he cares about you, too, or he wouldn't have gone through all this trouble. Get your head out of your ass, sis. I've been telling you for months it's time for you to move on. It's been a year and a half. You can't keep hiding inside this house and writing your little books you never do anything with. You need to put yourself back out there. It's been long enough. We've all mourned and suffered long enough, damn it."

Okay…I've listened long enough. I need to step in here and stop this. I walk around the corner and poke my head in and ask, "Hey guys, can I come in? Everything okay?"

Jason looks over at me, and then smirks to his sister. "See, I told you, good guy, coming to check on you!" He starts to walk out of the room with a head nod in my direction and says, "Do not make me regret supporting this relationship. I like you and I want that to continue, but if you hurt her….

MAN…"

I nod, "I know. Thanks, Jason." He leaves us after smacking my back.

I look over to Alexis. "Sweetheart, you want to tell me what I've done, so I can go ahead and fix it?" She looks sad. I'd do anything to see her smile. But I don't know how yet.

"Garrett, I'm okay. Can we just talk about this after the company leaves? I've been very rude being gone so long," she says as she starts walking out of the kitchen with the pitcher of tea.

I step in front of her. "Yes, babe, we'll talk as soon as were alone, but I can't go a minute longer without a kiss. Give me those lips," I say to her, as I cradle her face in both my hands and kiss her with all the pent up emotions I feel.

She kisses me back. Then she pulls back, looking directly in my eyes she says, "I'm sorry I'm so complicated, Garrett. I'm so very broken. I'm not really sure I can ever be fixed."

I see her eyes getting glassy and I know the tears are about to spill. I've seen it enough times to know. I take the pitcher from her hands and place it on the counter. "Baby, you don't need anyone to fix you. You aren't broken. You're grieving and scared of things changing again. I get that, but you are whole, beautiful, and strong. We'll figure this out, Alexis. Give me the chance. That's all I ask." She nods her head once, looking at me eye to eye, but still says nothing.

She reaches for the pitcher and heads back to the table where everyone is chatting away. Court and Kate seem to be very involved in talking about pregnancy stuff. Kate looks up when we walk into the room and winks at Lex.

The rest of dinner goes as smoothly as possible. I'm still concerned about whether Alexis is going to make me leave tonight with everyone else, instead of having some one on one time with her. I hope not, because I know it sounds crazy, but damn, I think I might be in love with this girl. Actually…I've always been in love with her. I never stopped. I just didn't realize this is what it really was, until now. Not that I can tell her. Shit. She's already scared to death. I don't want to make it worse.

We say goodbye to our friends and family at the front door. I'm not really sure if Alexis is going to let me stay. She seems really frustrated. Alexis is wishing Courtney and Drew best of luck on the birth and safe travels back home, and saying goodbye to her family. Sierra walks over to me, as I am standing at the door next to Alexis.

"Garrett, can you pick me up?" Sierra asks in a small voice, very unlike the bouncing around and singing I heard earlier. I lift her into my arms. Her little head rests on my shoulder, as she inserts her thumb into her mouth and closes her eyes. They all immediately stop speaking and stand staring at Sierra and me. You would think I had just broken out into song, but I was just standing next to Alexis, holding Sierra like she asked me to.

Damn, it's just a cute little girl, who asked to be held. I'd do anything she asked me to, for the record, but what the hell is everyone staring at? Alexis finally looks at everyone saying she needs to get the little one in bed. Everyone leaves willingly, with huge smiles.

Alexis reaches up to take Sierra to bed, but Sierra objects saying, "Mama, I want Garrett to carry me." So I do. Alexis leads the way up to the room and I carry the little princess. I lay her gently in her bed and kiss her forehead.

"Goodnight, princess. I'll see you soon. Okay?"

She smiles. "Garrett, Mama, and I are going to Disney soon. Will you come with us?"

She wants me to go to Disney with her. I'm not really sure how that would work out. "You know what, sweet girl, I love Disney. Let me see what I can do about that. I'll certainly try." She nods her head, seemingly satisfied with my response.

I tell Lex I'll meet her downstairs, and she too nods her head. That damn head bobble she's been doing all night is driving me insane. I'm not sure how to read that.

I head downstairs to wait for Alexis. The caterers have packed up everything and cleaned. I pay, and tip them well, then send them on their way. I walk into the family room and I hear a little voice talking as Alexis helps her into her pj's. Then she's saying a prayer. "And God bless Mama, and Uncle and Auntie, all my cousins, my daddy in heaven, and Garrett."

"Yes, sweet girl. God bless them all," Alexis responds. "Let's sing your song together." And they do, while I listen over the baby monitor I find on a shelf in the family room. I don't know how much luckier I could be to have overheard that little conversation, and hearing Alexis sing to her little angel makes my heart feel very full. I haven't felt this before, but I'm becoming more and more sure as the time goes on that this has got to be love. I hear Alexis say goodnight, then she walks down the stairs toward me.

I'm standing at the bottom of the stairs. I need to make whatever she is feeling better as soon as possible. I've never wanted anything more than I want that right now. I'm desperate to know what she's thinking and what made her unhappy tonight.

She reaches the bottom of the stairs and walks into my arms. "Lex, I'm so sorry for whatever I did to upset you, sweetheart. Can we talk now…so I can fix it?"

She's frowning, as I pick her up and walk her over to the couch, sitting down to cradle her in my arms. I need to be close to her, so that she can feel our connection. I'm scared that if we break that touch she could forget what this feels like and push me away.

"Garrett, you didn't do anything. It was just an odd night - my family and your friends all under one roof. We meshed and everything is happening so quickly…too quickly. I feel like I haven't really been able to take a breath. And now Sierra thinks you've hung the moon. She's never asked anyone to hold her that way when she's sleepy. She usually only wants me." She sighs, pausing for a few moments before she continues, "Garrett, I'm really scared. You're making me feel things and want things that I didn't know were possible."

Shit, I understand that. This girl is making me feel things…more and more. She's making me want to be a person I've never imagined being, one worthy of a girl like this. A family man?

Chapter Fourteen

Alexis

I'M FRUSTRATED. I DIDN'T expect for some of the people closest to us to gather under one roof and for it to feel… well, right. Everyone was chatting and having a great time like it was always supposed to be this way. I thought having Jason & Kate over would give me a little bit of security and guard my heart from falling too quickly. But it backfired. They like him a lot and are pushing me to pursue whatever this could be.

Then there's Sierra… All night she would watch him carefully. She danced and sang with him. I almost lost it when she asked him to hold her when she got sleepy. I've never seen her do that with *anyone*. She's clung to him very quickly, and I'm not sure why that is. I expected that they would be fast friends, that's just her nature, but I never expected her to seek his attention and affection when she needed comfort. I'm not really sure what to do with that.

"Sweetheart, I get it. I didn't expect to see you last week at the beach. I didn't expect the feelings I had for you years ago to come roaring back to life, like they never died. I never expected you to have any interest in a guy like me. Lex, I'm confused, too, but damn, babe, do you think this kind of stuff happens to everyone? Hell no! We're lucky and we need to take advantage of this opportunity. You two girls are very special ladies, and you've quickly come to mean an awful lot to me. For the record, I would absolutely try to hang the moon if that little girl asked me to do it," he says to me with a wink and a crooked grin.

He's holding me in his lap. I'm not really sure why he feels the need to carry me and hold me so much, but since I like it, I'm not going to complain. It's been a hard day and the evening was best described as emotional. I'm exhausted. I lean back and lay my head on Garrett's shoulder. He adjusts me so that I'm lying in his lap. He leans down, kisses my forehead lingering a few extra seconds, and then reaches down to slip off my shoes.

I sense his desperation to move on from our conversation about what's happening with us. We're not prepared for what's going on, so leaving it for now seems a good choice. Garrett asks me about my day, wanting to know what happened at the parent/teacher conference. I tell him what the teachers said about Sierra being a great kid and her needing clearer boundaries, that and she can sometimes be a bit sassy to the teachers and other children. He laughs and says she's probably being honest, and they don't want to hear it!

We sit like this for a while relaxing and talking. He's going back to Nashville in a few weeks for a charity benefit performance. I would love to see him perform live. I've seen the videos on YouTube, but never live.

I tell him, "I want to see you perform, Garrett."

He looks at me with a little sparkle in his eye. I watch him as his eyes go glassy and lust filled. "Babe, I want to perform for you, but this performance is going to be a private one," he says.

He lifts me off the couch and starts walking towards the stairs up to my bedroom. We reach my bedroom and he lays me on the bed, looking me in the eyes. "You're going to have to drive again, babe. Tell me what you want, Lex," he says with a bit of desperation.

"Garrett, I want you and me," I say because it's true. He's making me want things I didn't think I would ever have. I can envision a family life to include this man. I never knew I could feel this close intimately and emotionally with anyone.

I sit up and he unzips my dress. I reach to lift his shirt over his head. He has an incredible body. I could touch and rub his upper body and arms all day and be content. He's lying on the bed beside me. I feel a little shiver travel up my spine. He pushes the dress down my body and I lift my hips, so he can slide it all the way off. I'm wearing just my bra and panties, and he's only wearing his jeans. He's deliciously sexy. He kisses me with all the intensity that we're both feeling. I could fall apart with just his kisses. His lips are made for kissing. His fingers glide up my body, reaching for the clasp of my bra to take it off. He pauses looking me in the eyes for confirmation. I give a little nod and before my next breath it's off, floating towards the floor.

He leans in and licks, then kisses my neck and chest, like he's been craving this all day. His hand is caressing my stomach and heading south to the place I want it to be. I reach over and unbutton his jeans, reaching into them.

He stops caressing me, raising his gaze to mine. "Lex," he gasps, "you don't have to go there, baby. I like making you feel good. That wasn't my goal in bringing you up here tonight."

It makes me happy that he doesn't have any expectations from me, but I do want this with him. I want to feel closer to him, because at this point, I can't get close enough. "I want this, Garrett. Please." He reaches down and helps me slide his jeans down his legs. He's not wearing underwear. Damn, that's hot.

"Commando?" I ask, looking with smirk.

"Yeah, babe, we didn't need any more layers of material between us. I wanted to be as close to you and your cute little ass as possible if you ended up sitting in my lap, but damn, I didn't expect this."

He's very well endowed and rock hard. I'm a bit intimidated by his size. It's been a while for me. My hand is gliding up and down his length. "Babe, we can just touch," sucking in a breath, between his clenched teeth, "it doesn't have to go any further until you're ready. You look scared."

I look at his eyes and see the concern. "It's just been a while, and you're larger than I imagined." He smirks at my comment, sits up, so that I'm tucked under him. He's holding all his weight, so that he doesn't crush me. He is completely naked and I'm wearing just my panties.

"Baby, I don't want to hurt you. I want to cherish your body. Can you trust me?" he hesitantly asks.

"YES…please."

He reaches down, but his eyes don't stray from mine. He draws my panties down my legs, all the way off, and touches me on the part of my body that has been desperate for his touch.

"You're wet, babe. Have you been wanting me to touch this little thing?" He asks, as he rubs his finger back and forth between the lips and up to my clit.

"Umm…yes…please?!" I'm begging not only with my words, but my body is reacting vigorously to his touch. His cock is twitching between my legs, occasionally making contact with my center. It's making the intensity even stronger. I feel like I'm about to explode into a million pieces when he starts sliding himself down the bed, kissing his way down my body.

"I know, sweetheart, I'm going to take care of it," he says when his head is hovering between my legs. The moment his tongue touches me, I feel myself flying off the bed. He gently holds my hips down and continues on his mission.

"OKAY, Garrett. Please, come back up here," I plead, desperate to feel his cock inside me. I don't care about the discomfort. I want him. "After, babe, let go. Let me see you come under my tongue." Then with those words, I do. I fall apart into a million pieces.

He lets the spasms subside, and then slides his way back up my body then places his cock at my opening. "Lex, look at me, sweetheart. Are you sure you want to do this?" he asks.

"Yes, Garrett. You promised me a performance, now give it to me, damn it."

He laughs, reaching into the back pocket of his jeans and pulling a condom out of his wallet. "Eager to please, Babe!"

Before he unwraps the foil, I say "Garrett, I have the implant, if that's what you're worried about." I'm trusting that if he feels the need to use the condom here he'll do so. Garrett wouldn't intentionally put me in harm's way. He looks from me to the foil packet, and then tosses it over his head.

He slowly slides into my folds. I feel myself stretching as he glides in. He stops half way to give me a few seconds to adjust before he slides in a little more. He's not nearly all the way in and I already feel very full. He's watching me, making sure I'm okay. His eyes are full of passion, but there's concern, also. He really doesn't want to hurt me, or scare me. But I'm neither. I want more. I want to feel all of him.

I moan, "Please, Garret, I want all of you."

His breath catches. "Alexis, you have all of me, sweetheart. You own me," he gasps, as he slides his full length into me.

My body accepts him easily. We are connected in a way I never imagined. My emotions are overflowing with fear and passion. This connection is foreign. I want more, yet I worry that giving more of me and taking more of him will break me. My emotions are already so wrapped up in this man, as is evident by the sheer number of times he has brought me to tears in the last week.

We make love slowly. He whispers in my ear, "You're so beautiful, Alexis. This is the most amazing thing I've ever felt, and I'm not just talking about making love to you, sweetheart." I understand, because I feel it, too. "I'm getting close, sweetheart. I want to go together. Come for me, Alexis," he commands, and with his words I feel the explosion building. He's in and out, in and that's it. I squeeze my thighs around his hips as I explode, gripping his arms tightly. Tears are welling in my eyes. Not sad tears, just an overflow of emotions that release with my amazing orgasm. He leans down and kisses every tear that trickles from my eyes off my face.

Chapter Fifteen

Garrett

I WANT TO ERASE ALL these tears off this girl's face, so I gently kiss them away. It wrecks me to see her cry. I would give anything in the world to kiss them away permanently. I'm not sure if these are the good kind of tears or the bad ones, but the amount of stress it causes me to figure it out is huge. I want to get rid of them quickly.

"Baby, I'm not sure I like tears on your beautiful face. Good kind or bad kind, they both worry me. Tell me what you're thinking 'cause I'm a little scared I hurt you."

She shakes her head. "I'm perfect, Garrett. Don't worry."

Rubbing her cheek with a sense of amazement I declare, "You are, sweetheart! You're perfect, even when you cry."

She shakes her head. "You're eyes aren't working, ace. I need to shower… Care to join me? Looks like you need one, as well," she observes with a decidedly satisfied smirk.

I pick her up and carry her to the large bathroom with an open shower. We don't speak as I place her on her feet on the ground next to the shower. I turn on the water and wait a minute, massaging her neck as the water warms up. We step into the shower, I put her directly under the water stream, and then I begin to wash her with the soap and sponge.

Making love to her wasn't what I expected tonight. I really wasn't sure what to expect two hours ago. I thought for sure she was about to send me out the door, along with everyone else tonight.

"Lex, I need to tell you. What just happened, I feel pretty confident, has changed the course of my life. Baby, I'm not sure it gets much better than that!"

She looks up at me and laughs...hallelujah…she is smiling again!

"So, it wasn't just me? It was pretty good, right?" She asks with a hint of uncertainty.

"Babe, that was fucking fantastic…not pretty good! It wasn't just you, sweetheart. But I can't wait to do it again with you."

We both rinse off and exit the shower. "Garrett, I don't really know what we are. I'm afraid to put a label on it, but will you please not do what you just did with me, with anyone else while we're together?"

What the hell is wrong with this girl? "Lex, are you shitting me right now? Do you really think that's the kind of guy I am? Babe, ONLY YOU! Got it? I want just you!" I'm kind of pissed she asked me that. She really has no clue about my life these days. I realize I haven't been forthcoming with information about my work and life, but seriously, I've clearly been consumed with her since that first night at the beach.

I hate the damn girls that flock toward the musicians on the road. Those chicks just want to say they banged a rock star. They really don't care who it is. They're nasty, and I've never had any interest in them. I guess it's something she wouldn't know, or understand, unless she'd been on the road with us. Maybe she needs to come to a couple shows and see how things roll. She needs to meet the rest of the guys, too. I'll have to work on that.

Right now, I need to work on getting her back into bed. I wrap her in a big fluffy towel I found rolled up in a basket by the shower. I wrap another around my waist. She goes to the wardrobe and dresses in a skimpy pair of orange panties and a plain white tank top. Growling, I declare, "Lady, you better climb your hot little ass into that bed and cover up quick, before I make you dirty all over again."

She runs to the bed and climbs in fast pulling the covers up to her chin, "I feel like Little Red Riding Hood."

"You should, babe, because right now I feel like the Big Bad Wolf." She slides all the way over, making room for me in her bed. I start putting my clothes on.

"Garrett, are you leaving?" Her voices quivers on the last syllable.

It wouldn't be my first choice, but I'm not exactly sure climbing in bed with her is the best decision either. "What would you like me to do, sweetheart?" I ask.

"I would like you to hold me. I'll set the alarm on my phone, so we can wake up before Sierra. Will you stay?"

I reach to the nightstand for her phone and look to her, "What time, sweetheart?" After I set the alarm for five o'clock, I climb in bed to hold her, all night, if that's what she wants.

When the phone chime wakes us up the next morning, we're knotted together with arms and legs wrapped around each other. Sleeping with someone's head on my chest and legs intertwined with mine has never felt as good as it does with Alexis. I've never slept the whole night with a woman. There hasn't ever been a woman that made me want this type of set up. Now that there is, I'm not sure how I can make that happen with Alexis, since her life is a little more complicated than the average woman, and mine is complex as well.

I've never had a desire to change a woman's name. I thought I wasn't the marrying type. After one night with this beautiful girl, I want to give her everything! Actually, I think I've always wanted to give her everything, and anything.

"Good morning, sweetheart! I like starting the day kissing you," I say, as I kiss her forehead.

"I like starting my day snuggling you. Don't get up, yet. We have a few minutes before she wakes," she says with a sleepy smile, as she settles herself against me with her head lying on my chest. We lay like this for several minutes before it's time to move, and time for me to scurry off, so these girls can get ready for their day. I wish I could be here to eat breakfast with them, but Alexis isn't ready to explain me sleeping over to Sierra yet.

This sleeping ritual becomes a bit of a routine over the course of the next few weeks. I come over to Alexis' house every night and spend time playing and hanging out with the girls together. Then after Sierra is down for the night, I play with Alexis. I sleep over every night and hurry out the door early the next morning, before the sun comes up, so Alexis can start the day with Sierra. It's getting harder and harder to walk out the door in those early morning hours. I'm becoming somewhat desperate for more time with them. I don't want to push Alexis too far, though. She's given so much over the past couple weeks.

Sierra is adorable. I'm as attached to her as I am to her mama. Falling head over heels for that blond haired, blue eyed little girl so quickly was unexpected. I haven't ever thought about kids in that way. I've always liked kids well enough, but Sierra is the sweetest little girl I've ever met. Her smile is as wide as the sky. Putting that smile on her face has recently become one of my life's missions. I would move mountains to see her smile light up! She's so much like her mama. They both glow when they're happy.

I have a benefit concert in Nashville in a couple days. I'm heading up there tomorrow for a few nights. I'm hoping Court will pop that kid out while I'm there, so I can kill two birds with one stone, and get back here to my girls. I've been trying to convince Alexis to come with me, but she is apprehensive about taking Sierra. I think it's more her issue, but she won't admit that. I'll continue to beg her until the minute I have to leave. I'm scheduled to fly out tomorrow night on the label's jet. I have just over twenty-four hours to convince her.

I take out my phone to send her a text. I know she has a busy day and she's having lunch with her best friend, Whitney, today. I usually don't hear from her much during the day. For some reason she won't ever text or call me first. It makes me feel like a stalker when I'm always the one calling and texting. It does make me feel like the 'Big Bad Wolf' as Alexis calls me.

Me: Hi, having a good day? I just wanted to talk to you about all the things we could take

Sierra to see and do in Nashville. I think you girls would have a really great time. Can we please talk about it? Sierra can come to the concert with us. I think she'll like it. (on knees begging)....can't imagine the next few days without you.

No answer...I check my phone every thirty-six seconds, and she doesn't reply.

Chapter Sixteen

Alexis

TODAY, I'M HAVING lunch with Whitney. When she called this morning I was having a complete meltdown. Garrett overwhelms me. His lifestyle overwhelms me. What we have overwhelms me. The fact that he wants Sierra and I to go with him to his show in Nashville overwhelms me. I can't seem to make him understand. This is happening so quickly. I have had very little of the time and space that I asked for when this started to wrap my head around it.

"Whit, I just can't seem to get the space and time to really make sure this is what I want and need. But it's not him, it's me. I can't stay away. I spend my day consumed with thoughts of him. And when I'm not thinking about him, I'm listening to his voice on my iPod. It's effecting Sierra, too. She waits for him every afternoon to come over and have dinner with us."

Whitney's looking at me, shaking her head in disbelief.

"Alexis, look at me, sweetie. I'm not really understanding the negative here. You like him. That's okay. He's great with Sierra, he likes your friends and family, and he obviously loves you. I've seen him watching you. You're falling for him, and that's really awesome. Choose to be happy, and stop looking for reasons this can't work!"

"Two things: First, HE DOESN'T LOVE ME." Then, lowering my voice, I continue, "He likes me and the sex is good. Second, you don't quite understand, Whit. I'm not famous. I can't pick up and leave to travel the country with him. I don't fit into his huge world and I can't expect him to shrink to fit into mine. He needs someone without such a set-in-stone life. I can't continue to believe that this life with me and Sierra will be enough for him. This is only temporary for him. I'm temporary. He's back on tour in just a few weeks. Then we'll just be friends…maybe?" Let the lecture begin. I can see the frustration all over her face. She's getting sick of talking me off the cliff, but I can't seem to stop climbing up there.

"*One*," she stresses, "you are insane, Lex, if you don't believe that man loves you. And *two* if he wanted what the other women had to offer, he wouldn't still be here. That's a man thing, sweetie. They don't do anything they don't want to do for very long. You need to talk to him. Does he even know you are freaking out?"

"No. What do I say? *'Garrett, I'm malfunctioning, sorry. I'm totally freaking out, because I like you and don't know if you like me?'* Don't be ridiculous, Whit! This is the real world where stories don't end with Happily Ever After. I think it's about time to get real with myself."

"Okay, Lex, Let's 'get real' as you say. Your compulsive self-destruction knows no bounds. I, for one, think you're making a monumental mistake throwing this away. I don't support what you're doing. I think that in the process of trying to guard your heart from loving someone again, you'll be breaking it on your own, and then you'll totally miss your Happily Ever After."

Could she be right? Am I hurting myself? Of course I am. I do love him.

Garrett texted this morning and begged me to reconsider Nashville. There's just no way I can take part in that. I haven't been able to think of anything else since this morning. Last night I couldn't sleep. I stayed up all night considering what was happening between Garrett and me, and realized this wasn't what we need in our lives. What we are to each other is lovely, but it's the wrong time. We're at such different points in our lives. Neither of us can be expected to give up what it will take to make this relationship work.

"Whit, I'm not what he needs. I realize it, even though, he may not yet, but he will soon! He needs the freedom to be '*The Garrett Freaking McKenna*' he was born to be, not my Garrett. Trying to mold him into my established life is unfair. Believe me, it will break my heart to watch him walk out the door, but it's time," I say, pleading that for once she'll see this my way. I need her to understand, and not keep pushing me toward Garrett. If my feelings for Garrett get any deeper, and things ended badly, I'll never recover. I'm not sure I'll recover now, but I'll be able to move on without having to pick up the pieces of my life. I'm not sure that will be the case for much longer. On top of that, I can't let Sierra fall anymore in love with him. She already expects him every night for dinner, for playtime, and for bedtime stories.

He'll be leaving for Nashville tomorrow. If I tell him today, then maybe he'll stay in Nashville. That would probably be best for now. Seeing him again will be far too hard for me at this point. But I can't ask him to stay away, he's done nothing wrong, except make me crave him in ways I didn't expect and wasn't ready for.

My phone rings, breaking the uncomfortable silence and the glare of my best friend. I'm desperate to answer it and talk about anything other than Garrett McKenna. I look at the caller ID and it's a call from Sierra's school. "SHIT… got to get this. It's the school," I explain. I answer the call. It's from Sierra's teacher. She assures me that Sierra is fine and tells me she'd like to see me as soon as possible to discuss some things she is witnessing. I tell her I'll be there in twenty minutes and disconnect the call.

The one thing Whitney understands and tolerates is me dropping everything to be there for Sierra. She'd never ask me to continue our conversation, even though, I know I'm not completely off the hook. I kiss her cheek and tell her I'll call her over the weekend.

She smiles a tentative smile and says, "Remember I'm here for you, even if you're totally screwing up. But please, Dear God, DO NOT let this be the thing to send you back into hiding. Text me and let me know what's up with Sierra." I nod.

I arrive at the school and am ushered into the early childhood office. The teachers here are very nice and have been supportive of Sierra and me, even though, Sierra wasn't in school when her daddy died. They know the history, and they are careful when handling situations where dads are part of the classroom or when there are activities involving crafts for dads.

"Hi, Mrs. Phillips. Thanks so much for coming in on such short notice," Sierra's teacher says when she enters the class. She's a wonderful grandmotherly type. I know her well, since I've had numerous conversations with her regarding Sierra's behavior. Usually, I don't have to come into the school right away. I'm hoping whatever has happened this time isn't too serious.

"Sure," I reply.

"Mrs. Phillips, today we had an incident I want to tell you about. I'm very concerned for all parties involved." I nod, accepting that I'm likely being judged as a horrible parent, who allows her four year old to act out. "It seems Sierra is targeting a child negatively in the classroom with bullying type behavior."

I'm shocked. Sierra is bossy and sassy at times, but not violent. What the hell? I can sense my guard going up, prepping to defend my child to the fullest extent. "Well, Ms. Davis, I find that a bit hard to believe. Maybe you can give me some examples of what you're considering bullying," I challenge, refusing to allow this lady to villainize my child. She's not a bad kid.

"The other child in this situation is the child of a single parent, a dad. It appears that Sierra has been harassing this child, telling her that her daddy will probably die soon, because daddies don't stay." She's waiting for a response from me, but she gets none, since I'm dumbfounded. "… and also, Sierra has created a club, and only the children with mommies can be included. Sierra is intentionally excluding this little girl. Mrs. Phillips, we aren't saying Sierra is a bad kid. We are concerned that she is dealing with her father's passing in a way that is adversely affecting her education and her peer relationships. We felt it was very important for you to know, right away, what was happening."

I feel the tears in my eyes and on my cheek before I can muster the strength to will them away. I'm heartbroken for my little girl. She is obviously hurting and I haven't seen it. Why didn't I see this coming? "Oh my…Ms. Davis, I'm not sure what to say except that I'll talk to Sierra. I'll do whatever it takes to help her deal with this in a more healthy way." She passes me a box of tissues and comes to sit in the chair adjoining mine. She rubs my arm gently and tells me it'll be okay. Although, I'm not actually sure it will be, I'll make it the best I can for Sierra's sake.

I leave the school and drive around. There's not a real reason to go home, since I need to be back to pick up Sierra in one hour. I just drive and drive. I find myself parked in the lot of a garden nursery. This is the nursery Jed & I came to with the landscape designer to map out the landscaping of our lot. It was a fun day. I had just found out we were expecting Sierra. I was blissfully happy that day. Jed was beaming at me all day, and I felt like the most special girl in the world.

I sit in the parking lot remembering, and crying about all the hurt my little girl must feel. This wasn't the life that Jed and I spent endless hours planning for. It's heartbreaking that, even though, we have so much, the one thing Sierra needs and wants, I can't give her.

When I pick up my perfect little girl, I slap on my happy face and put on her favorite music. I pop her into the car seat in the back of the Jeep. It's a beautiful day, so I've pushed the top back and blared the music. She smiles big. "Hey Mama, can we get ice cream?" she asks. She's adorable with her cute little braided pig tails.

"Anything you want, sweet girl," I say. We're riding down the road toward our favorite ice cream shop when she yells, "Mama, can we listen to Garrett?"

What the hell…I am playing her favorite Taylor Swift album and she wants Garrett's songs instead? This is exactly the problem. He's consuming us both. "Sure, baby girl," I say, reaching for my iPod to change the playlist.

I'm stressed beyond belief. I still haven't responded to Garrett's text. I need to have a serious conversation with him tonight, and then send him back to Nashville as soon as possible. I really don't have the time and energy to put forth to be in a relationship with all that's happening with Sierra. She'll need my undivided attention for now. I'm worried sick about her. I need to call Kate and Cami to see what they think. Maybe she needs therapy! I'm such a crack pot of a mother that I didn't notice this. I've been so wrapped up in Garrett that I'm screwing up my kid.

When we get home, Sierra runs upstairs to play, and I turn on the baby monitor that I keep downstairs so I can listen to her play. It makes this big house feel less empty. And since I need to understand what she's feeling and almost five year olds aren't that great at explaining their emotions without throwing themselves onto the floor and screaming, I'm eavesdropping on her playtime.

I suppose it's time to make that dreaded phone call, so that we can move on and I can focus on taking care of Sierra. I pick up my cell phone. It's been hours since I checked it last. Fifteen missed calls, six texts. UGH….

Garrett: Lex, are you intentionally ignoring my invitation to Nashville?

Yes…I totally was at the time, but after the conversation I plan to have later, he'll likely hate me. So it doesn't really matter. I'm such a bitch!

Garrett: U ok? Where are you, sweetheart? Worried :/

Doesn't he have other things to do other than check up on me throughout the day? I'm sure he has many way more important people vying for his time. I'm a distraction to him, too.

Jason: Hey sis. What's up? Haven't talked to you in a couple days. You good? Love ya. Call me tonight!

Damn…I need to call him. And I need to talk to Kate about Sierra.

Whit: What happened at the school? Did my feisty god-daughter tell the teachers where to go again? ;) Love that kiddo!

Nope…it's way worse… I'll have to call her tomorrow. I have enough to deal with today.

Garrett: If you're busy, can you just say that? Text me please…I just need to know you're okay.

He sounds a bit pissed in that text, which is surprising. He's usually so patient with me. I need to quickly text a reply, until I can make the phone call later. I need to mentally prepare for this conversation, and that will start with a nice bottle of wine.

Me: Doing Fine. Will talk later. Super Busy.

My phone chirps right away.

Garrett: Too Late…On my way! I'll wait until you have time.

Shit…Shit…Shit… I don't want to do this yet. I needed time to prepare. I need Sierra to be sleeping so that I can soak in my sorrows after I send him away. NO…He just can't come over now.

Me: Sorry…not a good time. Will call you later.

And then I hear the door bell and little feet running down the stairs. "Sierra, do not open that door. It could be a stranger," I say, but she continues toward the door anyway.

"It's not a stranger, Mama, it's Garrett. I saw his truck in my window." It would be so much better if he would go away for a few hours. I really don't need Sierra to be more invested in this than she already is.

"Baby girl, you go play. Mama needs to talk to Garrett," I say, as I open the door.

Instead of running up to play she lunges into his arms as soon as the door is fully open. He's kneeling down, because he anticipated her reaction. "Hi, Garrett, I missed you. Mama and I listened to your songs in the car."

He smiles at her and looks at me tentatively. "You did? Did you like them, princess?"

She nods her head up and down so fast her little body is bouncing. "Yep, they're my favorite," she says, before he places her back onto her feet and kisses her forehead.

"I'm glad, princess. You're definitely my favorite fan." She's skipping off to the stairs and back up to play, singing one of Garrett's songs as she goes.

Here I am thinking about just myself when what I'm about to do will likely hurt Sierra just as much. This is exactly why they say not to bring boyfriends into your kids' lives until you know they're going to stick. But he wasn't my boyfriend. He was a friend, and that's all I ever expected this to be. I certainly never expected things to progress so quickly with him. I hate this. I hate the whole situation. I hate that I opened myself up to whatever this is. I hate that I crave him so much that I have to restrain myself from climbing into his arms for comfort right now. In just a few short weeks he's become entrenched.

He looks at me. "Alexis, what's going on, sweetheart?" His eyes are pleading with me to spill my heart out, but I don't really know where to begin. It's been such a bad day, one of the worst I've had in a while.

"I'm not really ready to talk yet, Garrett. I tried to text you, but you showed up." He's wounded by my words. I can see it.

"Lex, I was really worried. I didn't come here to force you into a conversation. I just needed to see that you're okay. If you don't want me here, I'll leave, but please don't make me stay away for too long, babe. I have to head up to Nashville tomorrow, and I'm going to miss you like crazy for those few days."

I feel awful pushing him away, but it needs to be done before we're in too deep to recover. "I'm sorry, Garrett, but I don't think I'll be ready for a while. I'll walk you outside so we can talk more."

Chapter Seventeen

Garrett

THIS CANNOT BE HAPPENING. I knew something was up with her today when she wouldn't respond to my texts or calls. I was hoping she wasn't ignoring me, but now I see that she was. Damn it, I'll give her a few hours to sort this shit out, but if she thinks I'm going to be able to stay away longer than that, she's crazy. I can't. I won't be able to leave town knowing things aren't okay with her. I'm not sure what happened, but I'll damn well get to the bottom of it today.

"Lex, I don't know what's going on in that pretty little head of yours, and I'm worried I've done something to upset you. Shit, I'm pissed that you're upset, period. I want you to give me a chance to fix whatever's wrong in your world. If you're not ready to talk, you need me to go, I will, but please let me say goodbye to Sierra before I do." Her eyes are very full of unshed tears, and I can see she's holding onto them with everything she has.

I have no idea what's happened today. She was quiet this morning when I left. I know she had a lot going on. I'm re-playing everything in my head from last night and this morn-ing, analyzing every detail, trying to figure out what could have gone wrong. I can't think of anything. It's all been great! We've spent lots of time together. I'm here almost every night for dinner and I sleep in her bed every night. We connect like freaking magnets physically. Damn…what the hell happened?

"Sierra, can you please come her a second?" She calls out up the staircase. A few seconds later, I hear my sweet girl skipping along, singing one of my songs. It usually makes me feel funny hearing other people sing my music, but hearing the lyrics out of this little girl's mouth, I'm overjoyed. I'm also sad as hell, because I'm not sure when Lex will let me back in. She's pushing me out.

"Yes, Mama?" she asks.

"Baby, Garrett needs to go…he just wanted to say good-bye before he left."

Sierra sticks out her bottom lip and pouts. "But, Mama, I wanted to go swimming with Garrett tonight, and you said we could all finish our puzzle tonight and, and, Garrett is better at the bedtime stories, because his people have funny voices."

Damn, this sucks, but I can't let Alexis be the one to dis-appoint Sierra right now. I'm not sure she could handle that. "Listen, princess, I want to do all those things with you to-night, too, but I have to get ready for a big show on Saturday night. So would you mind if we did that another time?"

Her bottom lip is quivering and her little eyes are over-flowing with tears. "But, that's not what we were going to do tonight." I hate this just as much as she does.

Alexis stands to the side watching the interaction with her arms crossed, almost as if she was hugging herself. She has a few tears leaking down her cheeks, but she quickly sweeps them away. "I'm preparing a special surprise for the show in Nashville, Saturday. I'm going to sing a very special song and I'll send the video to your mama's phone, if that's okay?" I look to Alexis for confirmation and she nods her head.

"Okay," Sierra says giving in. I kneel with both knees on the ground and scoop her into a big bear hug. "I love you, Garrett." She says and I melt into a pile of gush.

"I love you, too, princess. I'll see you soon, okay?"

She's placated for now. I'm not really sure how long it will last. She's such a great kid. I've never really seen her upset or throw a fit. I feel bad that she's upset now, but I can't make it up to her mama if she won't tell me what the hell I did in the first place.

Alexis walks out the door with her arms still wrapped around her body. We walk to stand beside my truck. "I see that you're upset. Please, just tell me what I can do to make this better," I say to her, placing my hands on her arms, willing her to speak to me. And right then, she falls apart into a puddle of tears. I want to kiss all those damn tears off this girl's face. It wrecks me to see her cry. What makes it worse is I think I've caused them, but I don't know how. I would give anything in the world to make them go away and for a smile to replace that sad, lonely expression. She's sobbing, so I pick her up, open the truck door, place her in the driver's seat and stand in front of her, holding her. I'll stand here all night if I have to.

"Babe, I'm really worried here. What's going on?" She lifts her precious head and looks at me with eyes still full of tears. I kiss every tear streak I can see on her cheeks. I refuse to be the one who caused this, and not the one to try and make it better. At this point, I really don't care who caused it. I still want to be the one to fix it. I love this girl. I really, really love this girl, both these girls...Like crazy love them.

"Garrett, I can't do this. I can't," she's gasping through her tears, "anymore," gasp "not with you." Continuing to cry, "It's wrong, I'm wrong. We don't fit." Okay...so is this the cause of the tears? Because we don't fit? I can't imagine anyone fitting better in my life. What am I missing? This girl is the missing piece in my life. She's made my complicated life suddenly work in just a few short weeks. She's made me feel like I fit in, in the real world.

"Lex, look at me...I can't imagine anyone fitting better in my life, sweetheart. Tell me why you think that."

She shrugs her shoulders and looks at me. "It's just that you're Garrett McKenna, and I can't drop everything in my life to be a superstar's girlfriend. You deserve someone that can."

Did I ever tell her she'd have to give up her life to be part of mine? I'd give up my entire world to be part of hers. This is exactly what the guys and I have been talking about the last few weeks. "Sweetheart, I'd never want you to give up anything on my behalf. Baby, I want to add to your life, not take away from it. Is that the reason for all these tears?"

She shakes her head. "Just a few of them."

"Ok...what are the rest of these tears for?" She shakes her head forcefully.

"No, I can't talk about that right now." She says with a panicked expression. "Garrett, I know you are soooo special. And the girl that earns your heart eventually… the right girl… she'll be so very lucky. But I'm not her. I'm broken and not really fixable. I don't know if I ever will be. So what I need, right now, is for you to get in this truck and drive away before we wreck each other. I don't want to hurt anymore, and Sierra...I have to be more careful. I'm sorry...but...please," she pleads, as she slides out of the truck and out of my grasp. "I'm really sorry, Garrett. Please, forgive me."

I'm speechless. She's telling me goodbye...like permanently... not just for the night. Not on my fucking life...She can't... I won't let her... I love her.

"Sweetheart, are you pushing me away because I'm not making you happy, or because you think you're not what I need? I really need you to tell me before I make my next move, Lex." She looks to me, shaking her head.

"No, you are *'Garrett McKenna the huge star'*. The person you cherish in this life needs to be one that will move mountains to be beside you and take care of you. Not someone who you'll have to mold yourself around to fit into their already established life, especially not one that is broken and needs so much time and work to repair. You have no idea how broken I really am."

"Alexis, it's me who's unworthy, sweetheart. What kind of man is lucky enough to find the girl of his dreams ten years ago, screw up enough that I miss out on the chance of a lifetime, only for it to come back to me all these years later? Baby, it's you I want, just you, and that little blond inside the house. I want to cherish you both." I accidently let a single tear escape the tear fortress. Even grown men get emotional every once in a while.

"Garrett...I don't think you understand....I'm not....." She's not relenting. I can see in her eyes that she is still playing tug-of-war with her heart and her fear. I need to put a stop to this, quickly. I can't let her continue to tell herself, or me, that she isn't good enough. She's better than good enough. She's the best!

"Lex, shut the hell up! I don't want to hear any more about how unworthy of being in my life you are. It's insulting! If you think, for one minute, that I'm walking out that door because you believe, in that overly smart brain of yours, that you aren't what I need, you really have gone bat-shit crazy! There is no way I'm letting you push me away. NO.WAY.BABY! I'm staying. I'm keeping you, and I'm keeping the cute little blond upstairs, too. I don't know how many more ways I can tell you, but YOU are exactly what I need and want and most importantly, what I can't fucking live without!" She smiles. Thank Holy Christ! I've never needed to see someone smile more than right at this moment. Damn…I love this girl, but I can't tell her now… that could send her into another tailspin.

I've never wanted to give a girl anything, ever. Now I want to give her everything and anything she wants. Hell, she can have my last name if that would make her happy. I know for sure it would make me the happiest man in the world!

"Garrett, you make me feel things I'm not sure I am ready for, things I haven't ever felt before, not even with Jed. I've never connected with anyone else like this, and it scares me because you've made me need you. But at the same time what Jed gave in regards to parenting Sierra, I don't think she'll ever have that again. And that makes me sad, too. This is complicated, and I feel guilty for wanting what we have. You'll have to sacrifice so much to be part of us, Sierra and me. I just want more for you. Simple as that."

That's it! She needs to know how I feel so that she'll see what walking away would do to me.

"Lex, I love you like crazy, sweetheart! I was afraid to tell you too soon, and give you one more reason to run for the hills, but babe..." I pause to gather my nerve, "seriously, I think I loved you the minute I met you ten years ago. Your pretty little eyes have always seen right through me. You've always seen the real me, even when I didn't think anyone ever would see past the voice and guitar."

"Baby, all I want is for you to let me hold you, kiss you, and love you. I want that more than my next breath, it's not a sacrifice, sweetheart, ever," I say. "What you had with Jed in regards to parenting Sierra, no baby, you'll never have that again. It'll always be different. But different doesn't have to be bad. We can make it good. I don't know the first thing about little girls. I do know that little girl makes my heart sing in ways I've never known. I also know there's nothing in this world I wouldn't do to keep her from harm. Babe, she's a part of you. I instinctively love her with all my being, since all my being is wrapped up in you. I want to take care of you girls. Stop pushing me away and let me."

Chapter Eighteen

Alexis

WHAT IN THE WORLD JUST happened? I was breaking it off…and now he's professed his love for Sierra & me. How is it possible a guy like Garrett would want me? I'm not really sure what to say to his declaration. He wants us, in spite of the fact that I offer nothing to him except baggage. It doesn't seem fair, but I love him, too, and letting him go would irreparably break me. Whitney was right about that, but I'd never admit that to her. He does make me happy, and he loves my baby girl. He says he's keeping us, but I don't know what that really means. Even though I have so many unanswered questions, I'm trying to smile through the emotions and show him that what he's saying means a lot to me.

"I love you, too. I love you more than I ever expected. This scares the living shit out of me. *You* scare me. But I *will* try. You're going to need to be patient with me, though. My emotions are all going haywire. I don't know what the hell is wrong with me," I say to Garrett. I'm happy that walking away wasn't easy for him, but I feel like the amount he's going to have to sacrifice for us won't be worth the limited rewards. It won't be a fair trade.

He's holding me tightly, like he's afraid I'll disappear. As if I would walk away after what he just said. He's watching me closely. I'm trying to reassure him that I'm okay, but how the hell would he know that from the way I just acted. I pretty much told him to get lost, that I was a disaster area and he should run for the hills. Yet he stayed. I'm glad. I've grown to need him so badly.

I haven't even told him about Sierra and what's happening at school. I don't want him to think I expect him to step in as an instant daddy, but it's hard not imagining us as a family. I don't want to go there. I don't want to turn the tables and scare him away, or for him to feel obligated to take that step with Sierra.

"I'm so sorry, Garrett. I really did, kind of still do, think you would be better off. But I'm glad you want to be here with me, anyway."

He bends down and lifts me by my ass. I wrap my legs around his waist as we walk into the house. "Sierra," he calls out toward the stairs. "Come on, princess. We're going swimming and then we're packing for a trip!"

She's running down the stairs before he finishes the sentence. "Yay, Garrett, you came back!"

He places me on my feet and picks her up, walking out back to the pool. He sits her down and takes off their sneakers and socks. Standing up, he grabs her in his arms and jumps into the pool, both of them fully clothed and laughing.

"Come in, Mama. This is fun." And I do. We swim for a while before ordering pizza to eat by the pool. It's a perfect family fun night.

"Garrett, you know we really can't go to Nashville with you tomorrow, right?" I say to him, pleading for him to understand.

"No, babe, I don't know that. Why don't you go ahead and tell me your objections, so that I can figure out a way around them." He flashes a charming smile.

Then my little peanut pipes right into the conversation. "Mama, I want to go to Nashville, too," Sierra says, looking at me like I have four heads for saying we can't go.

I look to Garrett for help. "Will she really be safe at a concert? There will be a lot of people there." Now, Garrett's looking at me like I have four heads.

"Lex, do you really think I'd ever let anything happen to my girls? Babe, you'll both be on the side stage. I'll be able to see you the whole time and I'll have security doubled whenever you're around." Oh…security. Of course, he would have security. We haven't had to deal with that much here, but we've not really gone anyplace.

"Garrett, can I sing on stage too with the real life microphone?" Sierra asks. "I know your songs good," she entreats, batting her baby blues. She knows just how to work him.

"Sure, princess. I'd love that," he says. He's just made her dreams come true. I'm not really sure how that'll work out. We can resolve that tomorrow.

I tell Sierra it's time to get ready for bed. She kisses Garrett goodnight and he tells her he will be here to wake her up tomorrow. I take her inside to bathe. After her bath Garrett reads one of her favorite books, using all the funny character voices, just the way she likes. Then he says goodnight to her, leaving us to our private goodnight song and prayers.

I sing her the bedtime song, and then she says her prayers. As always, "God Bless Mama, Uncle, Auntie my cousins, Aunty Whit, my daddy in heaven, and all my friends, and one more thing God…could you please make Garrett my new daddy? I really want him to be, because he loves us and I love him and even mama loves him, too. Amen." Oh my…I don't say anything to that. There's nothing I can possibly say. I kiss her on her head and walk out of the room, closing the door behind me. I find Garrett sitting against the wall with his head in his hands and tears streaming his cheeks.

He heard… I warned him this would be too much to deal with. "Garrett, I'm sorry. Did you hear that? I'll talk to her, try to make her understand that you can't be her daddy."

He stands up, picking me up and carrying me to the bedroom. "Lex, shut up. You're ruining the best thing I've ever heard," he says, laying me on my bed, kissing me ferociously. "Sweetheart, I heard that she said she loves me enough that she thinks I could be her daddy, and that she knows I love you both. If she can figure this shit out at four, you have got to stop questioning it, too. Got it, lady? Today you told me that you love me, and, even though, you keep trying to ruin this for me by doubting what we have, this is the best day of my life, sweetheart. And I fully intend to finish it off with fireworks. Get naked fast, Lex. We have some making up to do!" He says right before he attacks me, tugging at our clothes. As great as that sounds, Sierra is right down the hall and there's no way she's sleeping. I want him, but we need to put it on ice for a few minutes.

"Garrett, wait….Sierra's not sleeping, yet. I don't want

her to come in here," I say, putting a halt to his plans.

"Shit, you're right." He stops and kisses me. "I have my bags in the truck. Let me go get some dry clothes and make you a cup of tea. Sound good?" I nod yes. "Climb in the tub. I'll be back in a minute," he says, as he puts his shirt back on and jogs out of the room.

I do exactly as he says and run a nice hot bath. Today was such an awful day. I never would have imagined that it would end like this. I take a minute to text Whitney and my brother, letting them both know all is well and that I'll call them tomorrow. Then I climb into the tub to wait for my man. Yes… my man. I have a man, and he loves me. He loves us. In spite of my crappy day, I find myself smiling. I'm too happy right now not to smile.

When Garrett comes back into the room, he brings my cup of tea and sets it on the ledge next to the tub. Then he's kneeling over the tub to kiss me. "I checked on Sierra. She's sleeping like an angel. Is there room in that tub for two?"

Nodding my head. "Absolutely, please, Garrett." He takes off his clothes and climbs into the tub, resting behind me, my back is to his front.

I need to tell him what happened at the school today and why Sierra is obsessed with daddies. I don't know what to say or how to start this conversation, so I blurt it out.

"The teachers think Sierra is acting out and being mean to one of the other little girls in class, because her daddy brings her to school every day. Apparently, Sierra told the little girl that soon her daddy would die and leave her, because all daddies leave. I hope she didn't mean to intentionally upset the little girl, but I suspect she did. That's how it worked out in her world, and either she doesn't quite understand, yet, that it doesn't happen to everyone, or she's bitter because it doesn't happen to everyone, but it happened to her." He tenses immediately.

"Damn, babe! When did this happen? Why didn't you call me earlier and tell me. I would've been there. Shit…what can we do, sweetheart? Please, tell me how to make her feel better. "

Shit. I can't believe I just put all that out there, and he still isn't scared off. What in the world have I done to deserve his loyalty? "Garrett, you can't drop everything you're doing to run to Sierra and me every time something bad happens. And, for the record, when I found out I was trying to send you off to your happily ever after. That's why I didn't tell you. But you wouldn't go." I'm sad and frustrated that I didn't foresee this, but at the same time we have Garrett here now.

"Damn right, I wouldn't go, and good luck with that the next time you try that shit. I know your system now. Sweetheart, always, always, always *call me*! I keep telling you that. I'll *always* answer your calls. I would have been there. I would've run to you and my princess. I've spent the whole day staring at my phone waiting for you to call or text me back, and nothing. I would've rather been there beside you, holding your hand, than any other place, Lex. You're smart, lady! Listen to me and understand my words!"

When I went in for that meeting I wasn't expecting for him to be sticking around. At the time, I wanted to break it off. In hindsight I'd give anything to do it over and have him there with me. That would've been quite comforting.

"Garrett, I wasn't telling you so that you could reprimand me for not properly filling you in on every detail of my day. I was telling you, so that you would come to a place of understanding about my emotional outburst and my actions earlier. I didn't want you to think I was completely crazy. I'm trying here, but you have to understand, I haven't had anyone in my life that required the amount of detail about my life, and day, as you do. You really need to give me a chance here. Plus, after Sierra's little prayer you needed to know why she's daddy obsessed."

He looks at me with eyes that are sympathetic, yet still trying to portray his seriousness. He's rubbing my shoulders as if he's trying to rub my tension away.

"I know. I don't really know what I'm doing in this relationship, either. I just know that I can't stand the thought of anything making you feel sad or frustrated, or not being there beside you. Honey, I want to be the one to make things better for you and Sierra. And I'm freaking taking her to school tomorrow. I don't want her sad because she doesn't have a daddy bringing her to school. Lex, if I can fix it, I will, and you need to let me. Okay?"

The seriousness of this conversation is wearing on me. I really need to move on to something more pleasant.

"Okay, ace, are you wanting to talk all night? Because, personally, I can think of some much better options."

"Grrr…" He says, as he lifts me out of the water and quickly wipes us down with a towel. "Move your ass, sweet cheeks. Time to make up with me," he says slapping my bottom as I run out of the bathroom toward the bedroom.

"Are you growling at me Mr. McKenna?" I ask, trying to play a bit of keep-away as I run from him. I know I won't win this game, but it's still fun.

"Yes, beautiful, I'm growling, and if you don't get into my arms immediately, I'll tie your ass down." He says, and I leap to him, jumping directly in to his arms and causing him to fall back onto the mattress. His hands are exploring my body.

Chapter Nineteen

Garrett

I WAKE EXTRA EARLY TO call Whitney. I know Alexis is struggling about going to Nashville. If I can convince Whitney to come along it will make her more secure, having someone familiar to be with her at the concert. I pick up her phone and dial the number. Whitney answers on the first ring. I'm grateful not to get voicemail, so I can have a definitive answer before Lex wakes up.

"What's up, chick? Why are you awake so early?" She greets instead of the standard 'Hello' you get from most people.

"Hi, Whitney, it's Garrett. I have a favor, and I'm hopeful that you'll help." I'm getting straight to the point.

"Hey. Spill it, g-man, anything to make my bestie happy," she says, and I laugh at the nick-name she's chosen to bestow upon me.

"We're headed to Nashville today for a benefit concert that I have to perform this weekend. I'm taking Lex and Sierra with me. We'll be there for a few days, a week at the most. I'm hoping that you'll join us. I know it will make Lex more comfortable, since she doesn't really like anything new," I say, trying to sound convincing without pleading. I damn well hate to beg, and in every other area of my life it's not a necessary task. But when it comes to my sweet girl, it seems this is my best tactic.

"Uh, g-man, I kind of have to work. I know it's a foreign concept to you rock stars and all," she huffs. I can practically see her rolling her eyes, "but you see in the real world people have to show up from nine a.m. to five p.m. for this thing called a *job*. If I don't show up, I get *fired*." She stresses the words job and fired, like I've never heard them before. "I can probably swing the weekend, but it's a no go for the week. I'm off work at five today. When are y'all leaving?"

Ugh. Everyone thinks because I'm a performer that I don't have a job or understand what it means to work. I hate that people perceive my career that way. But since I don't really want to piss off my girl's best friend before we all take a trip together, I'll refrain from putting her in her place about my career. I'll keep my damn mouth shut, and accept whatever time she's willing to give me.

"Whitney, thank you. We'll leave at six tonight then. I'll send you the information and have a car service pick you up, so you won't have to leave your car at the airport. I'll also have Josh, my assistant, contact you to make arrangements for your return from Nashville. I want my girls to enjoy their time in Nashville. I know having you there will definitely help with that," I say sincerely. I really would do anything I can think of to make my girls more comfortable. Having them by my side definitely makes me happy. I hope that feeling is mutual.

"You got it, Garrett. I'll be there! I hope you're getting us great seats for that concert 'cause I totally expect the royal treatment!"

Laughing at the insaneness, "Whit, I love these girls more than my own damn life. You really think I won't pull out all the stops to make sure they feel special. I promise you'll all be treated well, or I'll mount someone's damn head on the wall. Let me know if you need anything else from me. See you later."

"Awesome, g-man, see you later today. By the way, thanks for loving my best friend. It's been a rough time for her. She deserves greatness. Be great Garrett. Lex is as lucky to have you as you are to have her!"

Wow…did Lex already tell her what happened last night? She hasn't really had any time away from me for phone conversations…interesting. "Thanks, I'm trying my best. I promise." I hear movement upstairs. I want to go and say good morning to my girl. Start and end the day, that's my job! "See you later, Whit. Going to wake my girls now." We hang up, and I get moving.

I take the stairs two at a time, feeling anxious to get my hands on Lex. Touching her settles my nerves in ways I've never imagined. I reach the bedroom and see her crawling across the king size four-poster bed. "Hey there, sweetheart," I say from the doorway. She stops in her tracks and looks at me.

"I was just coming to look for you," she says sleepily. I walk toward her, climbing back into bed to hold her for a little while. "I just talked to Whitney. She's going to come to

Nashville with us for the weekend. I thought you'd be more comfortable having her around when I can't be beside you myself."

She visibly exhales and relaxes. "Yes. That *is* great. Thank you, Garrett."

She's sitting in my lap with her head on my shoulder. Her eyes are still very sleepy. I feel bad for keeping her up so late with our activities. But we needed to make up, and that is most definitely my favorite way to make up with her. Hopefully today will be an easy day and she can have a little nap. "Sweetheart, can I take Sierra to school today, so that you can stay in bed? You look tired. It's been a crazy few weeks for you."

She smiles. "I'm sure she'd love that, babe. Let's take her together, and then you can take me to breakfast." I grin at her suggestion, because I have a great idea.

I can do one better than mere breakfast. We'll take Sierra to school, and then I need to go back to my parents place to pack my stuff. I'll call mom and have her make us breakfast.

She's been asking about Alexis since I brought her to the wedding. I've been very vague in my answers. This'll make mom happy, plus I really want to officially show off my girl. I won't tell Lex now, though. I don't want to make her anxious, or give her the chance to say no.

My parents are really laid back. There's not a lot formal about my mom and dad, so they won't have issues with us dropping in without a lot of notice. Shit, it'll make my mom's day. I've never really brought any women around my family, never wanted to, until Lex. Mom knows this has to be something serious to make me stick around and not head back to Nashville for the rest of my hiatus. She also knows the history between Lex and me, and that Lex is a widow, since she followed the local news and kept me informed when it all went down.

We arrive at school with a very happy little Sierra. She's bouncing around, as we try and walk down the hall to her classroom. Walking this slowly is pointless. School will be over by the time we make it to Sierra's classroom. I scoop her up and place her on my shoulders, so that we can walk at a more manageable pace. She made me promise in the car that I would walk her in and let her show me the classroom. I intend to fulfill that request.

When we reach the classroom, I slip her off my shoulders and carry her into the class, setting her down when we're inside the door. Her teacher comes to greet us right away, looking from Alexis to me suspiciously.

"Good morning, Sierra. Who is your guest?" the teacher asks. She's an older grandmotherly type, but I immediately sense that she is very protective of Lex and Sierra, which makes me like her even more.

Sierra bounces with excitement as she answers, "Ms. Davis this is my new daddy, Garrett." Sierra says it before anyone else has a chance to answer.

Alexis looks as if she is about to pass out. "Sierra…no, sweetheart. You can't say things like that. We need to talk more about that, honey." Lex says alarmed.

But I kneel down to Sierra and give her a hug saying, "Show me around, princess. I want to see where you spend your days." And she takes me by the hand and walks me around, leaving her mother and teacher to watch in awe.

When Sierra is settled at the table to do her morning drawing, I make my way back to my still speechless girl and the teacher, so that I can be formally introduced to the lady taking care of Sierra every day.

"Hi, Ms. Davis, I'm Garrett McKenna. I'm Alexis' boyfriend. I've heard a lot about you. Thank you so much for caring for my princess over there. She's a great kid," I say, both ladies are still staring, not saying a word, although, Lex has very glassy eyes. I can see that she's getting emotional, so I wrap her hand in mine and pull her close to my side.

Ms. Davis looks again back and forth between Lex and me, and then finally says, looking a bit glassy eyed herself, "It's very nice meeting you, Garrett. I love both these girls very much. It's my pleasure caring for Sierra." She's trying to compose herself. "You two have a great day. I'll see you at parent pick-up," she says, dismissing us. Sierra looks up and Lex blows her kisses. Sierra reciprocates. I catch them all and give her a wink, watching her giggle at the interaction.

We walk to the car hand in hand and I help Lex into the passenger seat of the car and close the door. I'm so damn happy right now. I climb into the driver's seat of Lex's Jeep. The top is down and the sun is shining. I'm not really pleased with her choice of vehicle, because the safety ratings bother me a bit, but it definitely fits her personality. It's probably too early to start talking to her about getting a new car. I'll keep that one under wraps for a bit.

"Sweetheart, I have to go back to the house to get my stuff. I want you to come with me. Mom's been asking about you since the wedding. Is it okay if we eat breakfast there?" I can feel her glaring at me. I chance glancing at her. Yep she's glaring at me.

"Um…actually, no. I'm not going to your parents' house. That would be crazy. I can only imagine what they think of me. I'll just wait in the car or something."

She's out of her mind. Her little ass is coming in and eating the breakfast I promised her. She's nervous about what my parents think of her. If she only knew they're probably praying the same prayers as Sierra. They're desperate for grandchildren, and since Alexis is the first and only woman I've ever introduced to the family, or sacrificed any time for, I'm sure they're all hearing wedding bells.

"Lex, my mother is dying to spend time with you. She really wants to get to know the girl who's captured my heart. It's been almost a month and I haven't brought you around at all. They're a bit mad at me about it. Can we please eat with my parents? It's not like you're meeting them for the first time. You met them at the wedding. Isn't the second meeting supposed to be easier? Technically, it's the third meeting, if you count college."

Her eyes are shooting daggers at me. "No, it's not, because I wasn't sleeping with you then. They can't possibly think too highly of me for my actions. My husband died eighteen months ago and I'm a single mother. I have baggage that no mother wants for her only child. She's going to hate me."

Tears are welling up in her eyes. I hate that she is so insecure and doesn't see how incredibly amazing she is. My mother would never think any of those things about Alexis. She'll love Lex and Sierra unconditionally. She'd be a wonderful grandmother, and since I'm not sure Lex wants more kids, Sierra may be all she ever has, although, she'd be just as pleased with that.

Sierra doesn't have grandparents, which is quite a shame. I didn't realize Jed's parents died in an accident when he was a teenager. It seems Lex has constantly been surrounded by tragedies in the past. I'm hopeful I can bring some peace into her life. She deserves it, damn it! I pull the car over into the parking lot of a shopping center and park as far away from the other cars as possible. She's crying big tears again, and definitely not happy ones. Shit!

"Babe, look at me." She does without hesitation. "I love you, Alexis Nicole. I crazy love you, baby. I love you more than my next damn breath. I can't, I won't, live my life without you. I don't care what anyone else thinks. My mother and father are very clear on what you mean to me. They can see it in my actions, babe. I've never stayed around for more than a couple days. I've been here almost four weeks now. I go back on tour in less than two weeks, and I'm dreading the thought of being away." I slide my seat the rest of the few inches back, then turn to lift her out of the passenger seat, over the console, and onto my lap. I love that she fits so well against me.

"Sweetheart, I haven't been sticking around here for anyone but you and Sierra. My parents know you're important. They want to get to know you. I want them to as well, so they can be here for you when I'm not. Which is going to *suck*... *bad*!" She's nodding her head, but I really don't know what she's agreeing to, because she's still crying and ripping my damn heart out! "Babe, can you talk. Tell me what to do," I beg.

"Ok, I'll go to your parents' house with you."

Chapter Twenty

Alexis

I'VE AGREED TO GO BECAUSE it's important to Garrett, but how can they not think this is a train wreck for Garrett's future? I wipe my eyes and turn my head to kiss my precious man. He loves us so much. I know he does. How could I question that, especially after this morning with Sierra in the classroom? He was amazing.

He didn't flip out when she introduced him as her new daddy. He just hugged her and carried on with business as usual. I, on the other hand, was flipping my lid! I climb off of his lap and back into my seat. I buckle in and he starts driving toward his parents' house. It's a good thing I don't wear a lot of makeup, or else we'd be in trouble. At least I put a dress and sandals on today. It would suck if I were in my standard yoga pants, tank top, and baseball hat. I take deep breaths, trying to appear less anxious than I actually am.

We pull up to the gorgeous house his parents own in a very exclusive gated community. Garrett opens my car door to help me out. He puts his hand at the small of my back, guiding me toward the front door. I put my hand up to reach for the doorbell, but Garrett gently pushes it down. "No, babe, we can just go in," and he opens the door.

I step to the side once we're inside. I want to follow behind him. It feels a little uncomfortable, walking into the room ahead of him. The house smells lovely. I immediately notice the smell of homemade waffles. "Hey, Mom and Dad. We're here," Garrett calls out to his parents, taking my hand and walking toward the kitchen.

His mother is beautiful, and ever so sweet. She walks toward us, as soon as we come into the room, immediately wraps her arms around me. "Oh, gorgeous girl, I'm so happy he finally brought you around. He's been keeping you all to himself," she says, hugging me, looking over my shoulder. "Where's Sierra? I'm dying to see the little princess."

Oh dear, I wasn't expecting her to be so welcoming given my situation. Guess I could have slightly overreacted. "Thank you for having me over for breakfast, Mrs. McKenna. I'm sorry Sierra couldn't be here. We just dropped her off at pre-school. She has a few weeks left before summer vacation."

She nods her head in understanding, "Well, that's okay. Maybe I can meet her next week. And none of that Mrs. McKenna business, call me Elizabeth," she says, looking at Garrett for confirmation.

"Mom, relax. I know you're excited, but try to keep it under control. Let's eat. Lex and I are starved. "

Mr. McKenna walks into the room right then, as Elizabeth goes to the stove to start plating the food. This woman obviously loves to feed her family. Mr. McKenna walks over to us, and just as Elizabeth did, he wraps his arms around me and gives a good squeeze. "We're so glad you're here, Alexis. Did Sierra come, too?" He asks with all sincerity.

"Not this time, I'm sorry Mr. McKenna," I reply.

"Listen, young lady, it's James or whatever else you want, but none of that Mr. McKenna stuff!" He says in a tone so similar to the one Garrett uses sometimes. It makes me smile, because I've come to know that tone is filled with a lot of love.

We're sitting at the huge island breakfast bar that Elizabeth has set for us. I suspect that she had a lot more notice of this visit than I did. I need to ask Garrett about that later. He pulls out the stool and stands beside me as I climb up. He takes the stool directly beside me.

We're having a nice conversation about Garrett's upcoming tour as his mom continues the final preparations. The thought of him not being around as much in a couple weeks is hard to imagine. It's not that I don't think I can be alone, I totally can, it's that I've grown to like having him around. I'm sure we'll still talk every day.

I get a whiff of something on the stove…oh my, bacon…I love bacon, but for some reason, it turns my stomach a bit and I feel the need to excuse myself from breakfast for a moment. "May I use your restroom?" I ask quickly.

Garrett looks to me. "Sure, sweetheart, let me show you where it is," and he walks me toward the hall. "You okay, babe? You look a little pale," he observes with concern.

"I'm fine, Garrett. Just tired. It was a late night last night!" I reply, winking at him with a sly smile. He grabs me by the hips and pins me against the wall with his body, pressing my hands above my head, kissing me.

The nauseous feeling immediately subsides, quickly replaced with warmth. I can feel my whole body react. "You may need a nap today, sweetheart, 'cause I plan to keep you up late tonight, christening the bedroom and bathroom of my house," he says in a husky whisper in my ear. "Go to the bathroom, gorgeous, and lock the damn door, or I may follow you in there."

I'm laughing, as I run into the half bathroom and quickly lock the door. Just as he promised, I hear him jiggle the door handle. Maybe I should have kept it unlocked! No, what am I thinking? We're in his parents' home…how inappropriate can one person be?

I splash a bit of water on my cheeks. I love bacon. I'm not sure what made me have an aversion to the smell. That hasn't happened to me before. But that kiss sure made me feel better quickly.

I make my way back to the kitchen and overhear Elizabeth telling Garrett, "Sweetheart, we love her and we're so glad to see that you're happy. Of course, we'll look after her while you're on tour. You need to stop worrying so much. It's only a few weeks." Garrett has his hands in his hair. It's his typical move when he's worried or frustrated.

I walk in and they all look toward me. Elizabeth says, "Alexis, you're a lovely girl. I'm so glad you could make it today."

Smiling, I reply, "Thank you, Elizabeth. There aren't many things Garrett asks me to do that I won't willingly do. Sometimes it just takes me a minute to process."

Garrett looks to me and grins. "I'll have to remember that, sweetheart." And my face immediately heats up to what

I'm sure is a very bright rose color. He kisses my cheek and his parents move along, placing the plates in front of each of us.

Breakfast is very tasty. As I suspected she did make homemade waffles, which are my favorite. The conversation is engaging and they're interested in Sierra and me, our likes and dislikes, hobbies, and such. It's all very sweet.

After we finish breakfast Elizabeth shoos us out of the kitchen and into the guest house for Garrett to pack his things. He doesn't have a lot of stuff, which is kind of surprising. He gathers his things as I explore his space, picturing where he was sitting on the few occasions when we've been apart and talking on the phone.

I'm looking out the bedroom window, which overlooks a beautiful golf course, when I sense him behind me. He presses his body against my back. Immediately I recognize what I feel; my shirtless, beautiful man has a need. I wholeheartedly want to fulfill all those needs for him, because this man is more than just a fantasy come true to me. He's quickly become my lifeline. I love him. I love the way he loves me and my outspoken, beautiful daughter, without expecting anything in return. I have no idea what I've done to deserve this.

He wraps his hands around my waist, pulling my ass tight into his hardness. His heavy breathing in my ear brings warmth to my center. I too have a need…I can't stand not being close to this man. It's been an emotionally packed few days and I haven't had enough alone time with Garrett to assure me he's real, and what I'm feeling is real.

He's nibbling my ear. His hands have a good hold on my hip bones. I arch my back, pushing myself into his hardness, and a moan escapes me. He growls. "Babe, I want to feel you right now. I need to be closer," he says in a rough voice.

"Yes," I reply breathlessly. That's all I can manage, because my own need to be as close to him as possible is far too great. I want him, badly!

He turns me in his arms and lifts me off the ground. My legs instinctively find their place, wrapping around his waist. "Garrett, I love you so much!" I say, as I tighten my grip around his shoulders and neck. "I just didn't know I could ever love any man this much. Please, don't ever leave us." Small tears are leaking out of my eyes, dripping down his neck. He carries me to the bed and lays me down with so much care.

"Alexis, my heart feels like it's about to explode. I've never in my life felt this full of love. Baby, you and Sierra will never be without me. I'm here. I'll always be here, even when I'm away on that stupid tour. Babe, it's you that I'll be counting the minutes to be with again…and I won't be gone for six weeks at a time. I'll come here every break, so the most you'll be without me is three weeks. And, sweetheart, we'll be burning up the damn phone lines." He's kissing away my tears again. "You, my gorgeous girl, will be very sick of me. I promise."

I smile and sniffle. "That'll never happen. I love you too much. Make love to me, please?" I plead, lifting my hips to meet his.

"Lady, you never have to ask me twice," he says, as he lowers the zipper on the side of my sundress.

He removes my dress and lays it neatly over the footboard. It's very different from clothes being thrown haphazardly across the room, which is what normally occurs, but his lust filled eyes are still glowing with passion. He loves me and he's making love to me to prove it. He removes my bra and I reach to help him, trying to speed things up a bit. He smirks and shakes his head.

"No, sweetheart, this is my job."

I'm feeling a bit desperate for his hardness. My body is acting on its own. Every place his fingers grace is left with a trail of fire. "Ace, please, hurry."

He chuckles under his breath. "Shhh, we have all day, baby, and I want to enjoy this hot little body. I'm taking my time. Relax." This frustrates me a little, but I want to please him, so I will myself to be more patient. I know he'll give me the satisfaction I'm so desperate for.

He graces me with a trail of kisses down my body. He reaches my breasts, taking his time and offering each nipple equal time and affection. Then he moves to my stomach with little nips and butterfly touches that tickle a little, and he places two kisses on each hip bone with a little lick and nip. He loves my hip bones. He's always touching them and paying special attention to them. Then he's at my center. He's kissing and nibbling my inner thighs, and before my next breath I feel his hot tongue reach my clit. That's all it takes for my body to buck wildly. He presses my hips into the bed. "I know, sweetheart, I'll take care of it." And he does. First, he enters my center with one finger while his mouth continues its assault on my clit. Then he includes the second finger and I explode under his tongue.

"GARRETT, YES! I LOVE YOU! ALWAYS!"

As my body is spiraling back down to earth, he climbs up the bed, hovering over me, waiting for my eyes to open and look into his. "Babe, that's so fucking amazing. I love watching you fall apart in my arms."

I grin at him. "I didn't just fall apart, ace. You did *that* and I damn well exploded!" He has the most amazing chest and shoulder muscles, when he's perched above me this way, he's hotter than ever! I feel lucky because he's mine and I can see this...whenever I want! I feel his length at my entrance and he slides in.

"Damn, babe…nothing is better. Nothing will ever make me feel this good," he says in a groan of bliss.

He slides his length in and out, kissing me and carefully watching my expression. He's always so attentive to my needs. "Look at me, beautiful." He's telling me what he wants, "I want to see those hazel gems. Keep your eyes open." And I try, but he feels so amazing it's hard not to escape into the bliss. There's so much love and passion being passed between the two of us right now. I can feel my inner muscles spasm. I know I'm getting close, as Garrett increases the pace. I wrap each of my legs around his thighs and push him deeper with my ankles.

"Fuck …Lex, you ready, baby?" he growls.

"YES." I explode again, as he fills me with all his warmth.

He rolls over onto his back, taking me with him, so that I'm resting on his chest. He's not ready to separate from me, yet. He always likes to hold me afterward.

"Lex, why do you call me ace? I haven't heard that in years. You're the only one who ever called me that," he asks, while we lay still connected, regaining a normal breathing pattern.

"You always ace everything you do. I've always been so proud of you." He doesn't respond right away. He just stares.

Chapter Twenty-One

Garrett

WHAT DID I EVER ACE when we hung out in college? I wasn't successful then. Shit, when I finally made it to Nashville, I would have lived in my car had it not been for my parents making sure I always had a roof over my head. What is she talking about? "Sweetheart, I'm not sure that cleared it up for me. I wasn't successful then."

She just shakes her head. "Garrett, do you really think you being a superstar is how I measured your success? I thought you were amazing way before then. I was happy when the world finally figured out what I already knew. But, Garrett, I watched your talent and dedication far before your first number one track. You totally aced the music thing. You were smart and had tons of friends. You were kind and had swarms of girls around you. And, even though, you were constantly surrounded by girls, and I was incredibly jealous at times, I don't think they ever really understood you or saw your greatness the way I did."

"I was proud and that was my way of telling you. I'm sorry it wasn't clear to you back then. You aced life…music, friends, family, girls…you were amazing and it came easily to you, because you're such a great person. I'm proud of you, always have been."

Shit, she thinks I aced life. That couldn't be further from the truth, but looking at the crap ass life she's been dealt, I can imagine how it looks that way from her point of view. I feel like I've sacrificed so much for this life, and I've missed out.

"Baby, the only thing in this life I want to ace, is you and the little blond mini-you. I could give a rat's ass about the rest of it. I want you, and I don't want to screw it up. Please, don't let me," I say to her. I want to be worthy of this name she's given me, but I want it to be for something meaningful. I want to ace loving her. I want to ace being a good family man for her.

I lift her to the side of me and kiss her forehead. "Let me clean you up, baby." I carry her to the bathroom and place her on the vanity. I turn on the warm water, take a damp cloth and wipe her down. I see a bit of red on the cloth as I wipe her down. Is she hurt? "Damn, baby, did I hurt you?" Concerned, I ask.

She looks at the cloth and turns a bit pale. "Oh…I'm sorry, Garrett…It must be that time for me. I can never keep track, because the implant makes my time of the month erratic. Sometimes it never comes at all. Did I get blood on you?" She's concerned about me, yet she's bleeding.

I've never experienced a monthly cycle with a girl. I've never kept them around that long. I'm concerned. What happens now? Does this hurt? I've heard from the guys that it's torture. "Baby, I'm fine. Do you feel okay?"

She smiles to reassure me. "Yes, Garrett, I'm good. Can I use your shower and will you bring me my purse?" She says as she pushes away from my inspection.

"You can share my shower with me, lady. Together all damn day, I mean it."

I run to the family room to get her purse. She's started the shower by the time I get back to her. I watch her from the doorway, testing the water temperature. She's smiling and humming along to a song. She's happy, and that alone makes me feel like I'm on top of the damn world. I love her. She's the most beautiful girl I've ever seen. I could sit and watch her do anything and feel incredibly entertained. But most of all I love watching her smile, sing, take care of Sierra, and fall apart in my arms at the end of every day. This girl has completed my life in a way I never thought I wanted, but now I would damn near kill for it.

I walk into the bathroom, placing her purse on the counter, and going directly to her, wrapping my hands around her hips, so that I can caress her hip bones. I love them. I'm not really sure what it is about them, but touching them makes me feel a volt of electricity every time. She's hot. Her little body is the best I've ever seen. It does things to my eyes every time I see her naked. I see stars, and it feels amazing.

I reach out and test the water myself, before sliding us into the warm stream. She's careful not to wet her hair. "In you go, sweet cheeks," I say, as I nuzzle the spot behind her ear. I put her directly under the stream so she doesn't get cold. I can wait to be under the water, because being close to her makes me hot as hell. I take the clean cloth and lather it up with soap. I wash her body, massaging the lather into her skin, taking my time. I'm careful when I wash her between the legs. I'm not sure if she's sore. Instinctively I check for more blood, but there's none.

She looks a little embarrassed. "Garrett, stop. I'm fine. Women have dealt with this curse for centuries."

I shrug my shoulders. "But I've never dealt with it with a woman, let alone the woman I love," I say with a bit of chagrin. She kisses me, slides around, and then pushes me forward so that I'm under the stream.

She gets another cloth and takes her sweet, precious time rubbing me down with soap and rinsing my body. When she reaches my cock and feels how hot I am for her she drops to her knees in front of me saying, "Garrett, are you hard for me again?"

Shit... she's suffering and bleeding, she can't do this now. I should be taking care of her. "Baby, no, you don't need to do that now. But, I'm always hard for you. I can't help it. Let's try that when you're feeling better."

"Shut up, Garrett, I feel fine and I want to suck your cock right now. Are you really going to deprive me of satisfying my man?"

Well, when she puts it that way, hell no!

"I'm here to please you, lady. Have it your way."

She smiles, as she pumps my length in her hand, dropping to her knees and licking the tip of my cock. "Shit…" I say moving my hips forward. She opens her lips and my cock slides into her mouth. Her tongue is licking the underside of my length. I'm holding the back of her head and pumping into her mouth, as she wraps one of her little hands around the base of me. The other one is massaging my boys. It feels too good, and I'm going to lose my load, again. I can feel the back of her throat on the head of my cock "Baby, I'm gonna go…back up." But she doesn't let go. Damn… Did she not hear me? I can't hold it much longer. I try and guide her head back, but she takes me deeper into her throat. "FUCK ME…" I explode down her sweet little throat, pulsating in her mouth. "I love you so much!" I say, almost yelling.

She's giggling, as I find my way back to earth, looking down to her eyes. "Damn, babe. That was amazing," I'm telling her, as I lift her up and she wraps her legs around me. My girl loves being held. I take the towel and wrap it round her, taking her back to the bed to lay her down. I'm smothering her with kisses and tickling her.

"We can't sit around here all day. We need to get you packed up, and go back to my place to pack, if you want to make that trip tonight."

She's right, but I really wish we could just lay around naked all day. She pops up, taking the towel with her and wrapping it around her body. She picks up her clothes and walks to the bathroom. I get up to follow her, when she turns looking at me. "No, Garrett, stay there. A girl needs privacy sometimes."

I poke out my bottom lip, pouting. "I want to help you get dressed, baby."

She looks at me, smiling, "Another time. Go get ready, so I can go home and pack. It takes me forever to get our things together."

We leave my parents' house with all my stuff. I didn't really have a lot, but I'm taking it all with me in hopes of not returning to this house when we get home from Nashville.

"Sweetheart, can Sierra miss a few days of school? I want to keep you guys in Nashville for a few days and show you around. I'm also hoping Courtney will spit out that kiddo while we're there."

She shrugs. "I don't see why not. I know that I don't want to come back without you," she says, and it makes me so happy that we're on the same page about that. I know for sure I'd never be able to put the two of them on a plane to come home with me knowing I'll be leaving for the tour in eleven days. I'm dreading that. But I'll be spending the next eleven days giving them my undivided attention.

We say good-bye to my parents. They make us promise to visit and bring Sierra when we get back from Nashville. They know that this girl has captured my heart and is a permanent fixture. They couldn't be happier.

On the car ride back to her house Alexis is checking her emails and trying to respond. "Ugh…why now? I've had enough."

I hear her talking to her phone under her breath. "Sweetheart, everything okay?"

She looks at me, remaining silent for a minute, and then nods her head. "Yeah. It's fine. I'll deal with it," she says, clearly frustrated.

"Baby, I don't want you to deal with anything on your own. I want you to talk to me. Tell me what's upsetting you," I implore, but she just shakes her head no. "Grrr…Lex. What the hell is it? I'm going to be worried sick until you tell me." I'm not asking anymore. I want to know what the hell's upsetting my girl. I don't want or need anymore more crap getting in the way of her 'Happy Ever After'.

"It's my mom. She emailed. She wants money. I'm not going to deal with it. Jason will, but she doesn't usually contact me. It's just frustrating because she always picks the times in my life when things are going well to walk in and screw everything up."

Shit. No way am I letting that woman, who mistreated Lex for so long anywhere near her. I'll handle it once and for all. "Send me her info, Lex. I'll handle it," I say, but she screams at me.

"HELL NO GARRETT! You stay the hell out of this. This is between Jason and me. It's not anything for you to handle. If you even think about it…EVER…It'll be a deal breaker!"

Well, to hell with that. I'm not promising anything if Lex isn't safe. She can't put those kinds of restraints on me. "Lex, I'll let Jason handle it, as long as that woman poses no threat to you or Sierra. If that changes, deal breaker or not, I'm stepping in. Got it, lady?" She's looking at me with that little pissed off, hot tempered face, but I've got one to match, so it doesn't really affect me. "Call your brother, now," I order.

By the time we make it back to Lex's house she's called Jason, and he's agreed to handle the mother situation. I'll call his little ass tomorrow and verify it's done. I can't have crap like this upsetting Lex. She's been through enough, but I'm sure he'll agree.

We head right upstairs to start packing. I know we're running a bit behind because of our little after breakfast escapades and Lex's temper tantrum in the car. She's looking a little stressed and rushing.

"Sweetheart, you're looking stressed, still. What can I do?" I ask.

"Garrett, I have to pick up Sierra in an hour and a half, and we need to be packed before then, because we'll have to go straight to the airport from there."

"No, sweetheart. We have more than enough time. I'll go get Sierra. Relax. The plane won't leave without us. I promise. What can I help you with?"

Still looking stressed, but trying to relax a little she says, "Can you get the luggage out of my closet? I'll gather clothes for Sierra."

It does take a lot more time than I expected for Lex to pack, but it's because there's so much to gather for Sierra – a bag of things for the airplane to keep her busy (electronics, and stuff), a bag of clothes, her special blanket and favorite stuffed animal, a small bag of toys and things for Sierra to play with at my house. Then, Lex has a bag of clothes, a bag of toiletries, and her backpack with her laptop and stuff. I can't believe how much is needed for these girls to travel for one week. Not that I really care. I'd move the whole damn house to keep her with me for this week if she wanted.

I've called a limo service to drive us to dinner and the airport. I want to get my girls a nice dinner before the flight, because it'll be after Sierra's bedtime when we arrive. I know Lex likes to feed her early.

We leave the luggage by the door when we finish packing, with time to spare for a few kisses, and then we rush off to get Sierra. I'm excited to pick her up from school. I love that she wants to show me off. I've never wanted to be paraded around more. I love my little princess.

When we get to the school, Lex tells me to pull up in the line with the other parents, but I ignore her and go for a parking spot. "Garrett, we don't need to meet her at the classroom. They'll bring her out. Just go to the line." Again, I ignore her. Parking and turning off the car, I climb out of the Jeep and walk around to the passenger side and help my girl out. She's glaring at me. "You're going to spoil her, and she'll expect this sort of treatment all the time. Please, just stick with our usual routine. We both like it this way," she says with a snarky attitude.

"Shut up, Lex, you're ruining my moment. I want to get my princess from her class. It's only my first day on the job. I've missed her," I say. Her glare dissipates and is replaced with a glassy eyed smile. "No tears, Lex. We're all happy here, lady," I say, before kissing her senseless. Then we walk hand in hand through the school to wait in front of Sierra's class.

I keep looking into the window, trying to steal a peek. What's taking them so long? I see my little blond haired beauty gathering her things and marching to the door. When she looks up at the window and sees me, her face lights up. She's waving, pointing, and jumping up and down all at the same time. I wave back and hold one finger up, willing her to be patient, before she speeds out the door and into my arms. She's trying hard, blowing me kisses and mouthing something that I don't understand.

Lex is standing beside me watching the interaction, laughing. "You two are pathetic!"

"Hey guys, what are you doing in the school?" Kate, Alexis' sister in-law, asks as she walks toward us smiling.

"We came to pick up Sierra, and Garrett insisted we come inside. I was going to call you and let you know, we're going on a little trip today. I already told Jason earlier. Sierra and I'll be gone till next week," Lex tells a beaming Kate.

"REALLY? Where are you off to?" Kate doesn't even try to hide her 'I told you so' smile.

"Nashville," I say. "You guys want to come, too?"

Kate laughs. "Thanks, Garrett, No we are all good. Traveling with three little people is hard, not to mention Jason & I both have to work. Thanks for the invite, though. We'll take a rain check during summer." She's probably right. I can't imagine how much time it'll take to get stuff for three little people when it took almost two hours just for Sierra and Lex.

"Anytime," I say.

Just then the door opens and my little princess runs straight for my arms, while her aunt and mom stand aside watching us. Sierra launches right into a story about her day. Ms. Davis approaches us, saying goodbye to Sierra and telling her to have a nice weekend.

"Oh, Ms. Davis, I wanted to let you know Sierra won't be at school next week. We're taking a little vacation. I'm sorry for the short notice, but it just came up," Lex is telling the teacher.

Ms. Davis surprisingly looks very pleased. "Very nice Alexis, I do hope you all have a wonderful trip," she says, while patting Sierra's back.

I carry my princess out of school, while holding my girl's hand, and I've never felt so complete. Kate is walking us out before she has to go back into the school to pick up her children from the aftercare room where the employee's children go until dismissal is complete. She and Alexis are talking in somewhat of a code about her mother, but I get the gist of the conversation. Kate's also very pleased that we're going away together and that Lex is happily embracing our togetherness. I think she really is, finally. Yesterday sucked for my girl. It made her doubt how amazingly loveable she is. I don't ever want to see my girl that sad again.

Chapter Twenty-Two

Alexis

SEEING GARRETT AND SIERRA interact is precious. They almost speak their own language. It makes me so happy that he loves her. He told me yesterday that he loves her instinctively, and it's true. He's finding his way with her, and although, it's my nature to want to control this, I need to let go and let them form their own relationship without me taking over. Garrett wants this. Sierra needs this.

He's carefully buckling her into her seat. He double, then triple checks to make sure she's in snuggly. He kisses her forehead and tickles her neck, before jumping into the driver's seat to bring us home.

When we pull in the driveway, there's a hummer limo waiting in my driveway. Sierra is squealing with excitement! Trepidation starts to build again. "Uh Garrett, what is that doing here?" I ask.

He just shrugs. "Taking us to the airport, I suppose," is the nonchalant answer to my question.

What the hell! A limo? Can't we just drive like normal people? "You know, they do have parking at the airport these days. We can drive ourselves."

He shakes his head. "No...too much work and I don't want to leave your car there unattended that long."

"Okay," I concede, "but I don't want to bring Sierra's car seat." I laugh at his confused expression. "She's too old to have it on the plane, Garrett. She can be buckled in regular seats then. I don't think she needs one in the limo either. We'll just use a seat belt."

"Uh...no way lady, my princess will have her little pink throne," he says, winking at Sierra, as he takes her out of her seat and spins her around.

As soon as he places her on the ground, she's running for the parked limo. "Can I get in, Garrett?" She begs with unrestrained excitement.

"Yes, sweet girl, let me get your seat," he says, before climbing into the back of the Jeep and unlatching her seat.

Chapter Twenty-Three

Garrett

THE DRIVER OPENS THE TRUNK waiting for instructions. He's a big, muscled, well dressed guy, a lot like the security team we have on tour. I look him over and inform him, "Bags are by the front door." He follows Lex to the door. I pick up Sierra, putting her in the limo and leaving the door open, so I can watch her while she can bounces around on the seats. She can get some energy out before I snap her cute little butt into her pink throne.

I walk toward the house to help Lex. My lady is trying to lug bags, while the damn driver walks behind her, eye fucking her. Oh hell no! I walk straight to Lex, "No sweetheart, I got this. Go get in the car with Sierra." I'm glaring at the asshole standing behind my girl, studying her curves, and he hasn't noticed me, yet. Grrrr!

She smiles and kisses my cheek. "I'll get the car seat

settled," she says cheerily, not seeing what's happening behind her back, thankfully. She'd be a little embarrassed if she knew. I know my girl is sensitive about bringing too much attention to herself.

She walks off toward the car. I step right in front of this asshole and speak very low, so as not to alarm my ladies. "Listen, fucker, those are my girls. You keep those eyes of yours on the road and on the fucking bags, not on my girls. Got it?"

He's startled. That's good, because I'm pissed. "Sorry, Mr. McKenna. Didn't realize I was looking so closely. I'll get the bags, sir. I'm really sorry!" I feel a little better, now that I've put him back in his place. I've never had an issue with any of my drivers before, but then again, I've never had Lex and Sierra with me. I'll guard them with my damn life. I didn't think I was the possessive type, but I guess I am. She's mine and I don't want anyone looking at her that way.

I pull the Jeep into the garage, lock up the house, and set the alarm. By the time I get back to the limo, the driver is standing by the open car door staring at anything other than my girls. I nod my head in approval toward him and tell him where to take us for dinner as I climb in the back. I know Sierra would like the rotating restaurant on top of the airport. I've heard the food is good, too. So we'll have a nice dinner before our flight.

By the time we finish dinner and reach the plane, Sierra is winding down and getting snuggly. We pull up in front of the jet and the driver opens the door. Whitney's car arrives right behind ours. Perfect timing. Lex looks a little surprised….

"Garrett, where are we?" She asks staring at the jet, not moving. Scared.

"Sweetheart, we're at the airport, getting on the plane.

What's wrong?" I ask, reaching to hold her hand, but she is incredibly rigid and tense, gripping her knees with white knuckled fingers. "Talk to me, baby. You're making me nervous." She's got tears in her eyes.

Whitney reaches our car and opens the back door, irreverently joking, "Hey, guys, traveling in style? Huh?" Then she notices the look on Lex's face. "Hey, Sierra, come with me. Let's go check out the plane." She helps a clueless Sierra out of the car.

"Babe, are you afraid to fly?" I ask her.

She shakes her head. "No, I just don't want to fly in those type planes," she explains, pointing to the private plane. "I want to go in a regular plane, Garrett. Not a private jet," she pleads as tears streak down her cheeks.

Oh shit! Why didn't I think of this? Of course, this would be traumatic for her. I'm an idiot. "Babe, I can't take a commercial flight. It'll be a disaster, and we don't have security until we land in Nashville. Do you want me to book you on a commercial flight? Sweetheart, I'll do whatever you want to make you feel better. But I'd rather you fly with me, where I can hold you."

She takes several deep breaths, looking out the side window, watching Sierra climb the stairs with Whitney. She turns to look at me. "Is the weather okay?" She asks in a whisper.

"Yes, babe, I promise. We wouldn't be going if it weren't. I want to keep you safe. Always," I say with my hands resting on hers.

"But, are we safe, Garrett?" Her eyes plead for me to reassure her.

"Yes, baby, you're both always going to be safe with me." She nods, just enough that I see her acceptance, and starts to slide out of the seat. I grab her by the waist and hoist her into my lap. I kiss her with all I have. I want her to feel how much I care right now. She relaxes in my arms and I feel the tension begin to dissipate. "I love you, Lex," I whisper into her hair.

"Yes, you do," she says, and that's all I need to hear. I need her to know it's true. I slide us out of the car and carry my girl up the stairs of the plane.

She's putting on one of those fake-ish smiles, but I'm sure that's all she has to offer right now. We're settled in and doing the preflight stuff, as our bags are being stowed. Sierra is buckled into her seat. I've double checked both my girls' seat belts. I sit in the seat next to Lex and across from Sierra and Whitney.

Thankfully, even though the tension is high, Whitney's keeping Sierra very cheerful and distracted. They chat away about some television show and color in a book. The stewardess comes over to tell us to put the tray table away and I give her a clear 'back off' look, so she leaves and hasn't asked again. I want my princess to remain distracted from the tension her mama is feeling.

Lex lays her head on my shoulder and closes her eyes. I hate to see her stressed. I should've thought of this beforehand. I'll be damn sure to work out alternate arrangements for the trip home. I rub Lex's knee as we start taxiing down the runway. When we start for take-off I turn my head into Alexis' ear and whisper, "You, my beautiful girl, have made my life more complete than I ever thought possible. I love you more than my life. I'll do anything to keep you happy, healthy, and safe. Anything." She nods at my reassurance.

"Look at me, sweetheart." She complies quickly as we're speeding down the runway and I feel the tires lift. "I love you…like crazy love you, sweetheart!"

The corners of her lips lift. "Yes, Garrett, I know. And clearly you know how very much I love you, too. Right?"

I give her a little smile back. "Yeah, babe. I know."

The little one pipes right in then. "Well I love all of you, too!" She breaks the remaining tension that's still lingering as she points to the three off us and we laugh.

I pat her little head, saying, "Back at ya, little chick." She giggles adorably at that.

Chapter Twenty-Four

Alexis

I DON'T REALLY KNOW WHY I thought we'd be traveling on a commercial airplane. Of course, we'd be traveling on a private plane. I feel kind of stupid for expecting anything different. Garrett is quite an amazing man. I can't stop thinking about how incredibly fortunate I am to have him. He was strong for me when I was scared. Private planes scare me. I realize it's a fear founded solely on my own tragedy and not the actual statistics, but still…it's a big fear.

Jed almost always flew commercial, but on his last flight it was a private plane, because they had to make it for a meeting about a project. The weather was bad, and they thought they could fly around the storm. They were wrong and he paid the price for that. But it was just an accident. I have to remember that.

The plane lands safely in Nashville. We're gathering our

things when the cabin doors open and four huge men walk onto the plane, greeting Garrett. "Hi, boss, great to see you," the guy in front says.

Garrett signals for the men to keep it down, pointing to Sierra sleeping. "Grab the bags, guys. This is Alexis & her best friend, Whitney. How does it look out there?" he asks.

"Same as always boss, but the car's waiting," big guy number one answers.

Garrett nods, and points to Whitney and me. He's talking in a low voice, so I can't make out what he's saying. He speaks to the guy for a few moments. Then he flashes me a grin that looks more like a grimace, before dashing out the door with the other three guys. I look to the big guy and inform him I'll be ready as soon as I gather Sierra up.

"That isn't necessary, ma'am. We'll be pulling into the hanger for you to disembark." His tone is matter of fact, like he has this scenario down to a science.

What the hell? I guess Garrett wants to keep us hidden. I knew he would be ashamed to be seen with someone who wasn't from his rock star life.

The jet starts to taxi again. Whitney shoots me a confused look. I shrug and try to play it off, like she can't see I'm upset. She knows me too well. I should prepare for the interrogation as soon as we're alone.

Once the three of us and our bags are loaded into the car, the big guy, whose name I now know is Dan, slides into the back of the limo with us. He says, "Proceed," and the limo begins to roll forward. After we clear the hanger a low roar penetrates the windows. We stop and Dan pushes open the door, stepping out. The low roar becomes thunderous. The screaming, wailing, and shrieking are enough to make my ears bleed.

I immediately turn to check on Sierra. She's sleeping like a log. I should've known nothing would wake her up.

Garrett jumps in as soon as Dan clears the door. The door closes as the limo starts to move. He looks disappointed and worried. I guess he's concerned that his fans feel let down. Well, I didn't ask to be here. He begged. If we we're going to hamper him so much he should have left us in Florida. My anger is building.

I'm getting madder by the minute, and now that we've finally pulled up in front of Garrett's palatial home I'm even more pissed. Why didn't he give me a clue what it'd be like when we got here? Photographers, fans, limos, mansions, security team, being hidden…this fucking sucks! I'm about to throw a huge tantrum, but I'll hold it together until Sierra's in bed.

Garrett obviously senses my mood because he says *nothing* when I pick up Sierra and carry her into the house. He just opens the doors and leads me to the room where Sierra will sleep. He's prepared, because while I'm laying Sierra on the bed I see him switch on what looks like a baby monitor, but it's one of the new high tech camera kind.

I'm not sure where the other receiver is, but if he thinks I'm sleeping with him tonight, he's off his damn rocker. No chance of that. "Where are our bags?" I ask in a bitchy tone.

"They're coming up now, sweetheart," he says sweetly. I roll my eyes in his direction, intending for him to see. He does and the hurt look on his face doesn't even come close to making me feel better. It makes it worse. Sweetheart, my ass…you just wait and see how sweet I'm going to be about all this shit!

There's a light tap at the door as two of the security members hold up our bags. Garrett instructs them to leave the bags here. Then he follows the guys out of the room.

I'm searching Sierra's bag for pajamas when Whitney walks in. "Lex, you okay sweets?" She asks with concern.

"Nope!" I reply.

And then she starts in on one of her typical I know what's best for you lectures! "Lex, I get that you're pissed. It's been a shit evening. I get it. A lot of unexpected shit happened, but seriously…is it worth this amount of angst?"

Now I'm getting more pissed and my frustration isn't only aimed at Garrett. "Whitney, shut the hell up. I'm not discussing this with you now. Find a place to sleep in this big ass house and leave me alone. I cannot believe you're sticking up for him in this whole situation. You're supposed to be my best friend!" I say in the best whisper-yell I can manage, attempting to not wake Sierra.

"Alexis, you are so self-destructive it's ridiculous. I can't even begin to talk to you right now. Goodnight!" She says, turning on her heel and walking out of the room.

I change Sierra and myself into pajamas and climb into bed beside her. I imagine he wasn't expecting me to sleep in here, but I'll be damned if I'll sleep anywhere else. I lay in bed beside Sierra for what feels like hours, but it has only been just under one hour when I see the door open and the light around it expand. I see his silhouette, he's heading toward me. He bends down beside me and kisses my head, then lifts me out of the bed. "No," I say, but he ignores me and keeps walking with me cradled in his arms.

He takes me to what appears to be his bedroom and lays me into his bed. "Listen sweetheart, you can be as pissed off as you want in my damn bed, but you aren't sleeping apart from me. Build a wall with pillows, but you're fucking sleeping here!"

I'm pissed and tears are prickling my eyes. "Why? I don't want to be here. I want to go home, Garrett. This trip sucks and I've only been on it a few hours. Make sure we're on the next flight out!" He's hurt and angry, but I'm not the one screwing this up. He should be pissed at himself. He comes over to the bed where I'm sitting. I'm staring daggers at him, willing him to say anything else, so I can release all the hurtful crap I want to say.

"Lex, I'm sorry! I knew it would be chaos at the airport. I should've warned you. I should've put you guys on a different flight. I should've done this all differently, but I was selfish and wanted you beside me as long as possible, instead of arriving separately. I screwed up, babe. I get it." He's right in front of me, taking every dagger I'm throwing, face to face. "On top of that, Lex, I don't know what the hell I'm doing. I don't understand relationships. I'm trying and you said you'd give me a chance…Please?"

"Why yes, you jackass, that was a brilliant plan! Are you pleased with what went down? Are you worried we'd destroy your sex symbol image? You couldn't be bothered to let me know what was going on before you rushed out to greet your adoring fans? And this place…you said we were going to your home. This is a damn palace. And don't even get me started on the guys in monkey suits. You said we'd have security at the concert, not the minute we got off the plane!" I'm ranting and not quietly.

He leans in closer. "Are you done now?" He asks with a calm, even toned voice which only enrages me more.

"No you, asshole! I'm not done!" I yell, pounding my fists into his chest. I'm frustrated beyond belief, and he sits there calmly taking every single blow I deliver.

"Do your best, baby, get it all out, so we can make up."
He says in a strangled voice and that's all it takes. I'm done.
I've exhausted myself, and now I'm crying huge angry frustrated tears. I lay myself down on the pillow and close my eyes, crying myself to sleep. He lies beside me, but doesn't touch me or speak to me. He hates me.

When I wake the next morning the room is still dark, but I see the time on the clock sitting on the nightstand. It's after 9:30. I haven't slept this late in years. I look around the room and no one is here. I look at the baby monitor screen and it's been switched off. I jump out of the bed and run down the hall to Sierra's room. She's not there. Then I hear it – a guitar and her sweet, precious voice. They're singing…together. I sit on the top of the stairs to listen. I don't want to disturb the peace, and after what happened last night I'm sure tensions will be high when I enter the room. I stand up and start walking to the room Sierra spent the night in to start organizing our things to go home today. I'm not sure what time our flight is, but I'm sure after the way I acted he'll have us out of here as soon as possible.

As I'm laying clothes out for today, Whit comes into the room. "Good morning, sunshine. Feeling better?" She asks way too cheerfully for the situation.

I turn to her, feeling extremely remorseful. She's my best friend in the world. She didn't deserve the things I said last night. "I'm so sorry, Whit. I hope you know I didn't mean anything I said to you. You just happened to be in my line of fire." I jump up and wrap my arms around her shoulders. "Please, dear God, don't be mad at me. Forgive me?"

She looks at me with a big grin and a chuckle. "Like you

even have to ask? I forgave you the minute it happened. Lex, I know you well enough to know when you're spewing crap you don't mean. What are you doing now?" She asks, arching her eyebrow.

"Packing. We're going back home today. I can't stay here. Not like this," I say to my best friend, willing her to understand and not question my motives.

"Lex, you have got to stop running away from him every time things get hard, or when fans, photographers, air planes, or whatever else scares you happens. Eventually, he'll stop chasing you and that's really going to suck, sweets".

"I know…maybe this time he won't chase me. We'd both be better off, I think," I say quietly.

"You think, huh? Maybe you should go downstairs and see the man who is consumed with worry over you. Yet, instead of sitting in the corner waiting for you to scream at him, again, he's taken every measure known to man to make sure you sleep as long as possible, and that Sierra is taken care of like a little princess and that I, your best friend, am comfortable and happy in his home. Do you really think for one minute he's doing any of that to benefit anyone other than you?"

"Alexis, wake up! This man is jumping through every flaming hoop you place in his path, and yet, it's not enough for you. You really need to sit down and think this through before you throw away what could be the best thing in the world for you and Sierra," she says in a huff, before walking out of the room. "Let me know if I need to pack my stuff, Lex! I'll be in my room taking a bath and reading. Send Sierra up to my room if you need time to chat with Garrett."

I guess it's time to face the music. I walk down the hallway to the staircase and descend at a snail's pace. I'm scared to death of what I'm going to be faced with. As soon as I reach the bottom my little girl spies me and says, "Good morning, Mama. You were very sleepy."

I smile to her, "Thank you for letting me sleep. I was extra tired today." I look at Garrett and his face is blank. I can't read that look on his face, so I don't say anything. I just look away.

Chapter Twenty-Five

Garrett

SHE'S COMING DOWN THE STAIRS. I can feel her getting closer. I feel so bad about everything that went down last night. I knew Alexis was feisty when she was riled up. I remember that about her from college. She'd trample anyone who messed with her friends. I never expected what happened last night. But damn, she got her frustrations out on my pecks, that's for sure. I hated to see her that upset and frustrated. That was way worse than the actual physical side effects. My poor sweet girl…

Last night was a clusterfuck. When Dan stepped on the plane I immediately asked how it looked outside. I didn't want to alarm Lex, so as quietly as possible I instructed, "Keep them on board. I'll get off out here to distract the crowd. Pull the jet into the hanger, and then get them in the car. Once they're safely inside pull up, and I'll get in. I can't figure out how they always know when I'm arriving."

I thought I did the right thing to protect them from the madness. I thought Lex would appreciate the efforts to keep them from being exposed to the chaos, since she is adamant about keeping her life private. I don't know what I did wrong.

She's talking sweetly to Sierra, which is no surprise. She'd never take her frustrations out on a child. But she's not saying anything to me. I'm paralyzed in fear that last night will be the tipping point that makes this all too much for her. I don't want to do anything else that might upset her or make her want to leave. I need her here with me. I need to make up with her. I slept like shit last night. I just lied next to her, listening to her whimper for hours. Even after she fell asleep I was awake, watching her and searching for the right words to make this better.

When I woke this morning and found her still in bed with me, I counted my lucky stars. I closed all the blinds tightly, so it would be dark and peaceful in hopes that if she caught up on sleep she'd feel better, and then I snuck out of the room. She does look rested. I'm glad about that.

"Good morning, sweetheart," I say, searching for any emotion on her face. She gives only a small smile, and it doesn't even come close to bringing the sparkle to her eyes.

"Morning, Garrett."

I turn on the television to morning cartoons for Sierra. She's already had breakfast, so this should keep her still for a few minutes. I reach over to Lex. "Babe, come talk to me for a minute?" I tentatively ask. She nods her head.

We walk up the stairs to the master bedroom and she sits on the bed. Before she has the chance to say any of the things I know she's thinking, I speak. "Lex, I know I'm not worthy of you and Sierra. My life is complicated and frustrating. I knew better than to bring you into that last night without warning, but I was being selfish. I did the best I could to protect y'all's privacy when we arrived. I thought about trying to walk away a few weeks ago. But, sweetheart, I have these strings attached to my heart that are all wrapped up in you, and I just can't walk away without ripping out a vital organ. Babe, you now own my heart. What happens to it is up to you, and even if you try and give it back, I won't take it. I'm still going to have to follow you everywhere in life because of these damn strings. Please, babe. Don't push me away! Give me a chance to make this manageable for us. I love you both, so much."

She doesn't respond. She just sits there staring at me, dumbfounded, until finally she says, "You don't want us to leave? After the way I acted yesterday? I'm challenging and bitchy! I've been a puddle of tears since the day this all started. Why, Garrett? Why me?"

Why her…because, I love her. I've only ever loved her. And I'd do anything to keep her. Anything.

"Sweetheart, you had every right to say the things you did last night. Most weren't true, but I know you well enough to know you already know that. You're perfectly challenging. You keep me alert and on my toes. It's never boring! It's one of the things I love most about you. And your tears…damn, babe, they really wreck me. But they also tell me what is going on in that pretty little head when you won't talk to me." She's just staring at me and listening, but not touching me. "And, sweetheart, as for wanting you to stay…" He draws in a deep breath, "Babe, I always want you to be where I am. No matter how pissed you are at me. Please, stay with me. I love you," I plead, again, in case it wasn't clear enough the first time.

"I'm so sorry, Garrett. I was frustrated. You didn't deserve the things I accused you of…I do know that. A little warning would've been nice. I really hate surprises. I love you a lot, but your life is complicated and foreign to me. I love you enough to stay while you try and make it manageable. I just need to know that Sierra won't be harmed. Please, it's my job to keep her safe, and right now I'm scared."

This is the part I hate, because, damn…I'm scared, too. I don't want anything to ruin what I've got right here. "Sweetheart, I've learned my lesson. What happened last night won't happen that way again. I'll be prepared and you girls will be safe with me. It's my job, Lex, to keep you both safe, and I promise I will." We'll quadruple the damn security if we have to. I reach for her and she comes to me willingly. I kiss her face and spend the next few minutes just holding her. I'm a lucky bastard.

We spend the rest of the morning and afternoon touring the ranch. I'm glad Whitney came along. She calms Alexis and keeps Sierra busy every once in a while, so I can steal a few kisses. She's leaving tomorrow afternoon and that's fine, because I plan on spending the week in Nashville doing family things. Tonight is the benefit concert. I'll be leaving soon for the sound check.

"Sweetheart, I'll need to leave soon for the arena. Do you want to go for the sound check, or should I send a car back for you?" I ask. I planned for the girls to come to the sound check, but I don't want to assume that she's okay with anything after last night. I'm walking on eggshells, and that's okay, if it makes her feel more secure.

She looks to Whitney and Sierra walking ahead of us.

"I'd rather go with you. I'm afraid we won't be able to get to you later if people don't know who we are," she says, being sincere.

I laugh. "Baby, no one will ever be able to keep you away from me. But I'd feel better if you went with me, too. I need you close to me after last night. I hate when you're mad at me," I say as I pick her up and swing her around onto my back for a piggy-back ride. She nibbles my ear, and we keep walking and following Sierra, who's trying to find the horses.

"Sierra, we need to head back toward the house to get dressed, love bug!" Lex calls out.

Sierra turns around, sees her mama on my back and comes running. "I want up, too, Garrett. Hold me, too," she says, so I pick her up and haul the both of them, with Whitney in tow laughing her ass off.

We're all dressed and ready to leave. I decide to drive us to the show and have security follow. I'll have four security guys with the girls tonight. They'll be back stage. I don't really expect any issues, but I'd rather be prepared, and I think these guys will give Lex some confidence.

When we arrive at the stadium in my Land Rover, the band manger meets me at the back door. He's pissed off. I knew he would be. He has a folder with what I'm sure is a stack of internet articles he's printed. I already saw them all this morning, so I know what's coming. I see right away that he wants to talk. He's called several times, but I've been busy with my girls.

"Hey, Charles. Now's not good. We'll talk later," I say carrying my princess, walking right past him towards the room where the band members are hanging out. Charles follows, he's persistent. He better not start any shit that upsets

Lex. I'll kill him right after I fire his ass.

"Garrett, we need to talk." He looks over to Lex with contempt. "Privately… Now!" He says.

I pass Sierra off to Lex and kiss them both. "Give me a minute. I'll be right back," I say to them. He and I walk a little way down the corridor to assure a bit of privacy, but I'm keeping my girls in sight.

"Garrett, what the fuck do you think you're doing?" Charles asks. "You're Garrett Fucking McKenna. You don't have time to be playing family man. I don't even want to think about what your fan base will think if they see that you have a girlfriend. This is a successful tour and we don't need any damn distractions. Look at this shit." He shoves the articles printed from various gossip sites in my face. They have various titles, 'The Elusive Bachelor Captured…Finally' 'Baby Mama's Back' 'Garrett's child…paternity revealed.' What stupid shit this is? There are low quality pictures of us when we picked Sierra up from school yesterday.

Did Charles just call Lex a distraction? I don't want to make a scene right here, but I need Charles to settle his ass down. "Let me tell you something right now, Charles. You'll take care of this fucking tour and band like you've always done and keep your fucking nose out of my personal life. If you ever call either of those girls a fucking distraction again, you'll have much bigger problems to deal with. I promise you that!" I say, throwing the papers at him and walking back toward my girls. I'm pissed, and not just at Charles, the damn gossip sites are insane. I wish for once they'd print something real, but, no, that's too much to ask for these days.

I walk over to the girls and reclaim my princess in my arms, kissing Lex as payment. I feel better already. Distraction, she's more than a damn distraction. This is the girl that makes me forget my name when she looks my way. She's always had that power. I just never had the balls to tell her, but now, I want her here beside me more than I want my next damn breath. Lord, let's hope she wants that too. Otherwise, I might turn into one of those chest thumping barbarians. Caveman style is not my thing! What the hell has gotten into me? I'll be asking her soon to be my wife…mark my words! I'll need to make her really mine.

I walk them down the hall to the room where the guys are hanging out and I hear Courtney's voice. Good God, am I glad she's here tonight too. We walk into the room where everyone's hanging out chatting and snacking.

Courtney pushes herself up right away and waddles over to Lex and Sierra. "Hey, ladies, I'm so glad y'all made it! It's so good to see you," she says before hugging the girls and introducing herself to Whitney.

"Look at you, Courtney. You look fantastic. How are you feeling?" Lex asks as they walk over to the couch, chatting. I plug in Sierra's iPad and she makes herself comfy with a movie and headphones on my chair. I think she's a bit sleepy, since she missed her nap. It'll be good for her to relax in here for a little bit. Her sweet mama looks tired as well. I hate that this has been such a stressful week.

The guys and I discuss the set list and start warming up our fingers on the guitars. Lex and Courtney are still talking about baby stuff, while Whitney is talking to Jon, my lead guitarist. They are in their own little world talking about music and 'The great state of Alabama', where they're both from. Huh….that's interesting.

When it's time for us to go out onto the stage, we all walk

out together. I show Alexis where she'll be hanging out for the performance. Then I go to my spot and look back, making sure I'll be able to see them. I can. Perfect!

Chapter Twenty-Six

Alexis

WOW. GARRETT IS AMAZING live on this big stage. I'm really proud of him. Sierra is jumping up and down singing all his songs. She loves him so much. He keeps looking back at us, and winking every now and then. Sierra went out and sang one of his songs with him, but he didn't introduce her, thankfully. The crowd thought she was just a random child from the audience. She felt like a superstar for a minute. The show will be ending soon, and then we'll all head back to the ranch. I'm holding Sierra who's trying so hard to stay awake, but failing, regardless of how loud it is. We're all exhausted.

Garrett walks off the stage after the encore. One of the stage-hands passes him a bottle of water that he chugs as he walks straight for us. He kisses me, tells me he loves me for the thousandth time today, and takes Sierra out of my arms, which I welcome because my arms are so sore from carrying her.

Whitney is walking with Jon. He asks if he can take her out tonight and she agrees. Not really sure what that's all about, but she seems excited and Garrett says he's a good guy. He's quiet, but damn hot. Whit has never been interested in 'tatted up musicians' before. She's more of a 'hot business man' kind of girl. Huh…interesting.

Garrett is walking us out of the arena with security close by. His manager is following beside us, trying to set up meetings for this week, but Garrett has refused any appointments. His manager, Charles, I think, is getting very frustrated. Finally, Garrett looks at him and tells him he's not taking any appointments before he leaves for the tour in ten days. Garrett uses his stern voice that I've only heard a couple times when he's ordering people around. He glares at Charles in warning. Charles apparently gets the message and backs off.

He'll hear no complaints from me on this, since I intend to spend all of that time getting my fill of him before he's away. Tomorrow we're going over to Courtney and Drew's place to hang out with the band. That'll be fun I expect.

When we step out of the arena there are more fangirls waiting for Garrett. Even with four strong security guys it's a struggle to keep everyone back and make a clear path for us. But Garrett does a fantastic job shielding Sierra and she stays asleep through it all, again. I'm grateful, because this might have been a bit scary for her.

I relax once we're in the Land Rover and on our way back to the house. Garrett apologizes for the craziness. But I get it. I expected it this time. I'm over the top in love with this man. I need to accept that he'll be constantly surrounded by women, throwing themselves at his feet and willing to do anything to get a piece of him. Yet, here I am wanting more than anything to believe the things he says to me, that what I have to offer him will be enough. This is going to take a great deal of trust.

When we make it back to the ranch Garrett carries Sierra into the guest bedroom and turns on the monitor. "When did you get that?" I ask, while finding Sierra's pajamas to change her into.

"When I found out you were coming with me. I wanted her to be comfortable in this room, and to be able to hear her if she needed us. I had my housekeeper pick it up," he says as we quickly work together to dress her without disturbing her. We both kiss her little head and whisper 'I love you' to her.

When we walk out of the room he picks me up and cradles me in his arms. "Now, tell me what you thought of the show," he asks, while showering me with love as we find our way to the master bedroom.

"I loved it. You're amazing, but I already knew that. I prefer your private performances, though, ace."

He plants an evil looking grin on his face. "That's good news, since the next performance I have planned is only for you, sweetheart!"

He lays me on the bed and unties the halter around my neck. I lay still, watching him devour me with his eyes as he slides the dress off. I'm lying on the bed with only my cowgirl boots, bra, and panties. "Fuck, Alexis, too fucking hot!" He makes quick work of his boots, jeans, and t-shirt. He stands in front of me in just his tight boxer briefs. Yes...this is a nice game. We can both sit staring at each other. Although, I'd much rather have him on top of me. "Lex, you're perfect!

I'm a lucky ass man to get to do what I'm about to do, babe, and I know it," he says just before he pounces like a tiger onto his prey.

After the marathon make-up sex and love making session, I literally must have passed out. I don't remember it actually ending, but I wake up in the arms of my precious man. Half my body is draped over him, and I'm dressed in a tank top and boy shorts. I don't recall putting my clothes on. I look at him. His eyes are still closed, but I can sense that he's awake. "Good morning, Garrett."

He cracks open one eye. "Good morning, my sleeping beauty. You slept well, I see."

Smiling, "Yes, in your arms, how could I not?"

He grins. "I love you, Alexis."

"Yes, Garrett, you do…very much."

He nods. "Glad you know it, lady! Let me get dressed and go get our little girl. She'll be up any second. I can already hear her stirring. I'll bring her back in here to snuggle in bed with us and watch TV." Yes, I'm a very lucky lady.

"Did Whitney make it back ok last night?" I ask him.

He shakes his head. "She called *very late* to tell us she'd be back this morning sometime." He sounds very annoyed.

"Oh, that's not like her to stay out late with some guy she's just met." I'm curious.

"Yeah, babe, well…it's not like Jon either. But they're grown-ups and I don't have the time or the energy to babysit them, so they're on their own."

Um…that's my best friend and if she gets hurt by one of his friends, he's going to pay, along with his little friend. I'm just sayin'. "What the hell? That's my best friend! Your buddy better be on his best behavior, or I'll expect you to kick his ass for me," I exclaim, throwing a pillow at him.

He laughs, leaving the room, and then I see him on the baby monitor rubbing Sierra's back. Her thumb goes straight into her mouth as she turns her little head to Garrett. He sings to her. A song I haven't heard before. A song about questions children ask. It's precious. Sierra knows the song, because as she climbs into his arms and as he sings she's humming along with her thumb still attached to her lips. They keep singing all the way into the room, until he drops her right in between us on the bed. A TV rises out of the footboard. She snuggles in between us and doesn't say a word, as we all lay together in bed.

I'm not sure why I'm surprised by what I've witnessed. She loves Garrett and I think she's captured his heart as well. He's such a sucker for this little girl, and that couldn't make me happier.

It's ten in the morning before we hear the doorbell. I'm hoping that it's Whitney. I can't believe that girl stayed out all night. "I'll get the door, it's probably Whitney," I say, and he nods. It can't really be anyone else. I put my robe on and run down the stairs to the front door. I open it up and it's not Whit...it's Charles.

"Oh...hi, Charles," I say. "Garrett's upstairs. Let me go get him."

Charles looks me up and down and snickers. "I guess you're thinking you've hit a gold mine, huh?" He says, looking at me with evil eyes.

"What are you talking about? I want nothing from him except his love. I don't need anything else."

"That's what they all say. You're not even his type. How'd you snag him? Was it your sob story?" he asks. All I see is RED. I slap the living shit out of him.

"You, asshole! You don't know anything about my situation or me. Don't you dare try to tell me I manipulated Garrett! I love that man!" I yell.

Garrett is running down the stairs to get to me. He reaches me and looks me over top to bottom. "Are you hurt, baby?"

I shake my head, but my hand is throbbing. I'm rubbing it with my other hand. He looks at it, and then looks to Charles, who's holding the side of his face.

"That bitch hit me!" He screeches at Garrett just before he finds himself on the floor holding his nose. "You're done, Charles. I warned you. Get the fuck out of my house. I don't want to see you anymore. Am I clear?"

He looks confused. "Garrett, we've worked together for years. You can't really be serious that you're choosing this," he says, pointing to me, "over your career and all the success we've built."

Garrett looks at me and then to Charles. "Abso-Fuck-ing-lutely. She's the best thing to ever happen to me! Now get your ass up and get the fuck out of my house before I bury you in the horse pasture for hurting my girl," he threatens as he inspects my hand, flexing my fingers and wrist to make sure they aren't broken. Charles backs out of the house in a huff, tossing around threats of a lawsuit. Garrett ignores him.

My hand hurts, really badly, but I try to restrain from showing any signs of pain. I don't want Garrett to be any more upset. "I'm so sorry, Garrett. I thought it was Whitney. I tried to go get you, but he started saying some really awful things and I reacted. It was bad. It was my fault. I'm so sorry," I ramble, looking into his eyes.

"No, babe, I heard him. He deserved what you gave, but

I should've been the one to do it. I had to get Sierra settled. That's what took me so long to get to you. I didn't want her to see or hear the venom he was spewing. I'm sorry I didn't get here fast enough, and I'm sorry for the things he said. I'll take care of him later. I promise. Let's take care of you, now."

We go into the kitchen. He puts ice and water into a bowl and submerges my hand. I wince. He takes it out fast. Shit that hurts and it's cold. He kisses the palm of my hand then slowly submerges it again, keeping his hand in the water with mine.

Looking me in the eyes he says, "I'm so sorry, Lex. I should have protected you from that. Shit…are you really okay? Do you want to leave?"

I shake my head. Keeping eye contact I answer, "No. I'm not leaving, Garrett. I'm done walking away from you. I love you too much. I'm okay. I just have a sore hand."

He kisses me. "I crazy love you, sweetheart! You kind of made me proud in there, but next time, wait…let me throw the punches, baby. Okay?"

I shrug. "Okay…I think I'm done with that." And he kisses me some more. Then we hear the front door open and he starts to take off for the foyer, but Whitney makes it to the kitchen first.

It's Whitney and Jon. Thank God! They walk into the kitchen, and she looks at the bowl of ice water my hand is in and immediately asks, "What the hell went down here? Jon's phone was blowing up with calls from that guy, Charles. He's saying Lex attacked him."

Then Jon appears at Whit's side and looks at my hand in the bowl then to Garrett. "Shit, man. I think we need a new manager before the tour in what…nine days." Garrett just nods his head. "We'll deal with it, dude. Don't worry!" Jon says. Garrett still says nothing.

Later, we head out for the afternoon barbecue at Drew and Courtney's house. I'm nervous about going now, since all the band members know that the argument this morning with Charles was over me. I don't want them to think I'm a trouble maker.

Whitney is quiet about her night with Jon, but he's always close to her and she relishes it. When he's around, he fetches her drinks, rubs her back, and is always attentive. She likes him, I think, but she keeps telling me to focus on my own relationship and not worry my head about her love life. Crazy girl. She's avoiding it, but I can see something's there.

We say hello to everyone when we walk in. No one immediately talks about what went down this morning, even though, I know they all are in the loop. It's a big deal, because Charles is their tour manager, and they're supposed to be leaving in nine days for a six week tour. I really screwed things up, but Garrett isn't taking it out on me one bit. He just keeps saying it'll all be fine. I hope so.

I'm talking to Courtney, who tells us she's starting to feel Braxton hick contractions. She thought it was the real thing and went to the hospital last night, but they sent her home. She's really ready for the baby to come out. She's scheduled to be induced in two days if she hasn't gone into labor yet. She wanted to take the baby on the tour, but now it appears the baby will be too young, so she'll stay behind. Drew's planning on coming back for a few overnights, even though, he'll only be home for several hours, instead of a full night and day, but apparently it's worth it to them.

The guys all gather around the grill to have an impromptu meeting. They all agree that Charles was way out of line and deserved what he got. No one is upset with Garrett or me. These guys are like a little family. They stand together. The label will likely hire someone on a temporary basis, just to get them through the next several weeks. They'll deal with hiring someone permanently when they return. It's all settled. As for the lawsuit, it's not even mentioned. They don't really care.

The party was fun. Sierra had a blast being the only little kid there and getting all the attention. She's getting really tired, and a bit cranky, as the evening winds down. Two days in a row without a nap and staying up late are taking its toll. We need to get on a better schedule tomorrow. I mention to Garrett. He's quick to jump into action when I tell him Sierra needs to go to bed. He grabs our stuff and says goodbye to everyone with no questions asked.

Jon asked to take Whiney to the airport a few hours ago, so it's just the three of us for the remainder of the week. Garrett says we can do whatever we want. We'll make some plans in the morning over breakfast.

Chapter Twenty-Seven

Garrett

IN THE FIVE WEEKS SINCE I found her again, I've gone from a man that enjoyed spending most of his time in front of thousands of fans performing on the stage, to someone I can barely recognize. But I'm learning that I like this guy better. I like being a family guy, spending time with my girls. I never thought I'd ever be content doing normal day to day things. Honestly, I like having people who want to serve me breakfast, do my laundry, and clean up after me. But doing these everyday tasks with Lex is different. I like this time with her. I like doing damn near anything with this lady. Cooking, cleaning, playing, sleeping…anything, except fighting. I never want to fight with her again.

We're heading to the zoo today, and then to visit Courtney, Drew, and baby Gabe in the hospital. They're all doing great from what I hear. Drew completely flipped when Court's water broke. Now he's acting all crazy about leaving them in a week. But he'll be flying home every other day for a few hours. It's going to make a really shitty three weeks for him before we have a break, but I'm not sure I'd do anything differently than he is. I'm already trying to figure out how I can skip away for a few days, too, but it's a little more challenging for me, since I have more responsibility for the band than Drew.

Sierra is so much fun. She loves music, I think as much as I do, so touring Music City this week has kept her interested. We've also done a lot of kid stuff.

She's a great kid. Even though, I'm not her dad, and I would never want to take his place, I really like being whatever it is I am to her. I don't really know what name to put on it, yet. I'm still working on that. I don't want to discount the major role Jed had in the lives of these two. He was a good guy and he took great care of these girls. I can guarantee Alexis and Sierra were the best things to ever happen to him, because they damn sure are the best things to happen to me. But he's gone now, and he died a damn lucky man! I'm here, and willing and able to do whatever it takes to make them the happiest girls who could ever walk this earth.

We're walking through the zoo. I'm wearing my hat low and tying to be careful about being noticed. We're blending in pretty well. The security team is following closely behind us, but attempting not to interfere, unless it becomes necessary.

I'm standing behind Lex with her back pressed up against me. We're watching Sierra and Dan, our lead security guy, feeding the animals in a petting zoo. Sierra asked Dan to go in with her. She's so friendly with everyone she meets. The guys all seem to be taken with her too.

"Garrett, what's your type? I've never really seen you with anyone more than once. It's hard to tell if I fit into your perfect picture." My precious girl says, breaking me from my thoughts. Charles told her she wasn't my type. I heard him say it, but I didn't want the altercation to upset Sierra, so I had to quickly distract her before running to get that asshole away from Lex.

I knew she couldn't really be okay with all that he said. I spin her around and pull her chin up, so that she's looking me in the eye. "You, sweetheart! Your lips are the only *'type'* I want to kiss. This hot little bottom is the only one I want to squeeze. You, baby, you're my only *'type'* and the most perfect picture I could ever imagine!" It's true. I've never had a type until now.

She's smiling. "Right answer!" I kiss her, trying not to let it go too far, because it would suck to walk around the zoo at half-mast all day. Damn, I can never get enough of her.

"Garrett, do you think we can go back to your place after this and let Sierra nap for a bit? She's really off her routine, and it's going to be torture next week if we don't try and find some balance."

I squeeze her ass before kissing her again. "Abso-Fuck-ing-Lutely. I need a nap, too," I say, winking at her and she laughs.

"Sleep sounds great!" She says to me.

"NOT a sleeping nap, lady."

"That's what I want," she exaggerates with a yawn and a stretch, "aaahhh...I'm soo sleepy!"

She's such a little tease, and she knows it. I look around for a place to escape to privately, so I can show her how much she doesn't want to sleep. I see a door with 'employees only' written on it. "Don't tease me baby. I'll take your little ass into that room and do very dirty things to you," I playfully threaten.

She shakes her head. "No way, Garrett! Hands off until we're home. I don't want that shit online," she says, hitting me upside the head. I laugh at her, but my heart is jumping through my damn brain. She just said until we get home. Is she referring to my house as home? Fantastic! I love it. Yep, it's home. Our home. We need to make it so.

Courtney and Drew were over the moon happy when we arrive at the hospital that evening. It's a miracle, really. I've watched Courtney's stomach grow for months, knowing there was a baby in there. But then to walk in this room and see the basketball under her shirt deflated, and this little human in her arms…damn, it made me want something I never thought I would. I want to talk to Lex about kids. I need to find out if this is in her plans or not. I'll take her either way, but I'd do almost anything to have a baby with her.

"Garrett, where do babies come from?" Sierra, who's in my arms, asks me while Lex holds baby Gabe and talks with Court.

I'm stunned at first. I'm not sure how I should answer, but while I'm looking around the room it comes to me, "Oh… Princess…it's a miracle really…babies come from love – a whole lot of love. Look around this room. Can you feel it?" I ask her.

She looks around then back to me, "Yes, and that's how little babies grow too…lots of love," she says. What a wise little person; so much like her sweet mama. "Yes, baby girl, you are correct. You're loved so much that you'll surely be grown up in no time!"

Sierra falls asleep in my arms, as we're all hanging out and talking in the hospital room. She's had a busy day. Her nap was far too short and she's exhausted her little self. I'm thinking about the far too short nap time that I had with Lex today, and I grin to myself. There's never enough time for that. Lex looks over at us sitting on the couch. She's got the baby in her arms again. Apparently she loves babies, which happens to be great news for me.

"Garrett, I think it's time to take your little princess home." There's that word again. Damn, I love it! I grin and stand, putting Sierra on my shoulder. Her little thumb finds her lips as usual.

We're walking out of the hospital, and I'm thinking about what our life together might look like. It's amazing to picture these things. Alexis and Sierra are perfect. They make me feel like a real man. I like feeling like this.

"What are you thinking about?" She asks when we get settled in the car.

I turn to her, "Sweetheart, after spending the last several weeks with you, I want to write songs I didn't know I had the words or emotions to write. I want to sing about love, butterflies, and all that shit. Please, let me always love you. Let me feel what everyone has told me about all these years. Being with you makes me feel like a real man. And I fucking love it!" I say to her, and she climbs over the center console into my lap and kisses me with everything she's got.

"You are a real man, Garrett. I have to remind myself of that sometimes too. You are a dream come true for me. The crazy fangirls scare me, because I don't want you to decide any of those chicks are easier to love. I'm trying so hard to not let my fears tear us apart. I know you're a faithful man. You wouldn't do anything to hurt us…right?"

I take her face into my hands, "Never, lady! I don't want anyone else. Ever! Just you…always you!" She kisses me again and then squeezes the shit out of my neck. But I don't complain.

The week has flown by. We're headed back to Tampa tomorrow. Lex is feeling anxious about getting chores done before they roll into their normal routine next week. She's a bit on edge because of it. I have to leave in three days, but I'll fly out of Tampa and meet the bus at the first stop. I'm feeling more and more melancholic by the day just thinking about leaving. I'm going to hate this. I already hate being away from them.

We have a four day break after three weeks of touring and I'll see them then, but those three weeks will be torture! We've uploaded the video chat app to all the computers, but that can't possibly be enough.

Whitney has planned a girl's night for the day after I leave. I think Whit did it knowing Lex would need something to keep her distracted from me being away. There are two more weeks of school left for Sierra, and then she'll be home for summer vacation, although Lex is planning on sending her to camp with Jason and Kate's kids.

Lex has been in a funk for a few days. She's not feeling well and she's a shitty patient. She won't let me take care of her at all. She won't even tell me her symptoms. She's going to the doctor's this afternoon. I'm taking Sierra over to Mom and Dad's for lunch and to swim. Lex says she'll just meet us there after her appointment.

Chapter Twenty-Eight

Alexis

WE'RE HOME AND I FEEL LIKE complete garbage. I know this feeling and this is *really* bad. I'm not sure how it could have happened, since I have the implant. I have an appointment later today to see my OB/GYN. I can't put this on Garrett. I've already done enough damage to his tour by hitting his longtime tour manager and getting the man fired. I can't possibly tell Garrett that I'm pregnant now. I'll have to keep this under wraps for the next few weeks.

Thankfully, Garrett's taking Sierra to his parent's house for a little visit this afternoon. That'll give me some time to figure out a plan.

I'm waiting in the exam room after I've submitted my urine sample when Dr. Daniels comes in. "Alexis, it's so great to see you! I see you're already glowing." Was that recognition of the positive pregnancy that I'm already aware of?

"Looks like you're expecting, again. This is great news, I hope." Yes, I hope so, too.

I put on my fake happy face and say, "Of course, the best kind." It is great news…just not great timing. I've wanted another baby for quite some time, but I wanted to be married and have a real family. "Dr. Daniels, I'm confused, though. I still have the implant.

"Yes, you do, but it's only effective for three years and you've had it for almost four years now." Shit! He's right. I thought I was protected. I would have been had I done the damn math. I guess I lost count when sex wasn't really happening, and I forgot to reassess when Garrett and I happened.

Dr. Daniels pulls the sonogram machine over to me. "Let's see if we can get some pictures for you." I see the screen flick to life with the greys and whites. Then my doctor points to the tiny bubble with another confirmation of the tiny life inside me. I'm so deeply moved. This is happy news… for me. I hope that one day soon I'll be able to tell Garrett and he'll think it's happy, too.

Dr. Daniels tells me I'm about five weeks along and gives me several sonogram photos to keep. I take all my prescriptions for vitamins and head off toward home, stopping at the pharmacy on the way.

I have to be strong, and not tell Garrett during the next couple days before he leaves. I'm not convinced this news won't make him feel trapped. I don't want him to think I did this on purpose. I realize how this could look to others, but it was never my intention.

I'm not ready to be with company, so I'll make up an excuse to buy myself a little more alone time. I text Garrett.

Me: Hi, it's just a virus. Should be better in a few days. I'm going to head home and rest while the house is quite. Give my love to your parents and I'll see you and Sierra later.

He responds almost immediately. Which makes my guilt even worse.

Garrett: Good baby, go home and rest up. My mom is making you some chicken soup as we speak and Sierra is playing checkers with dad. I'll be home to take care of you later. I love you.

I know he won't want to sleep anywhere else, but I should at least offer him the option of not catching my so called virus. And maybe if he stays at his parents, he won't be around when I likely puke tomorrow morning.

Me: Garrett, it may be better for you to sleep there, so that you don't catch this bug before your tour.

Garrett: NO Alexis…I'm coming home to take care of you. If I get sick that'll be good news. Then I can stay with you longer. ;)

If he only knew that wasn't going to happen. I wonder how he'd feel if he knew the truth? He'd be running for the hills, I'm sure.

I'm home and I go up to my room to take a nice long bath. I need to plan how I can tell Garrett without making him feel like I've just imprisoned him.

I lay in the warmth of the water and suds. No wonder my emotions have been going haywire the last few weeks. Things are starting to become clearer. The smell of the bacon last week, my tears, and extra anxiety…I get it.

I'm not sad, I'm actually really happy, just worried about the repercussions where Garrett is concerned. I've been a single parent long enough to know how challenging it can be. Even when Jed was alive, he still traveled so often that I was on my own a lot in the beginning. It's okay. I know I'll be okay. If this is all too much for Garrett, I'll handle it. I'd never force him into co-parenting. He can be as big a part of our life as he chooses. But I won't tell him until the tour is over.

I relax letting my mind wander off, thinking about what our life could be like if Garrett knew what was growing inside me. If he wasn't *'The Garrett McKenna'* and just *'My Garrett McKenna'*, things would be easier. I see him as a proud daddy, loving us all and not loving this little person any more or less than my own little Sierra. He'd still be her special guy.

I feel someone rubbing my cheek and kissing my head. I realize it's him as I come awake. "Hello, beautiful girl, you're sleeping in the tub. Let me help you out of this cold water, before you give yourself a cold to go with your virus." The water is now room temp. I must have been sleeping for a while. My fingers are wrinkled and white.

Garrett removes his shirt and then lifts me out of the tub. I see that it's dark outside when we enter the bedroom. He lays me on the bed and goes to my wardrobe to get my tank and boy shorts. He dresses me, tucks me under the covers, then strips down to his boxers and climbs into bed behind me. He rests his hand on my stomach, pulling me in snuggly to him. That simple movement fills me with so much longing.

I desperately want to share this joy with him, but I know it's not possible, not yet. So I keep quiet but vow to remember the feeling of his hand on my stomach in case it doesn't ever happen again.

Chapter Twenty-Nine

Garrett

I LEAVE TOMORROW AND LEX is still sick. She threw up almost immediately after she woke up this morning. She's not really eating much and I'm worried about leaving her. I've called her brother. He's says he'll keep an eye on her and Sierra after I leave tomorrow, and he can always watch Sierra if Lex needs a few days to get over whatever this is. I started to postpone the first few dates on the tour, but she overheard my conversation and squashed that with one of her adorable temper tantrums. God, I love her.

"Sweetheart, what do you feel up to doing today?" I ask her. I don't really care what we do as long as I don't have to be away from her at all.

"Anything you want. I'm happy just to stay here and have a family day. We can swim, watch a movie, and play games. I don't really care," she says.

I've already packed all my stuff, so we can do all those things. I love creating these memories. I want to leave knowing we did make memories. I love family time.

Lex looks like she feels better as the day has gone on, she's just a bit tired and needing a little extra sleep, but she's been able to keep a little food down this afternoon. So I'm starting to feel a little more relaxed. I'm not comfortable leaving her, though. Truth be known, I wouldn't be comfortable leaving her if she were well. But I'm as okay about it as I can possibly get at this point.

She keeps saying how much she'll miss me. I love it and hate it at the same time. My lady is going to be sick of talking to me when I'm on the road. I'm upping our daily calls to the start of the day, before lunch, after school for Sierra, before Sierra's bedtime, and then end of the day at Lex's bedtime. I'm not sure if she's going to go for it, but I figure I'll just do it anyway.

Chapter Thirty

Alexis

HE'S LEAVING THIS MORNING. I'm driving him to the airport. Sierra is sad he's leaving, but he's promised he'll talk to her every morning and evening. He printed her off a calendar, so she can mark the days until he comes back. She's really going to miss him. We pull up to the plane. He looks at me, but says nothing before he gets out of the driver's seat of my Jeep and climbs into the back to hug and kiss Sierra, again. After their goodbye she focuses on watching a movie on the iPad, while I say goodbye to Garrett.

I get out, too, and walk around to the driver's side. He has his bags in his hands and he walks them over to the stairs in front of the plane before turning to me. His eyes are glassy.

It's taken everything I have not to tell him my secret this morning. I want him to stay so badly. But telling him now would be trapping him. It's unfair. I need to wait. If he stayed,

I'd want him to do it because Sierra and I were enough for him.

I know I'm seconds away from losing my emotional hold. I don't want to send him off with me crying and begging, but I have to tell him how I feel.

"Garrett, when you left me all those years ago for Nashville, I was sad. I missed my friend. But now, my whole being is wrapped up in you. You've made me desperate for your touch and your sweet words. Leaving us now is torture. Sierra and I need you here with us every day. We love you sooo much, Garrett. If you get on this plane, I can't promise her or myself you'll ever come back. Garret, my heart is breaking here! Please, don't go!" I cry out with tears spilling down my face. I'm scared to death. What if he doesn't come back? What if something happens to his plane? What if he meets someone on tour that's better suited or prettier than me? What if he finds out what I'm hiding and never comes back because he'll be so mad?

"Oh, sweetheart, nothing in this world could keep me from coming back to you girls. Alexis, I'll see you in three weeks and I'll talk to you every day, baby, so often that you'll be sick of me. When this damn tour is over, though, we're changing your name! I don't ever want to live without you and Sierra again. Be ready, baby. I'm giving you some time to wrap your cute little head around it. You girls are mine and this is going to be happening very soon. I love you more than anything, sweetheart!"

He says he's going to marry me? I'm sure it's to make me feel better. It wasn't a proposal or anything. I stand there staring at him, with tears falling down my face and him holding me, like always. I know he loves me, but will he still feel this way when he knows the truth? He's contractually obligated to be at these events. He'd have to have a damn good reason for cancelling. I still wanted to be enough for him to stay. I knew better.

I hug him again. "I love you, Garrett! We'll be here waiting for you," I say, trying to regain my composure before I walk back to the Jeep.

He walks me all the way back to the car, opens the door, buckles me in, kisses my head, waves to Sierra again, and closes my door. Oh dear Lord, I hope this isn't the last time I'll see or hear from this precious man. Losing him will possibly kill me.

Instead of going home we go to my brother's. I'm not ready to walk into that empty house, yet. It feels so wrong. Over the past few weeks my house felt full of life again. I loved it. I know Garrett's just on a trip, but so was Jed. This will never be easy.

Sierra is thrilled to visit her cousins. She hasn't seen them in over a week, since we've been away in Nashville. We walk through the front door and I smell my sister in-law's sauce and meatballs. It smells so good and I'm starving! Sierra runs off to play. Jason isn't home from work. I walk into the kitchen and Kate's sitting at the bar. "Hey, you. Was wondering when we'd see you. Did Garrett leave already?" I nod my head, but don't say anything.

She opens the cabinet gets out 2 wine glasses and starts pouring. "None for me." I say. She looks at me, startled. "No way," she screams. I can't deny it to Kate. She'll know soon enough anyway and she'll never forgive me if I lie. But she's the best at keeping secrets. I know she won't tell anyone. Not even Jason.

It's not like she keeps everyone's secrets from Jason. She doesn't. But sometimes it's necessary for Jason to not know things pertaining to Sierra and me, because it stresses him out; being the overprotective big brother that he is. This would certainly challenge his ability to stay calm. My brother worries too much about my well-being.

"Lex, start talking!" she badgers, replacing my glass of wine with a glass of ginger ale.

"Five weeks. I've been sick. He thinks it's a bug. He left an hour ago. I didn't tell him, but I begged him to stay. He says he's changing my name when the tour's over. Not sure he'll still want that when he knows what's growing in my belly." I spill it all out for Kate.

"Holy shit! When did you find out? What the hell are you doing keeping that from him, Alexis?" I know it sounds awful. If I were watching this play out on some lifetime movie I'd definitely be calling myself a stupid cow!

"I know, but I didn't want him to feel trapped. I'll tell him after the tour is over, but I'm scared he'll hate me! Please, don't tell Jason. I don't need him on my case right now." I beg, and she nods in agreement.

"I don't understand why you think he'd feel trapped. He wants a life with you. We all see that. He loves you, sweetie." Kate tries to reassure me.

I just don't understand why he loves me. I saw the girls last week falling at his feet. He could have any of them he wanted. "I know he does, but he deserves more than I can give him," I say sadly.

Kate huffs. "Honey, you have got to stop thinking that what you're offering him is less than anything else. You're giving that man one of the best gifts in the world. Give him the benefit of the doubt. He loves you and your daughter. He knows how lucky he is. Mark my words." I hope so.

My phone beeps.

Garret: I crazy love you! I crazy miss you! I crazy want to kiss your sweet face!

GUILT....GUILT...GUILT

Me: I love you, too. I'm at my brother and S-I-L's for dinner. Didn't want to go home without you yet!

At least this is true.

Garrett: Call me as soon as you drive home. I want to talk to you girls as you're going home. I want it to feel like I'm there with you. I Love You, Lex!

Going home with him on the phone will never feel as good as having him there, but I'll take what I can get.

Me: Ok. 1 hour. Love you way more, Garrett.

He doesn't have any clue that being so sweet to me right now fills me with anxiety, because I'm keeping such a big secret. Please, dear Lord, let this man forgive me for this one day.

I had a voice mail from Garrett's mom today wanting to know if she could have Sierra for a sleepover. They really love her! She's never had grandparent figures in her life, except for Kate's mom and dad, who've kind of just taken Sierra in as a package deal. I think I'll see if she wants to go there next weekend. I want to talk to Garrett about it.

Kate feeds all the kids at the table and she put two plates on the bar for her and me, since Jason is running late. She's drinking her wine and I'm still sipping the ginger ale. I sit at the bar, my plate in front of me, and the meatballs that smelled delightful earlier now make my stomach quake. "Oh no…" and I run off to the bathroom. For something that smells so good, it looks awful. I can't possibly eat that!

When I return to the bar, my amazing sister in-law has replaced my plate of meatballs and pasta with plain pasta and toast. This is more manageable. "Sorry Kate, I love your food, but not right now, I guess."

She's sympathetic, "I know. Just try and eat a little something. And keep drinking the ginger ale."

Jason comes home after we eat. He and I have a few minutes to chat about our incompetent mother, who contacted me asking for money last week. It's a really crappy situation, because I really just want her to fall off the face of the earth. But Jason, whose heart is sometimes bigger than his sense with her, keeps giving and giving and hoping for things to change. She'll never stop asking if he doesn't stop giving. Jason and I do agree that we don't want her as an active part of our lives, so she's never met her grandchildren. As badly as it sounds, I hope the day never comes that she does. I don't want to be anywhere near her. Jason's handled it he says, so for now she's on the back burner.

We stay for a while after Jason gets home, so we can visit with him. I haven't seen my bother in a couple weeks, which is a long time for us. It's been well over the hour I told Garrett, but I'll call him as soon as we get in the car.

We're walking out to the car and Sierra says, "Mama, can we call my daddy now?" Holy shit! Please, dear God, give me the strength to have this conversation with my sweet child.

"Sweetie, Garrett's not your daddy. Why are you saying that?" I ask, trying to remain calm, even though my heart is in my throat.

"Because, Mama, I prayed and God made him love me, so he's my daddy now," she says matter-of-factly.

"Baby, Garrett loves you because you're amazing. He doesn't need to be your daddy to love you."

She shrugs "I know that, but he *is* my daddy!" That's all there is to it. She's not going to see this any other way. She's just too young to understand.

I should talk to Garrett about this. I don't want her to catch him off guard. He needs to be prepared to tell her that he doesn't have to be her daddy to love her. He can just be her…. shit, I don't know, what is he to her?

Chapter Thirty-One

Garrett

IT'S BEEN OVER TWO HOURS. I don't want to bother her, but I'm getting worried. Leaving her today SUCKED! I'm not happy about being here. I know I've been a complete ass to everyone, but I don't really care. We're on the bus headed to New Orleans. Drew isn't any happier to be here, and even Jon's a bit pissy.

Eric, I think, is wishing he was anywhere else than here with us. He's a party animal, and the rest of us have zero interest in screwing around. We usually like to hit a couple bars with the roadies to start off the tour, but tonight we were all anxious to get on the bus and make our phone calls. Our first show is tomorrow. We had our band meeting with the new manager. He was a nice enough guy. At least he won't be giving Lex any crap. We won't tolerate that kind of shit. We're brothers first, band members second. Family is first…always!

My phone rings in my pocket and I damn near rip it out of my jeans to hear her voice. "Sweetheart, are you okay?" I ask in a panic.

"Yes, can I put you on speaker? There's this little blond haired, blue eyed girl following me around telling me you want to talk to her."

I can here the smile in her voice and it calms me. "Yes. I do, I'm missing my girls…bad! Are you home, yet?"

She sighs, "Not yet, we're pulling into the neighborhood now." She switches the phone to speaker, and Sierra starts telling me how she beat her older cousin at checkers, just like Pops, my dad, taught her.

It made my parents life to hear Sierra call them her Mimi & Pops. Talk about over the moon grandparents. Sierra's picture will be plastered all over their house by the time I get home.

The girls get home and keep me on speaker phone all through Sierra's bath time, story time, and bedtime prayers. Sierra asks me to sing her song with her mama for her, and I do, of course. But I'm still working on my own song to sing to her every day. I want her to hear my words, not someone else's. I've been playing with the lyrics and singing it to her. She seems to like it so far. I'm going to write one for her mama, too.

After Sierra is tucked in, Lex stays on the phone with me. I tell her about the show tomorrow night and how all the guys are doing. She asks how Drew's holding up without Court and Gabe. He's miserable, but it's not much different than what I'm feeling. I tell her he's constantly video chatting and waiting for photos from Court. Courtney doesn't do needy well, so she's going to blow soon.

She asks if I know anything about what's going on with Jon and Whit. I don't, but I suspect something, because he's texting constantly. Whitney's being vague with Lex about it, too.

"How are you feeling, sweetheart? Better?" I hope so. It worries me that she's felt bad for this long.

"I still feel yucky. I couldn't eat Kate's meatballs tonight, but I had a little plain pasta and toast."

Shit. I hate that I can't take care of her. I thought she was getting better. "Babe, do you want me to call my mom? You know she'd be there in a second to take care of you." It's the best idea I've had yet! My mom would kill to take care of her future daughter-in-law.

"Absolutely NOT, Garret, it's just a virus! I'll be better soon. Please don't call your mom. I have more than enough help right now." She's probably right, but I'd feel better knowing it was my mom. Shit, I'll wait and see how she is tomorrow.

"Your Mom called me today. She wants to have Sierra over for a sleepover. What do you think about that?" she asks curiously.

"Babe, I gave her your number. I thought if you want-ed to go out with the girls, she could take care of Sierra for you. They loved having Sierra over the other day. I wish you could've seen them!"

"Me too. It's nice that they like her. I'll call Elizabeth tomorrow." I pause, drawing in breath to give me strength for what I have to tell him next. "Garrett, I need to talk to you about something, but I want to preface it first with I have no idea how to fix this."

This doesn't sound good. What the hell? "Okay, Lex, tell

me and let's see if I can think of a fix, baby." I'm glad she's at least coming to me with a problem, instead of holding it in like normal.

"Sierra is calling you Daddy." She says nervously. Shit... is that what's wrong? Sierra's been calling me her daddy for days. How has Lex not heard it until now? I know she heard it at the school. What's wrong with that? I was thrilled! My parents have never been happier. I just don't know how to make it real!

"Baby, is that a problem, because she's been saying it for days? I know it's not real, but I like it, and I can't think of a better name. The only problem I see is I don't know how to make it true for her, yet. I don't want people to think I'm try-ing to take Jed's place in her life," I tell Lex, hoping that she won't say that Sierra has to stop calling me Daddy.

"So, it doesn't upset you? I tried to talk to her about it tonight, but it wasn't well received. I'm sorry."

Ugh! "Sweetheart. I love it. It makes me happy. You make me happy. She makes me happy. Please, let her just do what makes her comfortable. If to her I am Daddy, fantastic, that's what I want. If she'd rather me just be her friend and be Garrett, I can deal with that, too. But I got to say, babe, Daddy makes me feel good."

"You are a good man Garrett. I'm going to bed now, babe, I'm exhausted. Will you call me tomorrow?" I'll be setting the alarm to call her before school and counting the minutes until then.

"Yes, babe, as soon as you wake up. I love you, sweet-heart."

"I know. Love you, too," and she disconnects.

When I hang up the phone with Lex, Eric and Jon are

playing their stupid, blow shit up, video games. I'm trying to be a team player, but I'm just not fucking happy to be here. I miss my girls. I walk to the fridge and pull out a beer then slap myself down in the chair to pout like a damn lovesick teenager. Jon looks at me and laughs, making me more pissed off. "Shut up, Fucker! You'll get it one day and I won't feel sorry for you one bit."

Jon shakes his head. "Nah man. I can't let any girl get in my head that way. It'd make me crazy, dude!" I know damn good and well something's going down with Whitney, though. He checks his phone every ten seconds and is constantly texting. Right then his phone rings and he runs off to the bathroom in the back of the bus to hide.

"Yeah, in your head all right!" I yell out, and he lifts his arm over his back to flip me off. It's got to be Whitney.

"I'm going to bed, dude," I say to Eric.

"Damn, this tour is going to suck with all y'all pussy whipped bastards. I guess the only good part is I get first pick of all the hotties."

"You can have them all. I want them all to stay the hell away from me." I'll do everything in my power to keep all those women at arm's length. The last thing I need is Lex to have doubts about my commitment. My career already freaks her out.

I take my guitar and head back to the small room at the back of the bus. I need something to distract me from my misery. I want to be sleeping next to my girl, not here!

I start playing with some chords I've been working on about Sierra. That kid is too smart for her own good. She asks so many questions...really great ones. I'm often stumped by her inquisitiveness, but I always try to come up with an answer for her. I've been singing this to her in the mornings, and she's giving me more and more lines every day.

> *The other day, she asked me, where do babies come from?*
> *She looked at me earnestly, and waited for words of wisdom*
> *I said to her, my little friend, babies come from love!*

> *Questions That Children Ask, I never know just what to say....*
> *Who Is God? Where is Heaven? Why does that man look that way?*
> *I need some, some inspiration, I don't want to let her down...*
> *She looks to me for the answers...I do the best I know how.*

I'm working on the song, and Drew comes in with his box of cheddar crackers. "What are you working on? I like it!"

I don't even look up from my writing pad as I respond to him. "Sierra, that kid comes up with some crazy questions that make me damn proud!" I tell him about the hospital and her reference to how kids grow on love. She's amazing.

"Damn, dude. You'd think she was yours! You're like a big proud daddy right now," he says.

"Yeah man...I think I am!"

Chapter Thirty-Two

Alexis

GARRETT'S BEEN GONE OVER a week now. I miss him badly. We talk so many times throughout the day. He didn't lie about that, and also true to his word I've never called him and had him not answer. He's always available for Sierra and me, making anyone else wait for his attention.

Elizabeth picked up Sierra this morning to take her to The Lowery Park Zoo and spend a night or two with her and James. I'm still sick, so it comes as a welcome reprieve. I think I need to go back to the doctor's soon. This morning sickness has turned into all day sickness. I can barely keep any food down.

I'm supposed to go out with the girls tonight, but right now I have no energy. I'm going to have a nap before we go out. I'll call the doctor after my nap.

I crawl into my bed and snuggle up with Garrett's pillow.

It still smells like him. I miss him terribly. I need to ask him to mail me his pillow now, so that when this one loses it's Garrettness, I'll have a back-up.

My phone chimes, but I'm so tired that I can't even lift my arm to answer it. I fall back to sleep, telling myself I'll call whoever it is back in just a few minutes.

It's really dark in here, or maybe my eyes are still closed. I don't know which it is, but I can't bring myself to a conscious enough state to care. I need this sleep more than anything else. It's feels like I'm catching up from years of deprivation.

It's the phone chiming, again. I hope everyone's okay, but I still can't wake up enough to answer it. I fall back to sleep.

"Alexis…where are you?" I hear the yelling, but can't really comprehend what's happening. I'm half-awake, but I'm finding it really challenging to keep my eyes open. I'm being shaken gently. I open one eye half way. Whitney's standing over me. "Alexis, oh my God. You're so pale. Sweetie, I don't think you're okay. We have to get you to the hospital!" She's dialing her phone before she finishes her last sentence. "Kate, it's Whit. Lex is really sick! I don't know, but she's barely waking up…No…I can't carry her…I'll wait for Jason." She says. "LEX, where's Sierra?" she asks me.

"Elizabeth McKenna's," I answer, using the last ounce of strength I have. I'm too weak to deal with Whit's freak out. I'm fine…just really tired. I don't even have the energy to tell her that Jason will come take care of me before I close my eyes and drift back off to sleep.

Chapter Thirty-Three

Jason

MY STUPID, STUPID SISTER! And don't even get me started on my WIFE! I swear these women will be the death of me. For over a week these two have been hiding this from me. What the hell did they think I'd do? Flip out? Tell Garrett? Yell at my widowed, unwed, pregnant sister?

Severe dehydration. Exhaustion. Something about severe morning sickness. She's six and a half weeks pregnant.

Thank God Sierra was with Garrett's parents. My sister doesn't think about how her actions could affect those around her. She hasn't been taking care of herself. Even before this, everyone else takes priority and she's way down on the totem pole.

My wife, the love of my life, the greatest mother in the world, my best friend, kept this secret from me. She finally told me when Whitney called freaking out that Lex didn't show up for girl's night last night and no one had been able to get in touch with her all day. Whit found her at home in bed too weak to move. We had to call the damn EMTs.

Garrett's had the same problem. I just talked to him. I couldn't tell him the news, because my dear wife says it's not my place. She said it was just my job to get him here ASAP. So I did. He'll be here any minute.

As for Lex, she is knocked out, but she's going to be okay. She has a very healthy baby growing in her stomach. I saw it myself on the blurry back and white screen. The heartbeat was very strong. I love that my sister is strong, but I'll never understand her need to take on the world by herself. At some point this girl has got to learn to be happy about depending on the people around her that love her, and understand that we all need and want to be supportive of her.

I spoke with Garrett's dad a little bit ago. Sierra is great and having the time of her life. I told them what was going on, without spilling the beans that Lex is knocked up by their son. They were very concerned, but happy to keep Sierra there and distracted. She has school tomorrow, and Kate is getting them all sorted out about what to do.

Chapter Thirty-Four

Alexis

WHEN I WAKE UP, I'm in a hospital room. Jason is on the corner chair bent over with his head in his hands rubbing his temples. He's stressed out.

"I'm really sorry, Jason," I apologize, feeling awful that he's always having to pick up the pieces when I can't manage my own life.

He jumps up and is standing by my side. "Alexis, never EVER try to take on the world alone! You're my sister, damn it. You have me. Please don't keep me out, AGAIN," he's saying.

"I know, Jason... I'm sorry. How's Sierra? When can I go home?" I ask. Then I hear the stomping and yelling in the hall.

"I said what room, where is she?" It's him...he's here... does he know? Is he angry with me? I'm suddenly terrified, but I've missed him so much that my desperation to be wrapped in his arms overrides my fear.

"He doesn't know yet, Lex, but you have to tell him now, babe." Jason says just before the door bangs wide open and my big muscled cowboy runs over to the bed.

"My God, what happened? Are you okay? Babe…talk to me! Jason…" he's rambling, leaving no open air to have his questions answered. I reach out and touch his arm and he settles. "Sweetheart, I love you. I thought you were breaking up with me, again. But then Mom and Dad had Sierra. It wasn't making sense. Baby, I'm so sorry!" He's scared and exhausted. I can see the shadows under his eyes.

"Now that you're here, I'm going home to deal with my wife." Jason says to us, but winks at me, in spite of how hurt he is. I know it's because we kept a secret from him. He hates when Kate and I keep him in the dark. He kisses my cheek and leaves.

"You want to tell me what they're going to do to make you better. What kind of fucking virus does *this*?" He asks frustrated. I have to tell him. I know I do. It needs to be now or he'll find out from someone else. That would suck.

"Garrett…I'm sorry I didn't tell you sooner…" he interrupts me, kissing me on the cheek and investigating my body for anything out of place.

"No, baby, don't apologize…you're sick…where are the doctors?" He needs to listen to me now, before he starts an inquisition with the medical staff.

"Garrett, listen to me. I'm sorry I kept this from you, but….I'm pregnant." He sits on the ground…falls really… right on his ass and stares at the floor. Is he upset? I try and get up, but my arm is attached to the IV on the opposite side of the bed. "I'm so sorry," I cry in a panic…terrified that I've broken us by letting this happen and then keeping it secret.

Chapter Thirty-Five

Garrett

IDON'T EVEN KNOW IF I heard her correctly. She's pregnant...my girl is having my baby...half of me is growing inside her stomach. I'm trying to find my feet, my head, my words, but I can't grasp anything, nothing. The wind has been knocked completely out of me. Until I hear her sniffling. Fuck. She needs to be comforted and here I am on the damn floor. I have got to get my shit together. "Baby, oh my God. I'm sorry. Are you okay? Please, don't cry. I love you, Lex." I sit on the edge of the bed and try to hug her in this awful position. She sits up and crawls into my lap. That's better.

She feels so good in my arms. I hold her in my lap as we sit in the silence, taking it all in.

The nurse comes in. "Hello, Alexis, glad to see you're awake and that this man," she says looking at me sternly, "found his way to you without disturbing my other patients."

She comes over to the side of the bed and looks at me cradling Alexis in my arms. "You know this is a twin size bed. It's for one person, mister."

I shrug. "My girl needs to be held. I'm staying until she doesn't," I inform the nurse. I'm not screwing around with these people. They can take care of my girl with her in my arms. "What are you doing about this virus that's making my future wife and baby sick," I ask.

The nurse laughs. "Your baby is what's making your future wife sick, Mr. McKenna," she says almost like she is amused at my confusion, and I look to Lex.

Did she know all along? Is this why she was saying she was sorry. "Lex, how long have you known?" I ask, looking her in the eye.

"I'm sorry, Garrett." She's crying again. "Please, don't hate me. I had a good reason." Shit. We can work this out later.

"Ms. Phillips, you don't have any excess fluids to spare, my dear. None of that crying, please. Mr. McKenna, you need to be cautious about upsetting my patient. You'll have to leave if you can't keep her happy," she says to me with a no non-sense tone.

"Yes ma'am." I say with my eyes still pinned to Lex. No way is anyone going to make her sad…Fucking EVER!

The nurse leaves and I slide all the way into the bed, getting Lex into a more comfortable and permanent position. She drifts off to sleep, as I sing in her ear. I switch on the television and turn the sound to a barely audible tone and watch the Yankees and Sox game.

My phone rings in my pocket and Lex stirs a bit. I answer it on the second ring. It's Drew. I left the tour six hours before a show. We had to cancel the next few shows, but I could give a rat's ass right now…my girl was sick.

"Hey, dude, I can't really talk." I say into the phone in a whisper. I need to talk to him, but I don't want to wake or move Lex. She needs rest the nurse says.

"How is she?" he asks.

"She's amazing, but very sick. I'll talk to you about it later. Do you need me for anything specific?" I ask, wanting to speed this conversation up.

"No dude, we're cancelling the rest of the week. We'll reschedule in the fall. I want to get home to my wife and baby, too. You good with that? We need your confirmation," he asks.

"Abso-Fucking-Lutely cancel it. I'm staying here with my girls. We'll all talk tomorrow. I'm not going anywhere until she's better, let it be known now!" I say, and he laughs.

"Got ya. Be well, dude. Take care of your lady. We'll talk later."

"Will do, give my love to Court and Gabe." I disconnect and feel Lex stirring a bit.

"Garrett, did you just cancel your tour?" she asks in a sleepy voice.

"For this week, yes. We'll talk about next week after I see the doctor. I can't leave you in this condition, sweetheart," I answer.

"I'll be fine, Garrett."

"Are you kidding me, Alexis? Babe, you're sick because my baby is causing you trouble. I want to be the one to take care of you."

"Garrett, you can't cancel. I didn't tell you, because I didn't want you to feel trapped. I didn't want you to have to change your life. People are going to think I did this on purpose." She cries into my arm.

"Shhh…" I say wiping her face. "None of that, babe. No wasted fluids.

Sweetheart, what we have is once in a lifetime… I don't care what anyone thinks. I love you so fucking much, I can't even see straight anymore. You aren't trapping me, baby. You're changing my life in the most glorious way. I wished this on us. I want this life, really bad. This was magic, baby." I say to her knowing I've been writing songs, making plans, dreaming, and begging God to make this girl want me for the rest of my life.

Filling her with my baby wasn't planned just yet…but damn, I'm happy to have this baby. I just need to use some stern words with this kid about making his Mama so sick! Little man or woman needs to reign that crap in.

"Babe, you're making me a real man…more and more every single day," I say kissing her. I feel like the tin man who finally got his heart. I'm lucky. This lady has brought so much greatness and happiness to my life.

For many years I've felt like a cardboard cutout that people moved around the country to manipulate and perform. I felt fake and empty. It all changed so quickly when this beautiful girl came back into my world.

Chapter Thirty-Six

Alexis

FINALLY, I'M LEAVING THE HOSPITAL. Two nights in that place was torture. Garrett's home for rest of this week and I'm so happy about it now. I was worried at first that he'd feel like he had to sacrifice his tour to take care of me, but he hasn't shown anything except complete joy. Joy that I'm okay, joy that his baby's growing nice and strong, joy that Sierra is happy and healthy, just joy.

I'm so looking forward to getting home and wrapping my arms around my little girl. She didn't come to the hospital to visit, because I wasn't really sure how she'd feel about it, so she's been with Garrett's parents for a few days. They're thrilled about having her there, and I know that she's being very well loved. Kate's been helping out, too.

It'll be great to finally sleep in my own bed. It'll be great sleeping with my man in my big bed. Sleeping in this tiny bed has posed a bit of a challenge. But when I told Garrett I really just needed him to hold me so that I could sleep better, the man made it his mission to make sure I was snuggled. Even when the nurses came in giving him a hard time, he made it quite clear he didn't want to hear any of their crap.

Elizabeth is at my house with Sierra. Garrett had to let Elizabeth and James in on our little secret. I'm scared to see them. I don't really know what kind of reaction to expect from them, but it's far too late for me worry about how this looks. This is a bit of a done deal.

We're going to tell Sierra together, but not tonight. We agreed that it needs to be special, and I want to feel better for it. I already feel almost 100% better, but the doctor said I needed to rest a lot and drink lots of fluids. I have some medication that help ward off the nausea.

When we get home, I walk into the house, despite Garrett trying to convince me that carrying me in and putting me to bed was best. I hear my little girl come running for me. She's already seen Garrett several times, but I haven't seen her in three days. I've missed her like crazy.

"Mama…Mama's home…" she says, running around the corner.

I bend to scoop her up when Garrett takes my arm, shaking his head. "No way, lady. Go sit down. You're not picking up little girls in your condition," he says, intercepting Sierra and holding her up to me, so that we can hug and smother each other with butterfly kisses as we walk to the couch. He's hovering a bit, but I'm trying be patient with him because I know I really scared him, and he doesn't really understand how the whole pregnancy thing works. I've done it, but he hasn't, so he'll need a bit of loving guidance - not my typical approach. I'll give him a bit to catch up.

I sit on the couch and Sierra attempts to climb into my lap, only to be halted by Garrett. He sits next to me with her on his lap instead. Oh Hell NO…he cannot start acting all crazy and overprotective and stop me from holding Sierra. I'm pissed. I look at him sternly and reach to take her, and my stern look is reciprocated.

"Lex…" he starts to say something when his mother walks into the room.

"Garrett Michael McKenna, give her that child right now and don't you dare give her any hassles. Alexis is a very smart lady and knows exactly what her body can handle," she orders, walking over to the couch to hug and kiss me. She's wearing a very endearing smile.

"Thank you, Elizabeth!" I say, hoping she realizes I'm thanking her for more than just putting Garrett in his place. I reach my hands out and Sierra climbs into my lap and snuggles. Garrett scoots in closer to snuggle us, too. That's better. This feels nice.

Garrett's parents stay for dinner. His mother has cooked and stored enough food to last us weeks. She's done all the dishes and sorted out all the laundry. "Elizabeth, I can't thank you enough for all that you've done for me this week. I want you to know how much easier it was for me to relax and get better knowing you were taking care of Sierra," I say to her when we're finally alone in the kitchen. I'm sitting at the bar helpless, since every time I try to do anything someone escorts me to the nearest chair or couch.

Elizabeth comes to my side and holds both my shoulders, looking me in the eye. "You, my precious, precious girl have brought love to my son and life to this family. You're a gift from the heavens and I'm so thankful for you," she says with the corners of her eyes leaking tears. I'm amazed that this is the reaction she has to me getting pregnant, out of wedlock, with her only son's baby. But as amazed as I am, I'm so happy that there is no tension.

"Elizabeth…" I start to say and she interrupts...

"Mom or Mimi," she says, looking sternly and waiting for me to comply with either title.

"Mimi…" I start to say, feeling a little odd and uncomfortable, but then moving on to what I needed to say. "I know that you don't know me very well, but I wanted you to know, I didn't plan this…I didn't do this to trap him…I do love him very much." She looks at me with an enormous amount of compassion.

"Sweetheart, sometimes things that are meant to be can't be planned. They just happen. And for that we'll be thankful. The stars aligned properly, so that you and Sierra could come into our lives and bring us joy! "

I too have tears trailing from the corners of my eyes when Garrett comes into the room after helping Sierra with her bath. "Mother, no wasted fluids! What did you say to make her cry?" he screeches at his mom, running over to me to inspect me.

"Garrett, you idiot! She's pregnant. Everything will make her cry now. Her hormones are all out of whack. I love this young lady probably more than I love you today! Leave us alone. I was just telling her how amazing she is," she says scolding her son, and the fake wounded look on his face makes us both belly laugh.

James walks into the kitchen, holding a pajama clad Sierra to say goodnight, since he's already read her stories.

"What's going on in here?" he asks, telling Sierra he thinks they missed something very funny if it was a good enough laugh to bring tears to Mimi's and my eyes.

I take Sierra onto my lap and snuggle her close on the barstool, with Garrett standing closely beside us. I've missed my baby girl so much! Garrett's hovering again, but I'm trying to remember this is new to him and seeing me in the hospital was very hard on him.

Poor Garrett really struggled being told what to do and how to take care of me. I've learned in the last couple days that there are very few people in this world who successfully tell my man what to do. So far I've only seen Elizabeth, Sierra, and myself get away with any direct orders. The nurses at the hospital quickly figured out that:

1. He was not going to get out of my bed until I was properly snuggled.
2. He would not leave that room when the nurses and doctors came in to check me out.
3. Blood Pressure could wait if I was sleeping.
4. I wasn't eating their crappy hospital food when his Mother made homemade organic soup.
5. HE REALLY WASN'T GETTING OUT OF MY BED WHEN I NEEDED TO BE SNUG-GLED…NO MATTER WHO WANTED TO POKE AND PROD ME…. END OF FREAK-ING STORY!

Both his parents are beaming from ear to ear about our unexpected little secret, but are keeping it quiet so as to not let our little ears hear.

I'm quite excited to put Sierra to bed tonight, because it's been several days without our nighttime song. I'm sure she's missing it, too. Her birthday is in four weeks, and this is her last week of school before summer. I can't believe my baby will be starting kindergarten in the fall. She's growing up so fast, too fast.

I think and fully expect for Sierra to be overjoyed at the news of having a sibling. It's as much a dream for her as it is for me. Garrett has joined our life so seamlessly. I absolutely adore him for the happiness he's brought to our home.

The night winds down and we say goodbye to Garrett parents. I thank them over and over for all their help and support. Elizabeth and James promise to check on us tomorrow. They love Sierra, and the feeling is mutual. She says goodbye to Mimi and Pops, as she calls them, and promises to visit during the weekend. It's really quite precious and nice for her to be so freely accepted as their grandchild.

Garrett and I head upstairs to sing to Sierra, since it's past her bedtime as it is. I start to sing her song after she's said her prayers only for her to stop me. "No, Mama, I want to hear my song." I'm confused…that is her song. What am I missing?

But then Garret says to Sierra. "Baby girl, let's sing your song to Mama together."

*The other day, she asked me, where do babies
come from?
She looked at me earnestly, and waited for words of
wisdom
I said to her, my little friend, babies come from
love*

Questions children ask, never know just what to say
Who is God? Where is Heaven? Why does that man look that way?
I need some inspiration, I don't wanna let her down
She looks to me for the answers, I do the best I know how

What's it like to be someone else? To live in their bodies for a day?
Don't you wonder what they think? Or how they like to play?
Stumped again by my pint size kin, I say I wonder the same

Questions children ask, never know just what to say
Who is God? Where is Heaven? Why does that man look that way?
I need some inspiration, I don't wanna let her down
She looks to me for the answers, I do the best I know how

Daddy, are we rich? Why do we need money?
Money's nice I say to her, but the important things are free
Time with you, is the greatest jewel, I ever could possess

Questions children ask, Never know just what to
say
Who is God? Where is Heaven? Why does that
man look that way?
I need some inspiration, I don't wanna let her
down
She looks to me for the answers, I do the best I
know how

When they finish serenading me, I'm full of unshed tears. That's just the most precious thing I've ever heard. He wrote that song for her. I've heard her ask some of those questions to him over the last few weeks. He wrote her her very own song. "I love it, what a beautiful song for a daddy to sing to a very lucky little girl," I say to them both. I kiss Sierra's head good-night, and Garrett follows suit before we leave her to slumber.

I'm very much looking forward to climbing into bed with my man. I'm dying for him to get his hands on me. It's been far too long since I've fallen apart under his touch, and with all these pregnancy hormones raging, I'm a bit needy!

He cracks the door, as always, and we start walking to-ward our room when I'm overcome with a need to kiss him. He overwhelms me....I love him so much. I stop him en-route and climb into his arms, wrapping my legs around his waist as he supports me, holding my bottom. "Baby, as nice as it is to have you in my arms, feeling your warm little center pressed against me this way is making me crazy. You need to let me hold you another way or I'll lose my fucking mind, Lex. It's been over ten days..."

Yes, over ten days and that hiatus is ending tonight. "Yes,

Garrett. I need you. Please, take me to bed and make love to me." I ask in a whisper in his ear!

"Grrrr…fuck, Lex. You know I want you, baby, but we can't. You just got out of the hospital. You need to rest," he says, and I know this is going to be one of those situations where a direct order is the only way to get what I want.

"Garrett, you'll take me to bed, right now. You'll make love to me very thoroughly, and then I'll sleep. Otherwise, I promise to stay awake all night plotting bodily harm to you in ways I commit to seeing through! Got it?" He looks startled, but is still silent. "It's been over ten freaking days, Garrett. I'm pregnant and needy and in need of being serviced. You're the man who did this to me, now be the man to make me feel better."

With that he's trotting me down the hall into our room where he ever so gently places me on the bed, then roughly starts throwing off my shoes and yanking off my yoga pants and top, throwing them haphazardly across the room. He pauses, kisses my face, and runs out of the room. What the hell is he doing? Where's he going? Then I hear him in Sierra's room through the monitor. He's making sure she's sleeping. Yes… he's going to be a very Good Daddy!

Chapter Thirty-Seven

Garrett

MY GIRL NEEDS TO BE LOVED. She's made that pretty damn clear, with the threatening bodily harm and all. I did ask the doctor if making love to my girl was okay and he said yes, as long as she's feeling up to it.

She looks like she feels okay, but it was only two days ago that Whitney found her in bed unable to keep her eyes open. How good can she possibly feel up to sex now?

Three days ago, I thought I was going to lose my mind. I was calling and texting Lex, and she wouldn't take any of my calls or respond to the texts. I was sure she was pissed off that I was away and planning to boot me because of the damn tour. I was pissed and frustrated. I was just getting ready to book a flight and come back to check on things when I got the call from Jason.

Six hours before a show, we had to cancel. That sucked for the fans, but seriously, there was absolutely no way I would have been able to get on that stage knowing my girl was in the hospital, sick and barely conscious. Even though, everybody and their mother told me I needed to stay…in my heart I knew where I needed to be. She's my priority. When she needs me, no matter where I am in the world, I'll fucking be there, with her, always!

I had to check on Sierra before I let Alexis have her way with me. I wouldn't want my little princess to ever see what her Mama does to me, or what I'm going to do to her Mama. These pregnancy hormones are serious business.

I can't believe Alexis is having my baby. I can't believe I'm going to be a dad. My precious girl was afraid to tell me. She thought I'd feel trapped. For such a smart girl, she can be stupid as hell sometimes. I'm quite frankly pleased that she's knocked up, so she can stop second guessing what we have and stay put. What we have is PERMANENT! I'm staying, she's staying, we're all staying! I love her so much.

I walk back into the room throwing my shirt off and heading straight to my beautiful and very ready to be loved girl. "Alexis Nicole, I crazy love you, baby. Really. Really. Really." I say, standing over her and looking down at her beautiful body. Damn, I'm a lucky guy!

"You're incredible, lady! You're hot as hell and completely mine to play with, right?" I ask, knowing she'll let me do whatever I want to her right now. All I really have in mind is to fucking worship this woman and her body until she can longer keep her eyes open. Huh…threaten me with bodily harm and not sleeping. I'll show her cute little ass! She'll sleep after I'm done with her. I'll make sure of it.

"I'm going to be very fat and not at all 'HOT', as you say, in a few short months. Get your fill now, because I'll be hideous, soon," she says with a nonchalant attitude, but I can see she's worried, or at least not happy, about that part of being pregnant.

So I kneel down in front of her and proceed to run my fingers the full length of her torso. "Baby, this little body of yours will never be hideous. It's building the most precious gift anyone could ever receive," I say, locking eyes with her. "This baby is a dream come true. Your body can do whatever it needs to, baby. But it'll never be less than perfect in my eyes, since no other body has, ever, or will, give me anything as precious as Sierra and this baby. I'll worship your body for those gifts for the rest of my life," I say to a teary, glassy eyed girl.

"I love you, Garrett. You'll never really ever understand what it means to me to have you here, with me, to stay," she says, as the beautiful tears seep out of her eyes.

"No tears, baby. I'm here…to stay with you always. And even when I'm away sweetheart, I'm here. My heart is here with you, Sierra, and this new little person."

It appears she's much less in need of being 'Fucked' and will now allow me to make gentle sweet love to her. Glad I brought that shit down a few notches. Now, I can take care of my girl the way I know she needs.

I roll her over onto her stomach and massage all her back muscles. She's been achy from being in the hospital bed for a couple days. She was pretty weak from the dehydration and exhaustion. We're going to need to figure something out for when I leave next week. We'll need concrete plans to make sure that she has extra hands to help out around here, so she can get some extra rest. My mother, Kate, and Whitney have already been working out a schedule, which I know will make her pissy. She hates when people take control of her life. But, she's going to need to let them while I'm away, and then I'll be here.

I rub her up and down her shoulders, back, and legs. She likes it, because she hasn't said a word. I lean over her to kiss her cheek and her breathing is even and calm. My precious lady has fallen asleep on me. As much as I wanted to bury myself inside her, it thrills me to see her resting peacefully. I continue to caress her gently, careful not to disturb her, but wanting to make sure she's really out before I move her up to her pillow.

I hear a small moan escape her lips and I know she's stirring a bit, so I jump up, take off my jeans and pop back into bed with just my boxers on. I move in next to Lex, and slide under her, so that her head is resting on my chest. I kiss her forehead, whispering in her ear. When she returns the reply in a small voice, "I love you more. So much more." Her eyes are still closed, but she's awake. She's listening. "Never, lady!"

"Garrett, it's clear we're not doing what I wanted tonight, so stop trying to start an argument with this very tired pregnant woman," she says with a smirk and snuggles in closer, throwing her leg over my thigh.

"You're right, babe, no arguing, but I do love you more," I say with a kiss to her forehead.

I wake before the alarm in the morning and switch everything off, so that Lex doesn't wake up. I'm taking Sierra to school this morning. I want Lex sleeping. I head down the hall to wake up my princess. I'm singing the song I wrote for her when her little eyes pop open and she climbs to the end of the bed to sit in my lap. She sticks her thumb into her mouth and listens.

I help her get dressed for her day and she tells me about her golfing adventure with Pop, which was really just driving around in a golf cart. She had a lot of fun and my parents are convinced the sun and moon set behind Alexis and Sierra.

I want to make our little family official. I need to do it quickly. This is about the three of us. Not just Lex and me, so I want to do it right and include my little princess. I have a couple meetings this morning after I take care of Sierra.

"Breakfast at home or on the go, baby girl?" I ask.

"Home, Mimi made me the yogurt with berries that we picked," she says.

"Is it in the fridge?" She nods yes, her pony tail bobbing.

After her tasty breakfast of berries and yogurt and, of course, a cup of chocolate milk, we gather her things for school when I hear the angelic voice. "Good morning, I hope you two weren't leaving without me," she says, as she's walking down the stairs into the foyer dressed in a much too sexy running outfit.

If this lady thinks she's working out or running today, she's gone bat-shit crazy! No Damn Way! "Umm, babe, I hope you don't think you're working out today. Because I really hate telling you, no, but babe…" then I lower my voice whispering in her ear, so Sierra can't hear. "FUCK NO!" She laughs, just laughs…no acknowledgement of what she's planning.

She bends down to kiss Sierra. "What did you have for breakfast, sweetie?" she asks the little one, who promptly tells her exactly what she's eaten and packed in her lunch box. "Okay, sweetie, let's go get into the car and head off to school." Shit, I wanted her resting, but at least if she's with me I know she won't be running.

We walk out to the garage to get in her Jeep I open her door and she's standing there just starring. "What's up, babe? You okay?" I ask, confused.

"Yeah...sorry...just thinking....I guess I need to get a new car, Garrett," she says.

Fan-Fucking-Tastic! I'd thought about this, and wanted to mention it, but it is so much better that it's her idea. I'm thrilled! "Yes, sweetheart, you do. Do you want me to take care of it?" I ask, hoping she'll let me, and she just shrugs.

"I don't know...I guess, maybe." And she gets into the front seat, while I check Sierra's harness.

We drive Sierra to school and Lex stays in the car, talking to Whitney, while I walk Sierra into the school. While I'm here I also make sure the school has all my phone numbers on Sierra's emergency records. They were happy to take the information and will call Alexis to approve the changes.

When I get back to the Jeep, Lex is still on the phone, but I'm positive she's not speaking with Whitney. She's visibly upset and talking very sternly into the phone, almost as if she were speaking to a child, but I know immediately she isn't. "Listen, I'm not giving you anything. You have no right to call me. Why can't you just let me live a happy life? Please...stay away! I'm begging"

WHAT THE FUCK? She's shaking and I know that her strained voice is the result of trying to hold back her tears. I know exactly who she's talking to and all bets are off now. I place my hand on her knee and look into her eyes, as I reach to take the phone from her ear. "Sweetheart, you need to let me handle this, okay?" She's nodding her head, accepting my help. God, I love her.

I put the phone to my ear and hear the rough voice on the other end, not knowing that my beautiful girl has given me the phone saying, "Listen, you little bitch, you're going to give me some money, or I'll get to that little girl of yours and tell her all about her real grandparents and what a piece of trash her mommy is. Do you hear me?" the voice in my ear threatens.

I'm enraged. I've never in my life felt this amount of anger. "YES, I fucking hear you," I say into the phone. "Now, it's my turn. You come anywhere near my future wife, or child, and you'll need a hell of a lot more than money to help you. I want you to forget, and I do mean forget, this fucking number, or I'll make your life a living, breathing hell." The voice responds with an evil laugh.

"Ha, Ha. My life is a living, breathing hell already. I gave life to the most ungrateful little fucks on the planet and they won't help their mother. Now you, Mr. McKenna, wouldn't know anything about that, because you take good care of your family, but your little bitch of a girlfriend forgot who gave birth to her. She'll give me the money, or I'll make her life hell!" she says into the phone.

I open the door and step out of the car to continue this conversation without Lex hearing. "The fuck you will, woman! Since you know who I am and what I'm all about, you know that Alexis and Sierra are my entire fucking world. I'll do everything in my power to keep them safe. *Stay the fuck away*…or else you'll learn exactly what I mean by everything in my power," I say with all the anger and intensity I'm feeling before hanging up. If I could reach through the phone and thrash this woman, I would!

FUCK….I scroll through the contacts as quickly as possible, knowing Alexis is watching me and crying from the passenger seat, but I have to deal with this. I find Jason's number and press send. He answers on the first ring. "Hey, sis, you okay?" he asks a bit too cheery for my mood.

"It's Garret. And no she's not okay, because your mother called just now throwing around some pretty serious threats if Lex doesn't pay up. You want to fill me in, so I can get this shit taken care of. I can't have her dealing with this shit, Jason! I thought you had it handled?" ooompfh…I hear crap flying in the background through the phone.

"FUCK ME…WHEN? How did she get to Alexis? That's it! I'm killing her!" he yells at the top of his lungs.

"I'm taking Alexis home and settling her down, but we need to meet. TODAY! Meet me at the house," I say, and he responds that he's on his way.

Jason loves his sister, and I know he'll do whatever he can to protect her, but here, now, I have a little bit more power than he does. There's absolutely no way I can stay out of this. I just hope Alexis understands and lets me handle it.

When I get settled back into the driver's seat, she is climbing over the console onto my lap. She's crying very big unhappy tears, and I'm pissed. "I'm so sorry, Garrett. I wish I knew how to get rid of her. I don't want her causing you problems. I'll try and find a way…" she's rambling.

"Alexis, this isn't about me, baby. Stop being sorry. I'll fix this, sweetheart. Don't cry. I'll handle it. I'll be fine as soon as you take a deep breath and relax. I'm fine when you're smiling and calm, lady," I say to her in the calmest tone I can muster. "Baby, no one will come near you or Sierra. I promise. You're safe with me. Always," I promise, trying to settle her nerves. I feel her taking a deep breath. "That's it, baby, again," I prompt, and she does it four more times. She's relaxing a little. I lift her head off my chest so that I can see her eyes. "Sweetheart, you've got nothing to worry about. Let me handle this and you just be a happy mommy, taking care of our princess and the little one in here," I say putting my hands on her flat stomach. She nods and climbs back to her seat.

As soon as we start driving, I'm desperate to change the subject so I ask, "What kind of car do you want, babe?"

She shrugs again. "I don't really care. Something safe, I guess. We have some time." Yeah...we have time, but she'll be driving a new car by the end of the week and it was her idea. I didn't have to force this issue.

When we get to the house, true to his word, Jason is in driveway. He walks over to the car and opens Lex's door. Before she can say anything he starts apologizing, "Alexis, I'm sorry. I don't know how she got your number. I'll fix this. Please, don't be mad at me, or stress." But that's when I notice...she's pissed. She's mad at her brother, which is confusing. He didn't have anything to do with this.

"Jason, I warned you. You should never have fed the lion. I wouldn't be in this situation if you didn't. I TOLD YOU. Now she's threatening Sierra. This is your fault, Jason," she yells, as she storms out of the car and into the house. Shit...I don't know what's going on, but she's not holding anything back. "Have you told your wife, yet? You know that if she's going to try to get to Sierra, she'll be on your doorstep, too."

"I'll handle it, Alexis. Give me a chance." He's begging.

"NO...it's too late. I've given you a chance to get her out of our lives and she keeps reappearing, because you're allowing it. Why do you keep giving her a way in? She's never going to be okay. You have to stop this now, Jason. Anyone else in the entire world who poses a threat to me, you attack full force. But with her, YOU CAN'T! NO... I'm handling it. I'm calling the police and getting restraining orders. End of story. It's too much now, Jason. I have to protect my daughter," she's says, but there are no more tears. She's a woman on a mission.

"Sweetheart, we'll get the restraining orders and then I want you both to step aside and let me handle this. Clearly this is a bone of contention with the two of you. You need to let someone not so close to the situation take over," I say looking mostly at Alexis, because she'll likely be the one to object first. I know my girl.

And true to form "No...I DO NOT want you speaking to that woman, anymore. WE ARE DONE WITH HER!" she states.

I walk to stand directly in front of her, looking down into her eyes. "YES, lady. We are done with her and I can tell you right now the only person under this roof that will talk to her will be me or my attorneys. I mean it, Lex. You're not dealing with this shit. You got me?" I ask, seriously, because there's no way I can sit aside and allow her to negotiate with someone like that woman. She turns on her heels and storms out of the room, out of my eyesight. She can be pissed. She can stomp off all she wants. I don't care, but she won't be talking to that woman...end of story.

I say goodbye to Jason after getting all the necessary contact information for his mother. He's apologized. The man feels really bad. He hates that this is causing his sister problems, but it's clear that cutting his mother off completely is too hard for him. He wants to help her. He wants her to get better.

He's hoping she will someday, and he'll be waiting. But not my girl, she's never going to get past her mother abandoning them and leaving them with assorted relatives, or friends, over the years to party and live a life her children didn't fit into.

Luckily for now, no one except immediate family knows Lex is expecting. We need to keep it that way. I don't want anyone else harassing her right now.

After Jason leaves I go on a search for Lex and find her in bed, reading on her kindle. I go over to her, "I love you, sweetheart."

She looks me in the eye and I can see the unhappiness. "I know, Garrett. But I'm a big girl. I can fight my own battles. You can't take over."

"Sweetheart, we're a team. You'll never, ever, ever go into any battle alone. I'll always be there. Sorry, no more lonely girl on her own crap. I'm here and I'll try not to take over, but there will be certain things that I'll always want you to just let me take care of. Not because I don't think you can, babe, but because I love you too much to allow someone to say hateful, hurtful, and vile things to or about you. I don't want you or our children near it! Okay?"

It's a simple, single nod, but her eyes speak volumes. Not only does she get it, she accepts it.

"Thank you for being in bed resting. I like seeing you take care of yourself," I acknowledge. "Do you want anything?" I ask.

She smiles. "Yes, I'd like some of that yogurt your mom mixed up and a cup of tea."

Chapter Thirty-Eight

Alexis

I CANNOT BELIEVE THIS IS happening. My stupid mother has always chosen the best times in my life to reappear. I told Jason the last time this happened that we needed to cut all ties, but he started spouting the nonsense 'Keep your friends close and enemies closer.' Look what we're dealing with now. She's practically on my doorstep, threatening Sierra. She saw the tabloids from a few weeks ago with pictures of Garrett, Sierra, and me. She knows about us and is now threatening us.

Why of all parents did I have to be born to that woman? She's a piece of work and always has been. She's hated and resented me since the day I was born. Ugh. I'm stepping aside and letting Garrett handle it. As much as I don't want him near her, he's right. I need to take care of my babies. I can't allow her to get to me or under my skin.

She's met her match with Garrett. I've never in my life

witnessed a more enraged man. I think if she'd been speaking to him face to face I'd be visiting Garret in a jail cell. One thing's for sure, I know I'm safe, safe with him always.

He's downstairs working and having video conference meetings. He's super busy and I hate that my crap is being tossed on him as well. But truthfully, I'm exhausted and very ready for an afternoon nap before I have to get Sierra from school.

I hear footsteps and I'm sure he's coming to check on me again, but it's not. It's Whitney, Cami, and Kelsey! "Hey, chica. How are you?" they all ask with smiles before jumping on the bed. They have bags with them and Cami's holding four spoons.

"Please, dear Lord, tell me there's Ben & Jerry's in that bag," I plead, matching their smiles. This is such a great surprise. We were all supposed to have dinner together last Thursday night, and I was a no show because I was passed out.

I'm so happy to see these girls and catch up. "Soo… Whit, what have you been up to?" I ask, knowing she'll likely dismiss me.

"Thinking about possible names for my next god-child," she replies with a wink. Kelsey is ecstatic. Whitney is of course pleased. But my Cami is over the moon happy. She always worried the Sierra would grow up without siblings and it made her sad.

We all stay on the bed visiting and eating ice cream for a good while when I see my precious man at the door, laughing at me eating the entire quart of Ben & Jerry's out of the container with a spoon. "Thank God, they found something you can eat in bulk that doesn't make you nauseous." He winks, then walks over to the bed and kisses me hard right on the lips, giving them a bit of a little lick. "Yummy, babe," he says opening his mouth for a bite of the ice cream. I scoop out a big chuck and plop it into his mouth.

"I'm going to pick up our kiddo," he says, and I look at the clock. It can't possibly be time already, but it is. "Stay here with these girls, who should know they need to bring a pregnant woman good nutritious food with her ice cream," he says, looking at the three of them.

Kelsey pipes in, "Oh yeah, I did. Sorry, I forgot!" Taking a huge chocolate bar out of her purse and passing it to me, she winks at Garrett. We're laughing hysterically when Garret flips them off, before devouring my mouth with a full blown tongue kiss right in front of them.

"Okay. I'll wait where I am for you!" I say, mimicking a compliant child. And he eyes me with approval.

The girls stay only a few minutes after Garrett leaves to get Sierra. I decide to take advantage of the alone time and have a warm bath. I intended to that last night, but it never really worked out with all the company in the house.

I start the bath water and climb in, placing my phone on the ledge of the tub in case Garrett calls. I lay there feeling truly relaxed. I'm not really sure why or how I'm so calm in the mix of this insane storm of chaos, but I do know that Garrett said I wasn't going to battle alone anymore, and I know I'm not. He's got this all under control. I'm relaxed, calm, and insanely happy.

"Hi, Mama," I feel a little hand rubbing my cheek. "You feel better?" she asks. Smiling, I tell her I couldn't be better. I'm still buried in my tub full of bubbles and the water is still warm, so I haven't been sleeping long.

"Come on, sweet girl, let's go see what Mimi made us for supper and let Mama finish her bath. She'll come down and join us soon," Garrett says to Sierra and she bounces out of the room. He kisses my head. "Please don't sleep in the tub, baby. It scares me. Come join us downstairs when you're ready." His thumb brushes my lips.

I finish my bath and dress in my comfiest Capri sweats and tank. It's just the three of us tonight, so there's no need to dress up. When I get downstairs I see a large quilt on the floor. There's music softly playing through the stereo, but I don't recognize the song. However, I know immediately who is singing. He isn't, though. He's sitting on the floor with my adorable daughter in his lap. Both are staring at me with big grins. "This is nice. I love picnics," I say.

Sierra tells us both, "I know. I told Garrett, Mama likes picnics and he said we'd have a very special picnic tonight. Ta Da," she says, waving her hands around. Then I hear the song again. It's on repeat. I listen more closely…

Another week out on the road
Aw. That's just more time I spend away, away from
you
I know it seems like I'm always leavin'
Always a trip or taking care of something it seems
I must do

But know that you're always
You're on my mind
And that I think…I think about you, all the time
Please Love me. Love me and trust me, I'll be

home
Because You...you are the reason, you keep me
goin'

Lights on the tarmac they're always blinking
And I'm Wondering where you are and what you
are thinking
Where ever I go it's you I miss
Yeah but you really keep me going, oh...with just
one kiss

And know that you're always
You're on my mind
And that I think...
I say, I think about you all the time
Please Love me and trust me, I'll be home
Because You, you are the reason...you keep me
goin'

Well, How can I convince you of my faithfulness
When it feels, feels like it's always, some kind of
test
Please Love me, love me and trust me, I'll be home
Because you, you are the reason...I say you, you
are the reason
You keep me goin'

He's not singing, but he's listening with me and watching my reaction to every single lyric. I'm amazed...my precious man wrote this song. I think he wrote it for me. It ends. "You really keep me goin', baby!" he says, standing up, sliding Sierra around to his back and walking over to me where I'm still standing in the middle of the room. He takes me in his arms and dances and serenades me along with the lyrics. It's the most romantic thing I've ever experienced. There are no romantic television shows, or books, that could come close to being as precious as this. My little girl is clinging to Garrett's back. I'm in his arms, and we dance and twirl all around our family picnic blanket over and over again.

He's perfect. We're perfect. I will forever be grateful for the life that Jed started with me, the child he gave me, his advanced planning to make sure we were cared for, and for the countless other things he did. He was my best friend and I loved him dearly, but he was never the love of my life. I know that now. I think I always knew. But I had no idea what it would feel like to love and be loved this completely.

We sit on the blanket and eat the massive amounts of food I'm positive Elizabeth provided. "Did you two sneaky creatures stop at Mimi's house for take-out?" I ask.

Sierra chimes in, "It's the best, Mama. Mimi says we all need home cooked meals and she likes making our favorites. Pops said to tell you 'Thank you'!"

I know exactly what Pop's is thanking me for. He says 'thank you' to me every time he gets even a minute with Sierra, and he's so happy about the new baby. I look to Garrett thinking that maybe he planned this special night to tell Sierra our news. "Garrett, do you have some news you'd like to share?" I ask.

"Yes, actually, I do. I'll be right back." He runs off to the office and rushes back with two small packages.

Sierra is sitting in my lap, humming along to the song

still playing on repeat. Garrett sits down on the floor in front of us with his packages. "Sierra, this is for you," he says, giving her a box. She opens it right away and slides a beautiful Tiffany & Co. charm bracelet out. It has a great little collection of charms already. He starts explain them.

"Now, princess, this bracelet is special because this bracelet is our story," he says to a captivated almost five year old. He points to the first charm. "This crown is because no matter how old you are, you'll always be my little princess. Remember that." I'm watching this unfold and desperately trying to hold the tears back. I had no idea he was going to do this.

"And this star…is for your first time on stage with me. It was so much fun singing with you. This bear is to remember the day that I met you."

She pipes in, "Because you gave me the pink teddy bear."

"Yes, exactly! And this monkey was from our fun day at the Nashville Zoo. And this fish is for all the swims we take. I really like swimming with you. And this horseshoe is to remind you of our house in Nashville, with the horses, and the suitcase is to remind you that when I am away, I'm thinking of you." She climbs out of my lap and into Garrett's, so he can tell her about the last few charms.

"These last three are really super special. This heart that says 'I love you' on it opens up. Let me show you." And he stops to open the locket. Inside is a picture. Not a picture I was ever expecting Garrett to give to her. "Inside is a picture of your Daddy. He was really a very special and lucky guy. He loved you so much and I don't ever want us to forget about him. I won't ever be able to thank him enough for all the love he gave to help make you," Garrett says, looking at my tear streaked face with his own glassy eyes. But we're all smiling and happy.

"Garrett, are you my daddy, too?" she asks with a curious face.

"Yes, baby girl. For as long as you'll have me. I'll be your Daddy and I'll do my best to be a good one," he says, as Sierra jumps up and squeezes his neck.

"Thank you, Daddy."

"Now this next one is a bit tricky. See I need your help with this one. This one has a ring on it. Now guys like me get lucky sometimes and get to fall in love with really special girls, like your Mama. I love her so much and I want her to be my wife," he's speaking to Sierra, but looking at me. "So this charm is for what's in this next box, the box for Mama. I need your help asking her if she'll please, pretty please, with cherries on top, marry me. Marry me and make us a family," he says, pointing to us both. Then, he opens the box and it's the most perfect ring. In fact, I've never seen a more beautiful ring. It's gold with a solitaire in the center, and the bands are intertwining ropes holding the solitaire in place.

"Sweetheart, I told you a while ago that we were all tied up in heartstrings and I meant it. This ring symbolizes it. That center stone, it's my heart and all those ropes are wrapped right around your little finger," he says, sliding it onto my ring finger. "I love you, Alexis, and all these heartstrings are holding us together. Please make me the happiest and luckiest guy on the planet. Marry us?" I'm a puddle of tears and Sierra is jumping up and down. She's smiling so big and she's cheering me on with excited little giggles.

"Mommy, say yes. Please, say yes!" She's still cheering.

I look to Sierra and then Garrett. "Yes, I want to marry

us, too. Yes, Garrett. I will marry you," I'm saying through smiles and tears and excited cheers from Sierra.

We're all hugging and holding each other through our excitement.

Chapter Thirty-Nine

Garrett

I THINK I KNEW SHE'D SAY yes eventually, but I never imagined that she'd say yes quite that fast. Sierra did perfectly, as I expected. She wasn't in on it, but I knew pretty well what her reaction would be. I couldn't imagine proposing to Alexis without Sierra. Sierra is a part of who Lex and I are together. She needed to be here. It had all been perfect. I bought the ring, believe it or not, two weeks ago, expecting to give it to her at the end of the tour. But damn, if my wishing on all those stars didn't work out perfectly. I love these girls.

"Daddy, what about this charm?" Sierra asks. She and Alexis are both sitting in my lap now.

Alexis giggles…and I say, "Well, Sierra, that one is the best of all. Remember the day in the hospital with Courtney, Drew, and baby Gabe?" I ask and she nods her head. "That day we talked about how babies were made. Remember?"

She nods. "Yes, babies come from love," she recites.

"Yes they do...a lot of love. And we...Mama, you, me, all our family and friends had so much extra love to give that we, without even knowing it, made a baby inside your Mama's tummy." She looks to my stomach and rubs her fingers across my mid-section. "The baby is still growing and it'll be a little while before we can meet him or her, but you, my princess, will be the best big sister in the whole world," he says and Sierra cries her very first, in her whole life, happy tears.

"I love us soooo much!" she says, squeezing us all together.

"Yes, baby girl. I love us soo much, too!"

No one will ever understand what Jed must have been feeling the day that his plane went down. He had heaven here on Earth with these two special girls. I'm not sure why things work out the way they do sometimes. But I'm forever grateful to him for what he gave when he was here walking among us. He has given me the most precious gifts, and I'm committed to never letting his memory die in our home.

I want to be married as soon as possible. I hope Lex is on board for that. And I know exactly where we're going for the honeymoon. M.I.C.K.E.Y. M.O.U.S.E. ... I want to go to Disney World with these girls. I don't care if I have to buy out the park for the day. There's no other place that I'd rather take them.

Chapter Epilogue

Garrett
Seven months, Three weeks later

"**M**RS. MCKENNA, YOU'RE TEN centimeters dilated and ready to push," the nurse says.

"Do you really not think I'm ready to spit this little monster out? I know I'm ready. I've been telling you that! Move your asses, already. Get this thing out of me!" She's yelling at the doctor and nurses. My precious girl has been a trooper, but she's over it now. She wants to be all done with this pregnancy, labor, doctors, and hospitals, all of it. She wants to go home. She's told me this at least three dozen times in the last two hours.

"You're almost done," I whisper in her ear. "Want me to sing to you, sweetheart?"

She looks at me over her shoulder. "Yes," she says simply, in her most quiet voice. She's been so sweet to me today.

People warned me that she might say things she didn't mean, but she hasn't. She's said how much she loves me, that I'm her hero, that snuggling with me makes all the pain go away. She's been perfect.

Now with that being said, all bets are off for the poor nurses and doctors she's been outright nasty to, but you know what, they've all just taken it with a little laugh and been very helpful. I really have to commend them for their superior bedside manner.

She wanted me to play the guitar and sing to her in the delivery room, but I can't play the guitar and hold her at the same time, and I'm not letting go of her now. So I whisper the lyrics of the song I wrote for her into her ear. I'm singing it over and over, looking at her, watching her breathing exercises and her powerful pushes as she delivers our baby.

I hear the doctor say "one more time, Alexis" and then our baby comes into the world with loud cry. "It's a boy!" the doctor announces, and I kiss Alexis as they place my precious son on my wife's stomach.

"A boy," she says to me with a tear streaked face.

"A boy," I say, looking at my beautiful baby, counting his fingers and toes to make sure they're all there. "Thank you so much. You're amazing, Alexis. Look what you made for us, baby."

"Mr. McKenna, would you like to cut the cord?" the doctor asks me.

"Yes." He instructs me where to cut and I perform my first duty as the father of my son. I look at my wife and son and feel a slight pang knowing my little girl needs to be here.

The hospital wouldn't allow Sierra to be in here until after the delivery, when Alexis is settled into her room. I've already told the doctors, nurses, and anyone else willing to listen that this shit needs to happen quickly, so my little four-some can celebrate together. I'm so excited to go and get her. I need her to see this. They take my son off my wife's stomach, saying they're going to clean him up. They measure him, six pounds, and seven ounces, twenty-one inches long. Perfect. They stamp his little foot with ink, as he wails, but it's a glorious sound. He has nice strong lungs to serenade his Mama, just like his big sister and me.

"Mr. & Mrs. McKenna, we need to take baby boy McKenna for his bath and shots now," the nurse says, looking at my wife.

She looks like she's about to jump off the bed. "ABSOLUTELY NOT! Our baby goes nowhere without his daddy, or me, in tow."

The nurse is more than annoyed. "Mrs. McKenna, we cannot bathe him here and the pediatrician needs to look him over."

"Listen, lady," says my perfect, feisty little wife, "if you even think about taking my son anywhere without his father, or me, directly beside you, you are going to have some VERY BIG problems!" She looks to me and as sweetly as she's spoken to me all day, "Garrett, will you please escort our son, and THAT WOMAN, wherever it is that she needs to take him… and baby, please don't let our son out of your eyesight," she instructs.

The nurse is dumbfounded. My wife isn't a fan of doctors, or nurses, poking and prodding. She's not happy about being here, and on top of that they wouldn't let Sierra in the delivery room. This is her way of handling the frustration. They'll just have to take what she gives, because she's my little superstar today! I shrug my shoulders at the nurse and say, "Lead the way," after kissing my wife. We make a quick stop in the waiting room to tell the entire clan of family and friends waiting the good news. They're all crying and thrilled to meet Baby Boy McKenna. Sierra is crying more happy tears than I knew a five and a half year old had.

"Mama will be waiting for you soon. I'm going to help your new baby brother," I tell her giving her a big hug, as she waves to the little cart her baby is in.

Alexis

I CAN'T BELIEVE THE WHIRLWIND of this year. If you told me a year ago that I'd be married to an amazing man and delivering his baby, I would have thought you were on drugs, but clearly it is I who underestimated the power of heartstrings and wishes.

I'm finally to our room and it's empty. I'm waiting on my family to arrive and reminiscing about how far we've come.

Life is never perfect. We all have things that are challenging, that we need to work through and learn to accept.

My life has never been a walk in the park. I have a mother and father that are both addicts and have never been a meaningful part of my life. At least never in a positive uplifting way. I've chosen not to allow them into my life in any capacity. That's okay, though. I survived and learned some very valuable lessons from them. I learned to be the parent they weren't. I learned what I didn't want to be, and I think I have executed that as planned. I choose to accept those lessons and not feel badly about what I missed.

My first husband and best friend died when my daughter was three. We miss him. I think of him every day, especially when I see him peeking through our daughter's eyes. I'm grateful that he taught me to love and to accept love. I'm grateful for our daughter, who has brought more joy to my life than I ever thought possible.

I have family. I have an incredible brother, and as if being so amazing weren't enough, he went and married someone as wonderful as he is and then procreated, bringing three adorable kids into the greatness mix. They're my family and they were there for me when opening my eyes to the day was "a feat.

My best friends...I'm so very blessed that these girls love me in spite of all my stuff. They are the definition of true-unconditional-love. Keepers!

My adorable Sierra, this child has been the light in my world since the day she opened her eyes. There hasn't been a day in her life that she hasn't made me smile. The lessons she has taught me in this life far exceed anything any book or lecture could have provided. I'm grateful that she loves so willingly, feels so deeply, shares anything, laughs often, befriends anyone, and most of all calls me Mama. I'll never tire of hearing that sweet voice call me Mama.

My husband, I've never known a love like the one he's shown me. To say that you love someone is big. The words mean an awful lot, but to feel that you love someone and feel the love reciprocated....now that's really something. There are just no words to ever describe those feelings and emotions. That's what Garrett gives to me every day, feeling and emotions that I can never really describe. But we show each other how we feel.

Garrett wished us and we happened. He made me whole again. He made us all whole. I couldn't be more happy or proud of him. I love him so very much. And today, the day that I've given birth to our son, we've been married for six glorious months.

Our daughter thinks the sun and moon set behind him, and I couldn't agree more.

Acknowledgements

I must say first and foremost my family and friends are freaking amazing! They have been instrumental in helping me contain my insanity over the last several months. Can you imagine how crazy I could have been without that support? Aahhhhh....

Mike & Sky, I will try to cook for you more now, less takeout and turkey sandwiches, I promise. Thank you for allowing me to sacrifice family time to follow this dream. I owe you both everything and love you with my whole heart. You will never know how much I cherish the two of you and always will.

To my parents: I can't even imagine where I'd be in this life without you. I'm lucky to have such amazing role models to guide me. You taught me the meaning of unconditional love and then showed me how to live a life with meaning. I love you both so very much.

To my Nana, Catherine, I will never, LIKE EVER, be able to tell you how much you mean to me. You've changed my life. Your love and dedication to me throughout life has been priceless. You're my best friend and the first person I remember loving completely! Thank you for EVERY life changing sacrifice you've made on my behalf. I love you so very, very much!

To my big (almost real) brother Raymond, You are my hero. You will never know how much the love you've shown to me has impacted my life. You are an amazing father, husband, brother, uncle, son, friend and everything else you attempt. Thank you for writing songs that tell stories in my book but mostly, Thank you for being you and choosing to love me. Your beautiful family is my lifeline!

To my sister in-law Tabitha, I have lost count of the number of times you've swept into my crazy life to throw me a life preserver. You are quite simply amazing and I am so very lucky that you care enough to rescue me and take care of me. I will always be so grateful for you. (We need to plan an all night chat session again soon…that was too much fun)

To my mother in-law, Mary! Thank you for raising an amazing man. Thank you for always listening when I need to talk and thank you for supporting us. You and Benny are wonderful and we love you very much!

To the rest of my family… You know who you are. I love you more, always & Thank you! Aunt Glennis, Thank you for leading the pack! Aunt Toni, You are the sweetest person I know…HUGS…!

To my friends who I have skipped out on girls nights, trips, dinners, hanging out at the ballpark, whatever! I've been a crappy friend while writing this…I know. Thanks for loving me anyways and taking care of my kiddo when I was busy. I heart you all! Erica, Thank you for feeding me when I forget to eat and everything else you do to help!

To my editor Liz Aguilar, really… I never expected for you to talk me off the cliff when I was ready to jump. But you have so many times during this process. You're quite amazing and talented. Thanks for taking a chance on a girl like me. This book would be crap without you and I know it. Love you, Lady!

When I started this project I sought out knowledge and support through Facebook. I never in a million years expected so many authors and book bloggers to jump in to help little me…REALLY?! You guys are aMaZiNg! I'm so grateful to you all for the time and energy you've spent chatting with me and answering all my questions. Kelly Elliott (Because she's that awesome), Heather Gunter (my partner in crime), Southern Girls Author Event Planners – Chrissy & Jennifer (OMG…My BFFs…Can't live without you two, ever), Keshia Langston (amazing author and the other half of my brain) and so many others… Y'all are just amazeballs and keep be going everyday!

To Robin Harper at Wicked By design…still no words for how that cover makes me feel. Thank you! The cover and swag are perfect. I'm lucky that you were put in my path! <3 XO <3

To the Facebook community of friends on the author page! Every time I have a need, you fill it and quickly! You guys are the rock stars and the reason I finished this book! Thank you for the support and motivation! You guys have been incredible!

To the Picken's family, I sooo love you guys! Thank for very willingly forfeiting your names for this story. You will be paid generously in love! Whitney, thank for the encouragement. It was you who made me think maybe this was possible. XOXO

The Beta readers: Chrissy R., Darla B., Corinne B. and Luci N. You're critiques of my writing meant a lot to me.

Thank you so much for taking the time to read and give feedback! It was incredibly helpful and I hope to one day meet you all and give the huge hugs you deserve.

About the Author

Felicia Lynn is a transplanted Florida girl, born and raised, who lives just north of Atlanta, GA with her husband, daughter, dog and cat. She spends most of her days holed up in a cozy chair with a cup of tea and her laptop, writing about the characters that live in her head. When she's not writing you'll find her hanging out with her family and friends! She loves reading, taking long walks, chatting with her Facebook family, and listening to music, especially live music. A self-declared lover of all things baseball, she is obsessed with every aspect of the game!!!

Felicia writes contemporary romance, because love stories make people happy. Even in the midst of anguish and turmoil, true love can turn life around, and the process is beautiful. Most of Felicia's stories are based on real life experiences, which she embellishes to tell a story. She is currently working on her second novel, titled *Love's Learning Curve*.

http://www.facebook.com/FeliciaLynnAuthor

https://www.goodreads.com/author/show/7122637.Felicia_Lynn

14251638R00176

Printed in Poland
by Amazon Fulfillment
Poland Sp. z o.o., Wrocław